Also by S.G. Lovell

Bare Beginner

INAUGURATION

S.G. LOVELL

Copyright © 2014 Sandra Ghorbani
Cover Image Copyright © Maksim Shmeljov used under license from Shutterstock.com
Editing by: Kristin Anders 'The Romantic Editor'

First published in Linz, Austria in 2014 by Sandra Ghorbani

Warning:
This book is intended for adult readers, as defined by the laws of the country in which you made your purchase. The author makes no representations that her titles are appropriate or available for use in their locations. Those who access or read the author's titles do so at their own volition and are responsible for compliance with local law.

Disclaimer:
This book contains references to mental illnesses and treatments of such illnesses. All such references are products of the author's imagination or are used fictitiously and are not to be construed as medical advice. The author will not be responsible for any loss, harm, injury or death resulting from use of the information contained in any of her titles.

ISBN: 978-3-9503790-1-3
Printed by CreateSpace, Charleston SC
www.sglovell.com

INAUGURATION

Freedom

The New World was safe. Crime numbers were a sad statistic of the past, and humans lived in harmony and peace. Global warming had come to a timely halt, and the symbiotic coexistence between humans and nature was a reality rather than a dream. Economies flourished, increasing prosperity and wealth, while poverty and the Great War were a long-forgotten memory.

The guardian of this abundance of life was a brigade of Hybrids. Genetically superior to their ruling human ancestors and equipped with a microchip at the age of twenty-one, Hybrids were the next advanced, humanoid species that the Darwinian theory of evolution never anticipated.

Faster, stronger, and smarter than any other creature on the planet, there was one thing that humans could never allow Hybrids to be: *free*.

Chapter 1

Year: 2195
Location: Earth, AMEE region, Capital

"This is slavery." Ali ended the quiet statement on a hiss of pain, as the electrical current from the mobi on her wrist burned into her skin, turning her arm into a live-wire between one instant and the next.

The female Recruit beside her gasped in horror, her elbow hitting the hovercoach window with a dull thud in her haste to scoot away. "Speak no evil."

The whispered words were a blatant reminder of the Program's rule Ali had infringed upon, inciting the warning shock.

Ali heeded the advice only until her heart stopped palpitating. "What else can this be called? A whole race is forced into servitude."

"Peace?" Eyes wide in a striking, dark-skinned face, the girl sent a nervous glance past a dozen bleary-eyed Recruits, towards the watchful group of Marshals sitting at the front of the old, driverless vehicle.

Ali gave a mirthless laugh. "If there was peace you wouldn't fear them. If there was peace we wouldn't exist."

The girl flinched but couldn't deny it.

A human's vision to end the Great War by controlling an obedient super-army had led to the creation of their enslaved race of Hybrids, at the end of the Old World's inglorious twenty-first century. A hundred years later – despite the ruling Human Council's protestations that the New World was at peace – it was the Hybrids ability to quickly and quietly suppress any recurring violence that ensured their continued survival.

Without conflict, Hybrids were nothing. Useless pawns in a game already won.

Ali doubted her race would be out of a job anytime soon. The seven deadly sins were too deeply anchored in human DNA to allow long-lasting harmony and, despite a one-child policy that spanned all five regions of the New World, there seemed to be an endless supply of violent political insurgents who insisted that yesterday was better than today and the Human Council wasn't nearly the benevolent triumvirate it pretended to be.

The result was an illusion of the perfect world, rather than the perfect world itself. And the only thing keeping the seedy underbelly of society hidden from law-abiding, peace-loving citizens was their race of Hybrids, and a willingness of the Human Council to use deadly force if necessary, to keep the illusion alive. As a consequence, humans still died. Only now, they died in secret. Not what Ali would call peace, in any case.

"How about progress?"

The familiar reflection of Rob's face appeared next to Ali's in the hovercoach window.

"Slavery is progress?" she asked, groaning and clutching her arm when a second, stronger warning shock surged from her mobi straight to her chest, at the repeated use of the prohibited word. Ali exhaled a measured breath and reminded herself that speaking the truth was worth the pain.

"I think it can *facilitate* progress," Rob corrected, watching Ali struggle for control, his nimble fingers flying blindly over the touch-screen keyboard of the Data Interface Device on his lap. "After all, what could you strive for if you have everything you want?"

The supposedly tamper-proof electronic lock of Ali's mobi suddenly unlatched with a faint click, breaking the circuit running through the series of interconnected metal wrist bands that bound the paper-thin, rectangular computer against her unusually slim forearm. The warning shock ceased at once.

Ali couldn't quite suppress her whimper of relief.

For a moment, she stared in bewilderment at the darkened display of the deactivated device. Then her gaze darted to Rob's talented hands. They had ceased their endless typing and were now hovering motionless in front of a touch screen that displayed lines and lines of code…and in between, Ali's unique identifier, as assigned to her by Program officials.

Impossible.

The twinkle in Rob's caramel coloured eyes said he knew exactly what she was thinking. His expectant puppy look – entirely out of place on his handsome soldier's face – told her what he was waiting to hear. The words she had said a month ago, when he had first pinpointed her location at the Centre, amongst a crowd of fifteen-thousand Recruits. The same words he had since pulled off some of the most outrageous electronic stunts to hear again. "You're incredible."

With a grin that missed arrogant by a fraction and hit right on adorable, Rob sprawled back over three empty seats.

It was as close to strutting as he could get in the cramped space of the hovercoach, Ali realized, a smile tugging at her own lips. She wondered what he would say, if she told him he looked more like a beached whale than the powerful Recruit he was.

"You hacked a mobi." The dismal statement from the timid girl next to her pulled Ali back to reality. "The Marshals will punish us all."

"They may have the advanced eye-sight of Hybrids, but even they can't see through hovercoach seats," Ali said, slipping the mobi back onto her wrist, despite her words. "Of course, their hearing is pretty exceptional, too."

The girl snapped her mouth shut.

Ali nodded at Rob to reactivate the device and felt a pang of regret, when the display came back to life.

"Wouldn't you rather be free than incentivized?" Ali asked finally, picking up the original thread of their conversation.

"And do what? Work in security? Get a job in a technology company?" Rob shook his head. "You know as well as I do that the Program controls one hundred percent of the New World's law enforcement and technology market."

Ali had to grudgingly agree. Still. "Don't you ever get tired of blind obedience?"

"I think we just proved we aren't blindly obedient. Except for maybe…" He gestured towards the girl, who seemed to have regained her composure now that the mobi was once more lying flush against Ali's skin.

"Beth. Rt2030," the girl said, stating her name and unique identifier as required by Program introduction protocol.

"Except for maybe Beth. Mobis can be broken, pain can be endured."

An image of metal-clad fists flashed through Ali's mind and was squashed before it could take hold.

Pain *could* be endured. "But what about compulsion?" Ali asked.

Alone the thought of their upcoming inauguration as Hybrids had Ali shaking in her well-worn combat boots. "Do you not mind you'll be leashed like a dog once the microchip fuses with your brain, unable to fight any command a superior Hybrid – or human – might give you at a whim?"

She saw Beth's eyes narrow suspiciously and felt the sudden ridiculous urge to hide her face from the timid Recruit.

Rob's answer saved her just in time, before she could embarrass herself like that.

"I don't think anybody likes the idea of being so easily controlled. However, subservience is part of the give and take that is our life. The Program helps us to become the best we can be. In turn they feel entitled to use our services."

"With or without our consent," Ali said.

Rob shrugged his shoulders. "What do you want to do? Run away?"

Ali flushed. She had considered it a hundred times. She had discarded it just as often.

At the end of the day, freedom was an impossible desire. Even if she could get rid of the tracking beacon in her mobi, outsmart the New World's biggest law enforcement agency and somehow learn to live amongst humans – a race she was bred to protect but didn't understand – she would still be a fugitive for the rest of her life. On the run from the Program. Hiding where nobody could find her.

Where was the freedom in that?

**

The hovercoach came to a shuddering halt in front of the wrought-iron gate. *The Sanatorium*, a golden tag with black font announced discreetly on one of the stone pillars to the side. The six foot high barbed wire fence disappearing into the distance and Guards patrolling the perimeter - some alone and some in pairs or with a mean looking Doberman - weren't nearly as discreet.

It seemed they had finally arrived at their destination.

Ali felt unease creeping into her bones as the heavy metal barrier quietly lowered into the ground and the hovercoach chugged along. The next time she passed this gate she would be a Hybrid on her way to her first assignment, her free will stripped from her mind as surely as Trainer had tried to strip the dignity from her body.

"Look at all this space." Beth's amazed voice broke into Ali's thoughts, forcing her view to the parkland around them instead of the dark place inside her.

She was right. The landscape was stunning. Acres and acres of green space stretched to both sides of the access road. Beautifully manicured lawns vied with intricately designed flower beds. A small river curled like a silvery snake down a hill in the distance.

"We're in the middle of the sticks." Rob leaned across Ali's body to get a better look and ended up bracing his large, warm hand against the top of her thigh.

For a moment, Ali debated whether she should get offended at the uninvited touch. Control equalled power in the Program. She had fought too long and too hard for her place in the hierarchy to let a careless gesture tumble her back towards the bottom of the food chain. Then again, this was Rob. She seriously doubted he was trying to establish dominance in the backseat of a hovercoach.

"We're in the middle of the Capital," Ali said finally, having made up her mind to let the incident pass.

"The sticks of the Capital." He winked and lightly flexed his fingers once, to indicate he was but joking.

Ali felt her face grow warm at the intimate gesture. Maybe she should have told him off, after all.

She was glad when he retreated to his own seat and left her to turn back to the window…and a view that made her forget everything about the lingering sensation of his handprint on her thigh.

There on top of the hill, still half hidden behind the trees of a forest that formed a parkway just big enough for her to catch a glimpse, stood the most magnificent mansion she had ever seen. A relic from a different century, the grey stone building lacked the clear-cut lines and clinical precision of the New World constructions, instead inspiring visions of Victorian living, of the elegance and charm of a long lost world. Its huge bay windows were framed by ivy and vine, its array of old fashioned chimneys fought for space on the roof and competed with the spires in front for a touch of the sky.

Minutes later, the building loomed larger-than-life in front of them, as the hovercoach rounded the last bend and came to a stop in the middle of a busy concrete parking lot.

Multiple hovercrafts sat primly in the allocated spaces to their left, while a group of at least fifty Recruits in dark blue uniforms milled around a dedicated meeting point to the side of the hovercoach. It seemed Ali's group wasn't the only one arriving today.

Bright lights flared and the exit platform lowered to the ground with an audible release of air.

"After you." Rob gestured with his duffle bag for her and Beth to precede him. A wise decision, Ali realized as a blast of hot summer air squeezed pearls of sweat onto her forehead the second she left the air conditioned interior of the hovercoach.

"I read that temperatures in the Capital would be higher, but this is ridiculous." Beth groaned beside her. "The sun isn't even fully up, yet."

"At least you won't burn like us." Ali fingered her head with worry. It was shaved, as required for all Recruits and Hybrids by Program standards. It was also several shades lighter than Beth's own smooth, rich brown scalp.

"Just because you can't see my sunburn, doesn't mean I can't get one."

"Did she just disagree with you?" Rob asked, having braved the simmering parking lot behind them.

"Indeed."

Beth blushed to the top of her sunburn-able scalp.

"And that's what it will look like," Rob mused.

Ali bit her lip to hide her grin and busied herself scanning a picture of the mansion with her mobi. The requested information opened on the colour-ready e-paper screen, a moment later.

Built in the 19th Century of the Old World, the Program bought the estate twenty-five years ago with the vision of turning it into a dedicated inauguration centre. Renamed the Sanatorium, the estate is the twenty-second base for the Program in our AMEE region. It is the only base in the Capital. After its full renovation and upgrade, the Sanatorium is now considered the most advanced Hybrid centre in the New World providing our human investors with a generous return on their investment.

"You!"

Ali flinched, her gaze snapping from her mobi to the young man standing in front of her. A Marshal, she quickly deduced from his mud-brown uniform.

"Stand in line." He pointed to a spot in the queue that had formed at the entrance of the building. He couldn't be much older than Ali but, when he turned to call another Recruit to order, she could see the distinct Hybrid mark on the base of his head. A triple helix.

In a few days she would have a mark like that. Icy fingers trailed down her spine and she tried to look away, but the design held her captive.

Burnt into a Hybrid's skin with a laser right after inauguration, Ali knew the triple helix served a double purpose. One was to mark the location of the microchip implant. The other was to identify them as Hybrids.

Branded like cattle, leashed like dogs. Second class citizens.

The line finally started moving, breaking her stare.

Grateful for the distraction, Ali craned her neck to see if Rob or Beth were still around, but they had disappeared in the masses.

She slowly followed the Recruit in front of her along the stone path, until she reached the open double doors of the building. Mesmerized by how the rays of the sun reflected in a multitude of colours off the glass, Ali extended her hand but froze before her fingers could make contact with the polished surface. Not glass. She stared at the little rotating shape in the top right corner of her mobi. Diamond and steel.

The intricate work suggested that both materials had been assembled at the nuclear level into exactly this pattern. The same process was commonly used by AssemblyBots to fit the thin layer of diamond that protected the digital display of all New World electronic devices, into their steel frame. However, Ali had never seen it implemented in a project of this magnitude.

Extending her hand further, almost reverently this time, she ran her fingers along a vein of steel and felt the strength of the bonded materials vibrate through her body.

"Hands off!" The young Marshal glowered at her from the end of the line. He really didn't seem to like her much.

Ali slowly pulled her hand back, not giving him the satisfaction of seeing her intimidated, then revised her impression as he reprimanded three other Recruits in quick succession for nothing more than staring at him. He didn't seem to like *anybody* very much.

Ali finally stepped through the doors, grateful to leave the grumpy Marshal and the ever hotter burning sun behind.

Just like the entrance itself, the hall beyond was stunning. The investors had obviously gotten what they had paid for. From where she stood, Ali could see more diamond doors, marble floors and state-of-the-art electronic devices. Cool air, generated and circulated by a solar powered air-conditioning unit, whispered over her skin and her lungs filled with the inviting scent of smokeless incense.

Why someone would spend this kind of money on a prison was beyond her.

"They sure didn't do it for us." The Recruit in front of her tore his gaze from the three supermodel-gorgeous women behind the reception desks to look at her, and Ali realized she had spoken aloud.

"The investors inspect the property at regular intervals. Probably to make sure their puppies are well kept." He snorted. "Funny though, how they never turn up unannounced. I guess it wouldn't be good for business to confront them with the reality of life at the Program."

"How do you know?"

He shrugged his massive shoulders. "I helped with administration for the last two years. Every time a scheduled visit was coming up, orders went out to scale back training. No blood. No broken bones."

"You've lived here for two years?" She hadn't seen a Hybrid mark on his skin.

The Recruit shook his head. "I've lived at Centre 1-08, but the LiveNet spans all bases in the region. The Sanatorium's administration is disproportionately more time-consuming and they always need some extra help."

"Is it the same at the Centres?" she asked.

"The regular inspections, you mean?" Again, the Recruit shook his head. "The investors are only interested in us once we're inaugurated."

Ali wanted to ask more questions, but they were forced to split up then, as the single line filing through the doors divided into three; one for each reception desk. The separate queues continued to slowly move forward, the plush carpet on the floor swallowing the steps of a hundred feet, the quiet conversations going on at the front of the lines disappearing into the high ceiling above.

The walls to both sides of the hall were adorned with digital picture frames, showing a carefully selected collection of three-dimensional photographs of the estate, Hybrids in combat and...Dr Eric Young.

Ali quickly dragged her gaze away from the piercing brown eyes of a man she had never met and prayed she never would.

Elected as a board member for the AMEE region almost thirty years ago, word had it that he had taken the reins so subtly and with so much finesse that even the board members didn't realize they had been demoted to advisors, until it was too late. Word had it too, that Doctor – as he preferred to be called in and out of the Program – performed unsanctioned experiments on Hybrids.

"Next, please." The supermodel behind the reception desk motioned for her to come forward and Ali stepped into the small circle of raised marble stone, trying to ignore the sensation of eyes drilling into her back.

The small jolt of the BioDetect device piercing her right index finger helped marginally, as did the low humming noise that announced the processing of her blood.

Still, Ali didn't take a relieved breath until a soft chime announced the successful completion of the analytical procedure and the receptionist waved her through the body scanner, away from prying eyes.

The gentle vibration of her mobi indicated the receipt of her room number, seconds later.

Outhouse Q, Room 210. Opening the floor plan provided with the information, Ali dodged a number of Recruits who had checked in before her and made her way to the double doors at the back.

She stopped short as, for the first time, she saw the true expanse of the estate.

Hidden behind the mansion were at least ten separate buildings, each connected to the other by a simple stone path. All of them sported the same Victorian design that dominated the outside of the mansion, but Ali had no doubt that the inside of each one of them would be state-of-the-art.

Two solar heated outdoor swimming pools, an array of training courts and what looked like a circular obstacle course completed the assembly of man-made constructions.

Into this original layout of Old World structures, clever landscape architects had integrated New World technology in a way that enhanced, rather than diminished, the appeal of the Sanatorium's grounds.

A subterraneous irrigation system allowed plants to prosper even in the unforgiving heat of the Capital's summer. A water and air purification plant protected rivers, wildlife and Hybrids alike. Waist-high gardening droids travelled on solar panel walkways between greenhouses that were mounted at treetops for maximum sun exposure.

It was clear – even to the untrained eye – that the cost and effort it must have taken to turn an Old World Victorian site into this glittering jewel of New World real estate was substantial, to say the least.

Ali was all the more astonished that the sober-looking data warehouse in the distance didn't integrate with rest.

She turned her back on the architectural monstrosity of steel and glass, and located building Q a short way from where she stood.

She ducked into the lobby behind a small group of South African Recruits, and surveyed her surroundings.

Slightly smaller than the mansion's entrance hall, the lobby was nevertheless stunning, with marble once more dominating the floor and a thin, but undoubtedly expensive, red carpet leading to a couple of gold adorned elevators at the back. Ali dismissed them immediately. If the Sanatorium was anything like the Centre, the elevators would only be activated for members with medical conditions and visitors.

Instead she followed the Recruits up the stairs to her left, then proceeded to room 210 when she reached the second floor.

The door to her room slid quietly open as she approached, thanks to a tiny camera capturing, analysing, and recognizing her face in record time.

Impressive.

Her room was, too.

Drinking in the opulence before her, Ali walked along the short entryway to the queen sized bed and felt her mouth drop open when she saw the massive desk nestled into one corner behind a bend in the wall. Made of naturally grown wood, it effortlessly succeeded in striking the balance between the Victorian atmosphere of the estate and the pomp the Program was striving for, in every detail.

Ali trailed a finger over the beautiful randomness of grain and knotholes that defied the logic of even the most advanced AssemblyBots and wondered how many officials had to be paid to obtain a deforestation permit.

She opened the lid of the Data Interface Device that sat on top of the desk and felt more excitement streak through her. It wasn't just any Data Interface Device. It was a brand new DID Z2100, the most advanced intelligent agent the New World had to offer.

Barely resisting the temptation to power up the gadget, Ali scanned the rest of the room.

Large, inbuilt wardrobes framed both sides of the entrance. A fully tiled bathroom with sink, bath tub *and* separate shower promised a speedy recovery from difficult training sessions. But it was the balcony that overlooked some of the most beautiful parkland Ali had ever seen, that made her heart thump with joy.

Your luxurious new home for the next few weeks, Ali thought, when she was once more standing in the middle of the room. She could've done worse. But then, she would do worse soon.

Ali wondered if the splendour was the investors' way to sweeten the bitter pill of inauguration. Humans, she had learned, had some strange beliefs about redemption.

But surely even they had to realize that all sugar coating in the world didn't change the outcome? Did they truly believe that living in wealth was worth lifelong slavery?

Ali closed her eyes against the stab of desperation she felt every time she thought of her life after inauguration and drew in a calming breath. What she wouldn't give to be one of *them*.

Chapter 2

The lunch hall was as extraordinary as everything else Ali had seen of the Sanatorium so far. Instead of one large hall, it was designed as a set of connected rooms. Huge windows overlooking the park outside allowed golden light to spill over antique chairs and tables, while the buffet was set up in a shaded area near the entrance of the hall.

"Looking for someone?"

The voice at her ear made her jump a split second before she recognized it.

Had he been standing there waiting for her, all along?

Rob pushed a plate full of food into her hands.

That answered her question. At least one of them. "How much do you think I eat?" Ali eyed the overflowing dish in disbelief.

He ran his gaze along the length of her body, until she had to suppress an urge to squirm.

"Not enough. You're too skinny."

Ali felt her stomach plummet. She hated it when people reminded her how underweight she was. She wanted to *be* human, not look like one.

She must have been a weak Hybreeder, a Medic had once said about her Hybrid mother, when Ali finally mustered the courage to ask him why she was so different than everybody else.

The accusation had hurt, even though he had accused her mother and not Ali. She had felt the overwhelming urge to protect the woman who had given birth to her. A woman she didn't even know. A mother she missed all the same.

It was unusual for a Recruit to miss their mother. Indifference was the norm. In the Program where Hybreeders were forced to continuously produce highly competitive, resilient offspring in a process commonly referred to as hy-breeding – where after artificial insemination and the initial prenatal development of the embryo inside the womb the foetus was transferred to an incubator to free up the Hybreeder for the next pregnancy – there was little time for a bond to form between mother and child.

Rob must have seen her face fall, because he dropped a single red cherry tomato from the buffet onto the mountain of food. "Don't worry," he said, giving her an encouraging smile. "Just join me for food a few more times and I'll fatten you up real quick."

Ali slapped his hand away. "Thanks. That's every Recruit's dream, after all. Fat instead of muscles." But she couldn't deny the quip had the desired effect.

Rob knew it too.

He guided her to an empty table at the back of the hall.

"Have you seen the DID?" he asked, when they slid into their seats.

Ali popped the tomato into her mouth, flavour exploding onto her tongue as she bit through the skin.

"It's nice," she said, just to see his reaction and because she felt she owed him at least some form of payback.

"Nice?" His eyes narrowed. "The new Z2100 isn't nice. It's brilliant. Outstanding. Awesomely futuristic."

Ali swallowed the squashed vegetable to hide her grin. "Awesomely is a word?"

"That's what you picked up on? Really?"

Her façade cracked.

"Little devil." But his words held no heat.

Suddenly his face turned dark.

"What is i—"

"Don't."

But it was already too late. The fork in Ali's hand clattered onto her plate the same time as the male Recruit behind her hit the gleaming parquet floor.

Shouts of surprise and horror erupted around the hall. A yellow-clad Hybreeder at the entrance started to cry.

A couple of Assassins in red uniforms attempted to turn the large body over, but stopped immediately when they saw the blood trickling from the male's ears, pooling in an ever growing circle around his head.

Ali swallowed hard. She had never before seen a Recruit die like that.

No, not a Recruit, Ali realized as her gaze snagged on the triple helix burnt into his skin. A Hybrid in Recruit uniform. But that didn't make sense.

A Marshal rushed towards the commotion, just as a frantic Medic stormed into the hall.

"Where is he? Is he—?"

Ali could see the Medic's mouth still moving, but no words left his lips at the sight of the motionless body. Eyes wide open, he stared at the dead male on the floor.

"Anthony is going to kill me," the Medic finally said, his voice trembling almost as much as his hands holding what looked like a helmet with electrodes. "He is going to kill me, no doubt."

Older – and calmer – than the Medic, the Marshal took over the situation in an instant. "Recruits, clear the hall."

Chaos ensued as everyone rushed to follow the Marshal's order, giving the casualty on the floor a wide berth.

Feeling like her stomach might revolt, Ali steadied herself against a table and was glad when Rob grabbed her elbow in a firm grip.

"Just hold onto me."

Thoughts of maintaining the pecking order didn't even occur to her for a single second. Unresisting, she allowed Rob to guide her out of the hall and past a distraught Medic who was still quietly muttering to himself about the dead Hybrid and his black soul.

***

Sitting in front of the desk, Ali regarded her brilliant-outstanding-awesomely-futuristic DID with sombre eyes. The casing was shiny with a slight purple tinge that shifted back and forth as she adjusted her viewing angle. The display was covered by a pane of thin diamond with an antireflection coating. The lack of a keyboard suggested that eye movement tracking and voice commands were the two main input methods, although a touch screen option was probably inbuilt as a fall-back procedure.

Of course, all that was obsolete once a Recruit was inaugurated. One of the advantages of the inauguration chip was direct communication with any electronic device. Hybrids could literally control DIDs with their thoughts. Until then…"DID, wake up."

Earlier, Ali had been excited to try out the gadget. The incident at lunch had dampened more than her appetite.

"What a way to die."

"My apologies, Rt2120, but I am not familiar with this command." The voice that flowed softly from the DID's speakers was pleasant, but nondescript. Genderless.

Ali sighed, rubbing her temples. "Never mind, DID. Please guide me through the setup process. And please," she added after a second, "call me Ali." She hated her identifier. Trainer had used it whenever he had punished her.

"Of course, Ali. Do you wish to follow the automatic or manual setup process?" the DID asked.

"Automatic." She just wanted to have it done and over with.

"Setup process initialized. Step one, generate appropriate DID identifier. The next available identifier is DID1589. Do you wish to proceed with this new configuration?"

"Not really," Ali stared listlessly at the letter-number combination on screen. "Can I give you a name?"

"You could if you chose the manual setup process. Do you wish to change to the manual setup process?"

"Yes." It seemed she didn't have an option, if she wanted to have her way.

"Very well. Please choose an appropriate DID

identifier."

Ali tried to think of a name. It was more difficult than she had anticipated. The names sounded either too clinical or too…human.

"Electra." It was perfect.

"I am Electra. Do you wish to proceed with this new configuration?" the DID asked in a suddenly female voice.

"Yes, I do."

"Opening input calibration tool now. Do you require an introduction?"

"No, Electra. I'm familiar with the input calibration tool."

The first white dot appeared on the left of the screen, the second on the bottom. The next one flashed on the right. More dots kept appearing all over the screen and Ali tracked all of them with her eyes, one after the other, until the screen went black again.

Then a single white dot appeared, along with Electra's command. "Click."

Ali contracted her pupils to pinpoints for the briefest of moments. Controlling her iris sphincter muscle was one of the first things she had learned in *Biofeedback Studies* when she was a child. It had been difficult back then. Now it took less thought than even breathing.

"Double-click."

She allowed her pupils to pulsate twice.

Other challenges appeared on screen along with Electra's commands. "Scroll horizontally. Scroll vertically. Zoom in. Zoom out." And finally. "Calibrating now."

Ali waited while Electra calculated her accuracy in

tracking the objects on screen and the degree of her pupils' dilation and contraction, as well as the way her eyes stroked the screen in a straight or circular motion.

"Testing now."

A number of buttons appeared on screen next to each other and Ali 'clicked' each one of them, then tried scrolling and zooming a text.

"I'm happy with the responses, Electra."

"I'm pleased to hear that, Ali."

Ali thought she detected a trace of pride in the voice, and wondered briefly if Electra was advanced enough to feel real emotions. *Unlikely*, she thought. Maybe a link to the word *happy*, instead.

"What's next?" She had never set up a DID from scratch.

"We will now set up my security," Electra said. "I will guide you through the process."

"I shall follow. Launch the program."

Hours later, Ali retraced her steps to the lunch hall for dinner.

It had been a long process to configure Electra. It had been an even longer process to look through the welcome pack that had waited for her in Electra's inbox.

Most of the information, Ali already knew from her research at the Centre, but the estate layout document had been new.

According to the provided map, the Sanatorium's grounds stretched much further than Ali had originally realized, with the complex they stayed in only taking up a small portion of the actual grounds. The rest of the land was largely wilderness covered in forest.

The sticks of the Capital indeed.

A description of security measures, implemented to keep the whole area safe, had been attached to the document, probably for reasons of deterrence.

It had confirmed what Ali had suspected since she first laid eyes on the Sanatorium's front gate security force. Only someone insane – or insanely desperate – would ever attempt to escape the Program by running away.

***

"I think the microchip exploded in his head. There was definitely some brain mixed in with the blood. I saw it. Like custard and raspberry sauce blended together."

Ali gagged and pushed her plate away.

Opposite her, Rob shovelled another forkful of mashed potatoes into his mouth, undisturbed by the gory horror stories circulating the lunch hall.

"We can sit at a different table," he offered, using his knife to cut up a piece of meat on his plate. Pink juice seeped from the medium-rare steak.

Ali looked away. "It's the same everywhere," she said.

The only way to escape the rumours would be to go back to her room. But that, the Marshals wouldn't permit until mealtime was over.

Ali closed her eyes and tried to think of something else. Anything.

It didn't help. Her thoughts kept circling back to the Hybrid on the floor.

Not that the body was still there. Even the blood stain had been removed completely. It was the first thing she had – reluctantly – checked when they had entered the lunch hall, half an hour ago.

"Hybrids. Recruits." The Marshal, who stepped forward with an officially branded notepad in his hand, waited until a hushed silence fell over the hall. "I can now formally inform you that Rt1917 died of a rare, *non-contagious* illness. His death has been ruled a tragic accident by the investigating Medic. His status has been set to deceased on the Program's database as of 1:32 p.m."

Ali sucked in a breath.

Her mother's death had been ruled a tragic accident too. The only case in Program history of a foetal extraction gone wrong. No other Hybreeder had ever died releasing a foetus for further development in the incubator after the required three months of pregnancy. The low mortality rate of mother and offspring was one of the reasons Hybreeders had replaced artificial surrogates for the initial development of embryos in the first place.

"Why does the deceased have a Recruit identifier? He was inaugurated." Rob's quiet question pulled Ali back to the present.

She looked back at Rob, surprised. He was right. The Hybrid's identifier should have denoted his designation. Tr for Trainer. Gd for Guard. Ms for Marshal. Anything, but Rt for Recruit.

"A Hybrid without designation," Rob mused, his eyes narrowing suspiciously.

"That's impossible," Ali said.

"As is hacking a mobi." Rob winked, his fingers drumming a quick staccato on the table, bored without a touch-screen keyboard to manipulate. "I wonder if there are more of them. And are they all doomed to die?"

Chapter 3

The beeping sound from her mobi woke Ali at five-thirty the next morning, fifteen minutes before her first training class at the Sanatorium.

Physical training was an integral part of every Recruit's daily schedule, from the moment they learned to walk. As the future peacekeepers of the New World, it was their duty to develop a body that left no doubt as to their ability to handle any situation with confidence and efficiency. Once they reached full Hybrid status, their intimidating physical appearance served as a source of comfort to law-abiding citizens. It was an effective deterrent for everyone else.

Increasing her heart rate and basal body temperature with a simple exercise from her *Biofeedback Studies* to shut off the alarm, Ali rolled out of bed and winced as her muscles protested the movement. Maybe using her hour of idle time to train herself to exhaustion in a bid to sink into dreamless slumber afterwards hadn't been such a good idea after all. Now she was barely able to move. A condition the new Trainer was unlikely to approve of.

The thought gave her pause.

What if he punished her?

She squeezed her eyes shut as memories tumbled through her mind. Trainer at the Centre excited to teach her a lesson. The corners of his lips twisted into a sneer, his plump human face a mask of barely suppressed anticipation at the thought of humiliating her, until she begged for mercy.

Her hands flexed of their own accord, fingers curling around an imaginary throat.

She had tasered him within an inch of his life for his efforts to break her.

Would she be required to do the same again?

No. Not everyone in the Program was a sadist like Trainer at the Centre had been.

Forcing her fists to open, Ali realized she had squashed the biodegradable tooth gum that she always picked up from her bedside table immediately after rolling out of bed.

Get a grip.

Plucking the soft mass she used to clean the impurities from her teeth with from between her fingers, she flung the gum into the waste disposal unit and went through the motions of the rest of her morning routine without the usual effectiveness she had cultivated over the years.

The click of her tongue sounded loud in the quiet room.

"Good morning, Ali." Electra's screen flashed awake.

"Good morning, Electra. Our new wake up command seems to work well."

Electra chimed her agreement.

"Show me the location of the training hall for today's morning session."

The estate layout document opened on Electra's screen.

The flashing red dot highlighting the left corner of one of the outhouses immediately drew Ali's attention.

"What's the estimated walking distance to the hall?"

"Seven minutes."

The clock said she had five.

Ali cursed the fact that she had allowed panic to make her late and quickly committed the route to memory. There was no point in losing additional time looking it up on her mobi on the way.

She slipped into her uniform and grabbed a bottle of water from one of the wardrobes.

She would have to run to make her class. Maybe a good thing, considering her muscles could do with the extra warm-up.

"Sleep." She heard Electra's soft chime of acknowledgement then the quiet click of the electronic lock as the door to her room slid closed behind her.

***

Entering the training hall, Ali took a quick look around and breathed a sigh of relief when she couldn't make out a single green uniform amongst the sea of blue. She was right on time, but the attendance indicator on the wall next to the entrance suggested that she was the last one to arrive.

The devil takes the hindmost.

Not today, she thought grimly, quickly crossing the expanse of empty floor to the electronic equipment in the back and settling into an easy rhythm on one of the treadmills without delay.

A moment later, she was glad she had hurried, when Trainer's voice rang through the room. "Recruits! Against the wall!"

Electronic equipment stopped at once and the clanging of weights was replaced by a hushed silence as everyone rushed to stand in line. Ali slid in between two particularly large male Recruits near the end of the hall and pressed her palms against the slightly rough fabric that covered the lower third of the walls.

The tiny hairs on her arms rose as Trainer passed her a second later, pacing the length of the line…giving her a good look at the triple helix etched into the base of his head.

Fear clogged Ali's throat.

She knew her reaction was ridiculous. Despite their outstanding reflexes, denser bone structure and higher threshold for pain, Hybrid Trainers were no more or less dangerous than the Marshals in the lunch hall. But it wasn't logic that had Ali pushing her fingers against the wall until her joints started hurting. It was what Trainer represented. A faster, stronger and more powerful version of the man who had nearly succeeded in making her crawl.

Ali forced herself to take steady breaths, until the ringing in her ears finally subsided.

"From today until your inauguration I will be your Trainer. I expect timeliness." His eyes landed on her and Ali shrank back. "Hard work and obedience. I will not permit disturbances, laziness or insubordination. Your days as Recruits are numbered and I expect you to step up your game. Your senses, agility, and performance are better from birth than any human's. The microchip that you receive during your inauguration will further enhance your abilities." He stopped to look at each Recruit in turn. His voice when he spoke held a quiet promise. "Rely on your natural superiority and you will find yourselves at the mercy of those who set out to challenge our regime. Recognize them for what they are – anarchists who will stop at nothing trying to disrupt our peace – and you may stand a chance." He glared at them. "Is that clear?"

Ali joined her not-quite steady voice to the chorus. "Yes, Trainer."

"You will train longer and harder than you have ever trained before and you will do so with the dedication and commitment befitting a future Hybrid."

"Yes, Trainer."

"In a moment, I will ask each one of you to step forward separately. I will assess your fighting skills in a thirty second free style fight, after which you will proceed to the treadmills for an endurance test. We only have a few days together, but we will make the most of it. You!" He motioned the first Recruit forward.

Ali winced. Trainer's blows were so powerful and fast that his limbs started to blur in front of her eyes. His fighting style was completely unpredictable. The Recruit didn't stand a chance.

When it was finally Ali's turn, her heart was lodged firmly in her throat.

"Fight."

Her centre of gravity dropped a split second before she attacked. Trainer blocked. A lash of air hit her shoulder, then her thigh. He was too big. Too fast. Within seconds he forced her to defend instead of attack. Touches feathered across her middle, head, and limbs, exploiting every weakness they could find. If this was a real fight she would be unconscious by now.

"Stop." He motioned her through. "Next."

Feeling like her legs had turned to jelly, Ali headed for the treadmill. And she had thought leaving Trainer at the Centre behind had been a relief.

***

After breakfast, Ali and Rob made their way to the lecture theatre to attend the welcome seminar with the rest of the Recruits who had arrived with them the day before.

They had just found a couple of empty seats towards the front of the big hall, when the professor strode into the room.

Definitely human, Ali thought taking in the tuft of hair and bushy eyebrows. He reminded her of Albert Einstein.

The Recruits rose to their feet in unison to show their respect, a move required by the Program's rules but entirely ill-founded in Ali's eyes. As hard as it tried to fool everyone, the Program had never been about respect, but about fear and obedience.

At the gesture from the professor, they sank back into their seats.

"All hail and very welcome to the *Inauguration Basics* lecture." His greeting was typical for the Program, his overly enthusiastic attitude wasn't. Ali wondered what had brought him to the Sanatorium.

"Let's start with your inauguration schedule."

Ali's stomach dropped, before the fluttering wings of a thousand tiny butterflies picked it back up. She gripped the DID built into the desk in front of her and tilted it so she could see the screen and on it her inauguration date in bold black numbers.

Six days.

Six days, until the last of her freedom would be stripped from her. Dread settled heavily on her chest.

Ali wondered if she would have mourned the loss of her free will the same way, had she been inaugurated before her first conscious memory around the age of one. Could she have missed something she had never known?

She pushed the impossible 'what-if' scenario out of her mind. Everyone knew that inauguration could not happen before a Recruit reached maturity. Although her race possessed an enhanced nervous system with reinforced neural pathways, the risk of overloading an immature brain during the transition process and causing long-lasting complications or even death, was far too high.

Ali glanced back at the DID that had switched to a slide show and forced herself to listen as the professor explained in detail what this transition process included exactly.

"Upon inauguration you will receive the microchip implant that will take you from Recruit to Hybrid status. The chip will integrate into your brain in three stages. The first stage is the activation stage. This stage will automatically be initiated once the chip comes into contact with your brain matter. It establishes a primitive one-way connection to the brain, as well as connections to the bioservers here at the Sanatorium for energy supply and updates. The first stage will last up to ten minutes, depending on the individual. During the first stage, the chip's functionality is heavily restricted, although it can induce low level compulsion."

There it was. The word she hated so much. *Compulsion.*

"The compulsion will become stronger in stages two and three and is activated whenever you receive a direct order from a superior or are under the influence of your designation. The chip determines rank through voice recognition and the database of Program members that is stored on the chip's internal memory. This database is updated daily. We will cover microchip updates in another lecture." He squinted at his notes, before continuing. "The compulsion will also replace the pain controls you are currently used to from your mobis, as strong electrical currents in the brain pose a high risk of brain damage."

The slide on the DID in front of her changed.

"The second stage is the biofeedback stage. During this stage the chip will establish a full connection with the brain, changing from a one-way data transfer from the chip to the brain to a two-way data transfer from the chip to the brain and back. The length of this stage, again, differs for every individual and can last from a few hours to a few days. Once completed, you will be able to access the full functionality of the chip through your biofeedback, similar to the way you are currently communicating with your mobis. The Program recommends that you take a *Chip Communication* class after inauguration to receive mentorship on how to master communication with your chip. The schedule for these classes will be available on the LiveNet in due course and can be accessed using your DIDs. A completed stage two will also imply that the chip has integrated with your brainstem in a way that prevents removal. Any physical or virtual attempt to destroy or tamper with the chip will result in it short circuiting. Tests show that the chance of surviving a short circuit is less than one percent."

Ali definitely didn't want to know, how they had verified that particular fact.

"The third stage is the designation stage. As the name suggests, it is the stage when your designation will be activated. Your designation is an artificial improvement of your natural strengths to a level that allows assignment of a Hybrid to a pre-defined category, such as Guard, Marshal or Assassin. A full list of possible designations is available on the LiveNet and can be accessed using your DIDs. Please be aware that your designation will be hardcoded into the chip and cannot be changed. It will be determined during your formal assessment, which you will take in the days prior to your inauguration. After your inauguration, compulsion will ensure you behave according to your designation's code of conduct at all times. It will define who you are, for the rest of your lives."

The presentation finished with a quiet click.

"Any questions?" The professor's voice sounded incredibly loud in the deathly quiet theatre. He looked around. "Class dismissed."

***

The atmosphere at lunch was muted. Rob had been right; nobody liked the idea of being so easily controlled.

Still, there wasn't a single Recruit with quite the same expression of panic that had stared back at Ali from the mirror when she had tried to calm her frazzled nerves by splashing cold water onto her face in one of the bathrooms, after class.

Compulsion...for the rest of your lives.

"Compulsion my ass."

Ali turned to see a male Recruit sitting on the back of a chair, holding court for a small audience.

"If I don't want to do something, a piece of metal isn't going to change my mind."

A few members of the group around him nodded like well-trained puppies.

"Pretty stupid, isn't he?"

Ali turned to see the timid girl from the hovercoach sitting at a table near the entrance of the hall.

"Idiot," Ali agreed.

"You look like you're searching for a table?" Beth nodded towards the empty chair opposite her.

In reality, Ali had been searching for Rob, but it would be rude to refuse the invitation. She put her tray down and slid into the seat.

"I'll bet anyone that this whole compulsion thing is nothing but a farce." More nods around the male Recruit's table.

Really? Ali huffed. Did the idiot really believe what he said? And did they really have to listen to him for the rest of their lunch?

"You can't fight compulsion, dumbass. That's why they call it compulsion," another self-important individual, from a different table, chipped in.

"I'll bet any one of you." The Recruit's voice was almost as high as the colour rising in his face, at having his credibility questioned.

Ali watched as a few eager fools tried to take him up on the offer then quickly scattered when an angry Hybrid stomped their way.

"Praise the Marshal," Beth commented drily, eliciting a snort of laughter from Ali. "I guess there won't be much lost when this bunch is inaugurated."

Ali couldn't agree more. "What did you think of the welcome seminar?" She felt the overwhelming urge to talk to someone about it.

"I found it rather fascinating."

"You must be destined to become a Medic. Or some form of scientist."

Beth grinned shyly.

"Which one of the two?" Ali asked.

"Both."

"You can't be both."

"I can, if I become a Psychiatrist. *If* I become a Psychiatrist." A sliver of doubt slid into Beth's voice.

Ali remembered the scrutinizing look Beth had given her in the hovercoach and felt the pieces of the puzzle tumble into place. No wonder Ali had felt awkward. She hated psychiatric assessments.

"Of course you will." Ali touched Beth's hand reassuringly.

"I hope so. How did you figure it out anyway?"

"Only a Medic or a scientist could find brainwashing fascinating rather than terrifying."

Beth giggled. "Fair enough. How about you?"

Ali picked at her food. "I don't know."

Beth's tilted her head. "Haven't you taken a pre-assessment?"

"Not one. Three."

"And?"

"Inconclusive."

"Three times? That's—"

"Impossible. I know." The professors at the Centre had told her as much. "Doesn't change the results though." She speared a piece of carrot with her fork.

The pre-assessments were designed to give Recruits an initial indication of their future designation, and allowed them to pick lectures tailored to their individual strength. Ali had been unable to produce a valid result and had been forced to stick with the general curriculum for future Hybrids. It had given her a much broader education than most of the other Recruits. And had made one thing very clear. "I'm hoping for something non-competitive."

"But you're such a good fighter," Beth said. "I've seen you in morning training."

"Are you serious? My attack against Trainer lasted, what? All of ten seconds?" Ali swore she could still feel ghosts of air whispering over her body, where Trainer had struck.

"Some of the other Recruits didn't last five. I was dead before I even started." Beth gave her a level look.

"Fair enough. Still, I'd prefer something non-competitive."

Beth studied her for a moment. "You could be a...Mediator for intercontinental relationships. That's non-competitive."

Ali thought of Trainer at the Centre jerking uncontrollably as she wrapped her hands around his throat, tasering him again and again. The aggressive attack had saved her that day. She doubted it would be considered a suitable mediation skill, though. "Maybe not."

"An Ai Specialist?"

Working with artificial intelligence all day? That sounded more like Rob than Ali. It had taken her hours to configure Electra. "No."

"A landscape architect, then."

"There are no Hybrid landscape architects."

"So you get to start a new designation. How awesome is that?"

Ali laughed. She liked Beth's humour. "Landscape architect it is."

***

The evening training class came way too fast for Ali's liking. She had attended the afternoon lecture alone, as both Beth and Rob had been assigned to a different group. The professor, another member of the human race, had provided the dates for the formal designation assessments that, for Ali, would take place in three days' time. Afterwards, he had droned on and on about the methods used to calculate the perfect designation match for each Recruit. According to him, the assessment would analyse each Recruit's visual association to a tailored list of words, combine the results with the outcome from the virtual war games evaluation and apply a standardized set of formulas on the normalized amount of points reached. It was somewhere during that sentence that Ali had stopped trying to understand what he was saying and realized that nothing the professor told them would help her manipulate the assessment in her favour.

It had been an expected but frustrating realization. Her

fate was truly out of her hands. She could end up with any designation. Assassin would be the worst. Seeing dead people bleed from their ears was bad enough. She couldn't imagine being the reason for their untimely deaths.

Ali shuddered at the image and heard the weighted metal disks at the end of her dumbbells tinkle in perfect accord.

"That didn't look like a nice thought at all."

Ali glanced at the Recruit steeling his abs with a round of sit-ups next to her. "Hey, we've met."

The Recruit smiled, wiping the sweat from his brow with a towel. "Yes, in the entrance hall. I'm Jacob, by the way. Rt2853."

"Ali, Rt2120."

"Nice to meet you, Ali. Now, what was that thought?"

Persistent. But he had a nice smile. "It would suck to be an Assassin."

"Oh, but I hope not."

It took her only a second to grasp his meaning. *Damn.* Red suffused her cheeks.

His laughter rolled through her. "Don't worry, I won't tell on you."

She was still struggling for an appropriate apology when Trainer halted the warm up.

"Form three groups. Group one takes the treadmills, group two the bicycles and group three the rowing machines. Now!"

Ali slid into the seat of the rowing machine closest to her.

"This is a ninety minute endurance test. Highest settings. Use your masks."

She slid the transparent rubber mask that would measure

her breathing performance over her face and grabbed the handle that was resting on the angled iron rod between her legs.

"Go."

She pushed with her feet, bringing her arms up and towards her chest at the same time. The metal chain connected to the handle rattled then pulled tight, rotating the motor hidden in its casing at the front of the machine.

Ali exhaled a breath, fogging up the mask as moisture condensed on the inner walls. She allowed her arms and legs to collapse forward for a split second before pulling back again.

An hour and a half later, she barely kept from falling off the bike when Trainer finally announced the end of the round robin exercise.

Ali had been forced into regular endurance tests at the Centre, but none of them had been as long, or as hard, as this one. Trainer hadn't lied. He would push them to their limits.

"Recruits! Against the wall!"

She stumbled into line.

"From now on you will earn your right to leave training. Every morning and every evening, I will pick four Recruits at random. I will challenge each one with a single martial arts move. If you can block the move you are free to leave, if you can't you will be in pain...and you will earn yourself another thirty minutes on the treadmill."

Trainer stopped in front of Jacob, who had somehow ended up next to her. His face had lost the rakish charm and turned into a mask of concentration. His eyes never stopped moving as they followed Trainer's every movement.

"Each one of you is trapped on three sides." Trainer allowed his words to sink in, until a number of Recruits shifted nervously. "Your only way out...your only way to leave is through me."

The punch came so fast, Ali almost missed the movement.

Ali stared at Jacob's hand wrapped around Trainer's fist mere centimetres from the Recruit's face and felt her breath explode from her lungs. Trainer hadn't pulled the punch.

"Good." Trainer let his hand glide out of Jacob's grip, his shoulders relaxing. "You can go."

Jacob didn't move. He was still staring at the gap in front of him, where Trainer's fist had been a moment ago.

"Move!"

Ali barely kept from flinching at the harsh command, but it seemed to break the spell Jacob was under. He didn't look too steady on his feet when he left the hall. Ali felt her own legs shaking in sympathy. That fist would have easily broken his nose.

"Close ranks."

She shifted to close the gap and ended up in front of Trainer.

Her heart rate jumped, then steadied as she forced it back down with an exercise from *Biofeedback Studies*.

Ali explored her range of movement.

The wall at her back and the bodies on both sides rendered any attempt to evade an attack useless. There was no leverage to pull back or twist. Her block had to be straight to the front.

Trainer started pacing down the line.

The crunch of knuckle against bone had Ali's stomach turning as it echoed through the hall a second later. From her position against the wall, she couldn't see who had been hit, but the yelp of pain made it clear that the recipient of the blow hadn't managed to block in time.

Another yelp rang through the hall, turning Ali's head towards the sound.

Trainer had reached the end of the line and was pacing back in her direction.

"One more."

She saw his eyes travel the line of Recruits and snag on hers.

Ali caught herself praying.

His steps picked up as he neared her position. She tried to sink into her defence stance, but the wall at her back prevented any movement.

She knew first hand, from the assessment in the morning, how fast he was. A Hybrid. How could she ever...

His leg slammed into the thigh of another Recruit. A successful block, although Ali was almost certain the Recruit would have bruises from the force of the impact.

Trainer's eyes widened in surprise and, for a second, he looked almost disappointed. Then his features smoothed out.

"Good," he said. "Class dismissed."

Moving away from the wall, Ali's eyes searched the hall for the injured. A pale-faced Recruit was clutching at her shoulder about ten meters to Ali's left. The joint didn't seem to be dislocated, but Ali doubted that that was more than a small consolation for the female whose eyes were scrunched shut against the pain. Further down the hall, another Recruit had doubled over holding his stomach. She started towards him, but he saw her and waved her off with a weak gesture of his free hand. A second later, he straightened, his face contorting in pain. She caught his eye again, motioning to her mobi. He glanced at his own and gave her a thumbs-up.

No major internal bleeding. The steel band around her chest loosened slightly then tightened again, when she saw both injured Recruits staggering towards the treadmills. If every training session was like this she wouldn't have to worry about her designation. She'd be lucky to survive until her inauguration.

Chapter 4

"Pair combat."

It was the next day and her second morning training session.

Ali looked around. Rob had been assigned to a different training group late last night to even out the numbers, and a large male Recruit was heading in Beth's direction who, despite having a disposition to become a non-competitive Hybrid after inauguration, was required to complete a minimum amount of physical training.

Ali was about to consider the other members of their class when Beth stepped back, her eyes huge in her suddenly pale face. Wondering what had her friend so upset, Ali took a closer look at the male Recruit and felt her blood freeze. On his right cheek was a white puckered scar.

Chosen.

The word flashed through her mind along with a number of images she had seen on the LiveNet, all of them appalling in their violence. The fraternity of fanatically dedicated Recruits and Hybrids assimilated their members in the years before inauguration by inflicting a face wound with a corrosive blade – an induction ritual they thoroughly enjoyed. They considered violence as one of the main pillars to achieve their goals and often singled out weaker Recruits to bully and victimise. The Program put up with the fraternity simply because it was sometimes more efficient to compel a willing Hybrid to carry out a brute-force assignment, than allow the microchip to overrule the moral dilemma of a non-violent specimen.

Fear for her friend slithered through Ali's body.

Beth took another step back. The Chosen followed her. At least a foot taller than Beth, he towered over her as he chased her backwards through the hall. His large hand wrapped around her arm putting an end to her retreat, a few feet from where Ali stood.

"...you pair up with me."

Beth shook her head, frantically trying to twist out of his grip without causing a scene.

"Beth." Ali sidled up to the pair, before fear could hold her back.

"Ali." Her name was a plea on Beth's lips.

Still holding onto Beth's arm, Scar-guy dismissed Ali with a single glance.

"There you are." Ali gave Beth an encouraging smile, praying her voice would carry to where Trainer was standing, talking to Jacob. It did. Out of the corner of her eye, Ali saw Trainer frown at their little group then come towards them in big, ground-eating strides.

"Pair combat I said, not a threesome." His gaze swept over Beth, the Chosen, then came to rest on Ali.

Ali lowered her head, in an attempt to look appropriately

contrite. "I couldn't find my partner." She indicated Beth.

"Seems like your partner already has a partner." His eyes pointedly snagged on the hand locked around Beth's arm.

Ali stilled the nervous flutter in her belly. "The Chosen wanted to team up with Beth because she was weak. I overheard him say he couldn't be bothered to train hard today." And if Trainer ever found out she was lying...

Trainer's gaze narrowed as he focused on the Chosen. "Is she speaking the truth?"

But Scar-guy wasn't even listening. A vein had started pounding angrily in his forehead at Ali's words. His hand fell open around Beth's arm, as he advanced on Ali instead. Every instinct in her body told her to flee, but Ali held her ground.

"Maybe I should spar with you." The growl sent a shiver of dread down her spine.

No matter how this dispute was resolved today, she had definitely made an enemy. *Enemies*, she corrected herself, because the Chosen never stood alone.

More shivers skittered down her back.

Look him in the eye. Don't let him see your fear.

The pep-talk helped...as did Trainer when he suddenly kicked the Chosen's legs out from under him. "I've asked you a question. I expect an answer."

The Chosen looked surprised, although anger still radiated from his body. "She was free," he said between clenched teeth.

"So is Rt2853." The Trainer pointed towards Jacob who stood slightly off to the side, waiting to be assigned a partner.

"I'd rather take her." The Chosen jutted his chin towards Ali.

"And I say you spar with him."

Scar-guy finally rolled to his feet shooting daggers at Ali and Beth before turning his back and launching into a vicious attack against Jacob. Jacob blocked and counter-attacked with fluid grace.

Ali could hear Beth's relieved exhale of air and felt her own tension drain from her body. *For now*, she thought, because she knew it wouldn't be the last she had seen of the aggressive Chosen.

"You two." Trainer had clearly reached the end of his patience. "Start sparring. Now!"

They crouched down and were locked in combat a second later.

Beth launched a sequence that brought them face to face. "Thanks, Ali. But you shouldn't have done that." Ali parried a half-hearted kick then turned back to face Beth once more.

"Yes, I should have."

"We'll pay double next time."

"We won't." She was hopeful that at least Beth would be out of the limelight, which was good because she doubted the other girl could handle a fight with anyone even mildly serious. Beth was unbelievably meek for someone who had spent over two decades in the Program. There was no doubt in Ali's mind that the Chosen would eat meek for breakfast. "*I* will."

She saw Beth wince.

Yes, Ali thought, she would most definitely pay. But she would put up one hell of a fight. She had a lot of experience with that. She just hoped it would be enough.

"I'll manage." Ali said with a confidence she didn't feel, and attacked from the front.

***

Ali watched the professor rush into the hall, a sleek, black notepad clamped under his arm. His hair was even more tousled than the day before.

Next to her, Rob shifted almost imperceptibly. "Professor Tuft." His deadpan whisper travelled no further than her ear.

Ali bit her lip.

"All hail, Recruits and welcome back to the *Inauguration Basics* lecture. Today's lesson should give you a better understanding of the inauguration process."

The professor slid the notepad into the equally black docking station towards the right corner of his lecture console, connecting it to the inbuilt DID he had previously used for his presentations.

"DID four sense recording, open."

The blinds on the windows lowered to block out the daylight and a hologram appeared next to the professor, turning the front of the lecture theatre into a stage.

Ali's lip slid from between her teeth, all urge to laugh fleeing her body as she took in the first scene of the recording in horrified amazement.

A male Recruit was strapped facedown to a reclining seat, his arms and legs immobilized by shackles that forced his wrists and ankles against the padding of the chair. Light glinted off a metal ring that wrapped around his head, holding it in place for the MediBot standing at an angle behind him with a deactivated laser in one steel-plated hand. Off to the side, two Medics in matching white coats alternately studied the electronic notepads in their hands and the steady line of the Recruit's heart rate displayed on the wall-mounted Biomonitor on the opposite side of the seat.

Ali had seen four sense recordings before, but none of them had been as real as this one. The three-dimensional image was crystal clear, all items and people weighted to perfection. The smell of disinfectant – so closely entwined with Ali's memories of the medical facilities at the Centre – wafted in her direction. Tension crackled in the air with every intermittent beep of the Biomonitor that cut through the thick silence.

It was easy – too easy – to imagine that she was indeed sitting in the inauguration room, watching the Recruit, bound and helpless, waiting for the implantation of the microchip. Only the fact that she could see the recording from three different angles at once reminded her that what she saw was a recount of the past rather than a live event.

The Recruit suddenly jerked in his shackles, sending his heart rate skyrocketing before it plunged back down as he forced his body under control.

Ali drew in a sharp breath. She had thought he was anaesthetised for the procedure. Obviously, she had been wrong.

How long has he been lying there, motionless, before fear got the better of him, she wondered, feeling the small hairs on her arms rise as goose bumps covered her body.

The Medics lifted their heads simultaneously at the commotion, their gaze sliding expertly over bonds and shackles, before dismissing the struggle as insignificant. One of them turned towards the audience, his flapping white coat hitting the professor's leg, who quickly stepped out of the way.

"All hail, Recruits." The Medic's eyes swept the room in an eerily accurate arc, belying the fact that he was merely talking to the recording device that had captured the scene. "We are now ready to start the inauguration procedure. MedicaOne, commence."

The MediBot, which had stood motionless up to now, came to life, bending over the Recruit and lifting the small laser. The instrument activated, a low hum vibrating in the air as it approached the smoothly shaved base of the Recruit's head. A beam of light shot from its pen-like tip, cutting through the tissue on the Recruit's scalp in a neat line, until the smell of burnt flesh permeated the air. On the Biomonitor, the Recruit's speeding heartbeat drew an increasingly jagged line.

Taking shallow breaths to keep the sickening smell at bay, Ali felt her body recoil at the dispassionate look in the Medic's eyes when he turned his face towards the audience once more.

"As is standard for the inauguration procedure, the patient is not under anaesthetic. Thanks to the advanced breeding of Hybrids, the area at the base of the head contains a minimum number of nerve endings and, as a result, is mostly numb from birth."

Ali probed the spot above her neck with trembling fingers, first stroking then scratching when the lighter impression didn't register. The Medic was right. She couldn't feel any pain. But that didn't divert from the fact that the Recruit in the inauguration chair was barely holding onto his control.

In the recording, MedicaOne had finished making the incision and was now sliding the microchip out of its protective plastic sleeve. MedicaOne's robotic arm hovered over the Recruit's head.

"Fit the chip."

The Recruit's fists clenched, and the heart rate indicator on the Biomonitor leapt even higher as the chip slowly disappeared into the brain matter.

The Medic surveyed the reading. "Upon contact with the brainstem, the microchip automatically activates phase one of the inauguration process, causing a temporary drop in heart rate and brain activity."

Sure enough, the indicator for the heart rate dipped a second later.

As if on command, the Medics unbuckled the Recruit's restraints, while MedicaOne finished closing the wound.

"Stand up." A command from a Medic, something the Recruit wouldn't be able to refuse for the rest of his life, if the chip worked correctly.

It did. The Recruit pushed to his feet.

The Medic held out a surgeon's circular saw. "Cut your palm."

The words were spoken with an utter lack of emotion, so different from the desperation in the Recruit's eyes that it sent tingles running through Ali's body.

The Recruit's pupils dilated, his arm reaching instinctively for the powered-on instrument. Fighting with every cell of his body, the Recruit curled his fingers away from the saw. They opened back up a second later, as if pulled by invisible strings. The Medic shoved the instrument into the Recruit's palm, satisfaction gleaming in his eyes when the Recruit's hand automatically closed around the handle.

The tingles in Ali's body grew worse, and she belatedly realized that she was holding her breath, starving her body of oxygen. She sucked in a breath, and the warning shock triggered by her mobi's survival support module, ebbed off.

Ali forced herself to keep her breaths measured while she watched the Recruit's left hand slowly unfurl, exposing the unprotected skin of his palm to the steadily advancing metal teeth of the rotating blade.

Gleaming beads of sweat rolled down the side of the Recruit's head. He tried desperately to pull the saw away from his palm, realizing with every inch it moved closer – despite his efforts – his resistance was futile.

The blade bit into his flesh painting his skin red with blood.

Ali flinched and curled her own hand.

"Release."

The saw clattered to the floor as the Recruit stared in shock at what he had done. Horror dawned a second later at the realization that his mind, body, and soul were no longer his own.

"Transition to Hybrid status stage one successful."

The hologram froze.

Ali gulped to keep her breakfast in her stomach. In another five days, it would be her getting up from that chair, realizing that the little freedom she had known in her life was taken from her forever. Realizing with finality that they could give her any command and she would be unable to resist.

She fisted her hand harder, feeling the flex of strong fingers against her palm. Her eyes dropped, and she realized with a start that she was clutching Rob's hand in a white-knuckled grip.

***

Ali still felt slightly queasy when she walked to the training hall, hours later. She had finished her lunch at Rob's insistence, but regretted giving in the moment the professor mentioned compulsion in the afternoon study class and her brain recalled the horrified look in the Recruit's eyes as he stared at his hand dripping with blood.

"Look who we have here."

The slow drawl froze Ali's body mid-stride, even before she saw the two Chosen blocking the hallway in front of her.

"If that isn't the little Recruit who gave Otis so much trouble in the morning." The taller Chosen advanced on her, crowding into her personal space. Chosen number two circled to her side.

Ali took a step back and to the side, angling her body to keep both Chosen in her line of vision. Fear throbbed through her bloodstream. Only her years of training kept her from diving head first into panic.

"Don't you know better than to mess with the big guys, little girl?" Tall-guy asked, his voice a mixture of curiosity, hostility, and some sadistic quality that made Ali's stomach clench in remembrance of Trainer at the Centre.

Her fingers curled involuntarily.

Steady heart. Steady breathing.

Her body responded to the unspoken commands. The Program had trained her well. But, unless she wanted to attack, all she could do was retreat. Her shoulders hit the wall.

The Chosen smirked.

"Hey, Jay." He ran his gaze down the length of her body, sneering at her size. "I think the little rat here needs a lesson."

Jay's grunt of agreement was right in her ear making Ali jump, before she could suppress the reaction.

"What do you say, Rat?"

His hand reached out, tracing the side of her face, down her neck.

Ali tensed her muscles. "And what if I give you a lesson instead?" She jabbed at the Chosen's eyes, before he had a chance to process her words, forcing him to step back. His hand fell away. She had just enough time to crouch before they attacked in tandem.

Ali blocked a punch, then another. The blow to her wrist was so fast she didn't stand a chance. It looked almost casual when it happened, but the pain exploding through her arm with a second's delay was anything but. Tears sprang to her eyes, blurring the Chosens' movements, making her easy prey. A fist connected with her ribs driving the air from her lungs, another hit her vulnerable side.

Ali doubled over.

"That's enough, Jay. Otis wants to play with her too. Move."

A push against her shoulder punctuated his order.

Ali allowed her legs to give out and crumpled to the floor. Let them carry her.

"You stupid—"

The ringing in her ears drowned out the rest of the profanity as a large hand backhanded her across the face.

Ali tasted blood.

She felt, more than saw, being hauled up by two strong arms and propelled towards the training hall at the end of the corridor. Grasping for balance, she stumbled into the side wall. Her wrist twisted to absorb the impact, sending searing white-hot pain shooting up her arm. Light exploded behind her eyes. Ali exhaled in agony.

There was no way she could fight Otis like this.

Ali checked her mobi. The digital display swam in front of her eyes. She squinted. Not broken. The pain could have fooled her.

Forcing herself to relax the muscles in her arm, she flicked her wrist hard and heard the satisfying pop of bones, muscles, and tendons realigning even as another lightning bolt of pain almost brought her to her knees.

Jay growled next to her, grabbed her around the waist and shoved her through the open doors of the near-empty training hall.

For once, Ali prayed to see a green uniform amongst the sparsely scattered blue, but Trainer wasn't there.

The clock on the wall said it was still ten minutes early. Would she last that long? Her wrist throbbed.

Unlikely.

"Hey, Otis."

The Chosen turned from where he sat on one of the benches in the weights area.

"We've brought you a present."

An unholy smile lit up his face. "Well, well, look at that." The dumbbell he had been holding dropped to the floor with a resounding thud. "Where did you find that lovely present, Mace?"

Mace. Figures.

"In the hallway, looking for trouble."

"Was she now?" Otis cracked his neck. "It seems I get to have an extra special warm up today." He came to a stop in front of her, and Ali fought to stand her ground. The fact that Jay and Mace stood half a step behind her helped.

"No permanent damage." Mace's voice brooked no argument, but did little to alleviate Ali's fears. There were a lot of painful possibilities between perfectly healthy and permanent damage.

Ali felt Mace and Jay retreat, but didn't dare turn her back on Otis to watch them leave. It was the right choice, because a second later his fist angled straight for her nose.

Ali blocked.

She barely had time to duck before another punch, this one aimed at her already bruised cheekbone, cut through the air. She counterattacked, but Otis dodged in time.

Where were the other Recruits? Why didn't they help her?

Enemies, plural, Ali reminded herself. Retaliation would be swift. Nobody wanted to chance pissing off the Chosen. Except for maybe Jacob, but he wasn't here yet.

Her fist connected with Otis's ribs, driving the breath out

of his lungs. Not waiting for him to recover, she followed up with a three-kick attack. He staggered back.

She almost had him, when she suddenly saw a movement in the corner of her eyes. Ali turned just in time to block a punch to her kidneys. *Mace.*

There was no way she could win against both of them.

Otis came at her again. Punch. Kick. She blocked, the sound of flesh on flesh loud in the deathly quiet training hall. In the back of her mind, Ali registered that the other Recruits had ceased their warming up and had formed a circle around them. *Cowards.*

Another series of blows rained down on her, one of them hitting the side of her head with the force of a sledge hammer. Ali staggered, caught herself. Dizziness swept through her.

She felt her limbs grow heavy, her reaction time slowing. Her wrist throbbed in time with her rapid pulse. Otis grinned, seeing her struggle.

Mace kept in the back, only intervening when Ali seemed to get the upper hand. He wasn't interested in the fight, Ali realized. He just wanted to make sure that Otis got his revenge.

"Aim for her left wrist."

Not helpful, asshole.

Punch. Smack. Her whole body hurt, but she was still blocking. Then, Otis managed to swipe her wrist.

Pain exploded.

She saw the next attack coming, but this time she was a split-second too slow. She deflected Otis's kick, but her balance was shot. The world spun. The floor rushed towards her. She took the fall on her side, her wrist curled against her belly. Her temple hit the floor.

"Now you'll pay, bitch."

Ali used her good arm to push herself into a sitting position, ignoring the nausea tightening her throat. A carousel of faces whirled in front of her eyes. She silently pleaded with all of them. Didn't anybody here have the decency to step in and help her?

Anyone besides Beth, Ali thought, surprised and horrified when she saw her friend struggling in Jay's grip.

"She's next." Otis's smile was pure evil.

"Let her g—"

His kick missed Ali's jaw by a fraction. Time slowed. Otis used his momentum to shift almost imperceptibly, and Ali knew he was through playing. His next strike would force Ali to use her injured wrist in a defensive move. Then he would follow up with a kick to her unprotected middle. It was a classic combination. One she was defenceless against, from her position on the floor.

Aiming for damage control more than anything else, Ali used her good arm to block the first strike, turning her side to Otis. She barely had time to curl into a ball, before she heard the thump. But the pain never came.

Carefully, she lifted her arm from where she had thrown it protectively over her head and felt her eyes widen in surprise.

Otis was lying on the floor clutching his chest, struggling for air. An Assassin loomed over him, anger shooting like fire from his deep blue eyes.

Not any Assassin, Ali realized with a start, when the

yellow arrow on his left pectoral registered. Unique identifier A001. The leader of the Assassins. Her breath caught.

All anger drained from his face when he looked at her cowering form. "I'm Sam," he said, ignoring Program introduction protocol. "Can you stand up?"

"I can try." She hesitated only a second before she grabbed the hand he offered. He pulled her to her feet with ease. When he let go, Ali saw the floor fly towards her. A strong arm grabbed her, pulled her upright then wrapped around her shoulders. "Are you alright?"

"Dizzy."

Sam steadied her gently.

"Better?"

"Yes." She didn't trust herself to nod.

"Can you stand on your own for a few seconds?"

"I think so," she said haltingly.

He loosened his hold carefully, and Ali was relieved when the world swayed only a little.

"Good girl."

She followed him with her eyes as he made his way to where Jay was still holding onto Beth's arms with a death grip.

"You might want to let go of her, boy."

A fine tremor shook the Chosen's body.

"Now!"

Jay's hands fell open, and Ali saw the Assassin's jaw clench when he noticed the bruises on Beth's skin. His shoulders bunched.

"Thank you." Beth wrapped her arms around Sam's body

and buried her face against his chest, before he could take a swing at Jay.

The Assassin stood, stunned for several seconds. "You…You're welcome."

"This isn't over yet." Otis had regained his feet and looked at Ali with unadulterated hatred. "You think one Assassin is going to keep you safe from the whole fraternity?"

"One Assassin doesn't have to." The voice, coming from the doorway, was quiet; the black-clad man it belonged to almost invisible in the shadowed hallway. Except for the yellow arrow blazing across the left side of his chest. "My squad will."

The Chosen blanched.

Ali gulped a big breath. There was only one squad in the Program.

Tasked to protect the board and any high risk targets in the human population, the Protection Squad was known to undergo the harshest training of all designations, even before their tailor-made microchips turned them as close to super-hybrid as physically possible. Virtually invincible individually, the members of the Protection Squad were a close knit group that made the Chosen fraternity look like a few loose threads of cotton stitched together. And they all bowed to the command of one man. P001, the leader of the squad.

The man who had just declared she was under his protection.

The Recruits in the hall took a collective step back. Ali would have too, if she hadn't worried about falling flat on her face. She averted her eyes instead and saw Otis slink back to stand with Mace and Jay.

"Thought so," P001 said, and it sounded like rolling thunder.

"I think Aiden has the situation handled." Sam winked at Ali, extracting himself from Beth's grip. "Let's get the two of you out of here."

"But Trainer—" Beth started.

"Aiden's going to handle him, too."

Ali sneaked another glance at the man who commanded obedience with his mere presence. She had no doubt he could – would – handle the Hybrid Trainer with ease.

The crowd parted in front of them as Sam led Ali and Beth out of the training hall.

***

Ali leaned back in the reclining seat and closed her eyes. The low hum of the handheld body scanner gliding over her head was starting to give her a headache.

She was glad that Sam had been with her when they had arrived at the medical facilities. The Medic on duty had taken one look at the leader of the Assassins and had waved them straight through the full waiting area and into the examination room.

"I think I've cracked my skull." Ali didn't know why she said it. The scanner should pick up on the fissure soon enough.

"No cracks," the Medic disagreed with her assessment. "You have a concussion, though."

Impossible. "I'm sure I've cracked my skull."

"Your skull is perfectly healthy, Recruit. You have a

simple concussion."

Anxiety gripped her. "I don't." Was that really her voice? Her head throbbed. Why didn't he listen to her? "I have a fracture," she insisted.

"Rt2120, you have sustained a concussion and it is clearly affecting your emotional state. I need you to calm down now."

He was wrong. He had to be.

Something sharp pricked the soft skin on the inside of her elbow, but Ali couldn't stop looking at the Medic. "I know I have a fracture." The words sounded slurred. Why couldn't she speak properly? Her tongue felt too big. Her lips were numb. She had to tell him. It was important. She didn't want her brain...leaking through her skull. "I have a fracture," she repeated, desperately trying to hold onto her train of thought. She had to make him understand. "I see the crack...when I close my eyes."

Her world went black.

Chapter 5

The scent of steel and disinfectant tickled Ali's nose when she sank back onto the pillows with a groan the next morning. Sitting up was a bad idea. Her whole body hurt.

She turned to scan her injury report on the Biomonitor, for the fifth time in the last half hour, and wished the damn device would stop beeping in perfect synchrony with the throbbing in her head. Maybe then she could remember what it said about her condition long enough to feel reassured.

Or not, she thought, looking at the list filling half the screen with words like concussion, sprained wrist, split lip, and at least twelve mentions of bruises on various parts of her body. Nothing severe – or so the last line item tried to convince her. It still hurt like hell, thank you very much.

The worst of it all was that even bruised and battered, she had to count herself lucky. If Otis had managed to carry out his last kick, if Sam hadn't saved her, and if…Aiden. Ali suppressed a shiver. She had only managed a couple of quick glances at the Protector, but it had been enough to convince her that everything they said about the Protection Squad was true. Aiden looked like he bent iron rods for fun.

"Ali?"

The room circled around her, then circled some more after her head stopped moving in the direction of the door.

"Hi, Rob." She had never before realized how difficult it was to smile at a moving target. "How did you know I was here?" He hadn't been in the hall. Or had he? Wasn't he in a different training group altogether? Ali fought to sort through the jumbled memories in her brain.

"How could I *not* know you were here when everyone talks about the Recruit who took on three Chosen at the same time?"

"Yes, that was a pretty stupid idea."

He pressed his lips together as if he wanted to agree, but was worried he might upset her in her fragile state. His gaze glided over her body, touching briefly on each bruise. "I heard you put up one hell of a fight."

"I tried." Ali gingerly touched the considerable bump at her temple. "I failed, in the end."

Rob winced. "So it's true? Two leaders rescued you?"

"Yes."

"Amazing." He sank down onto the bed, next to her thigh, shaking his head.

The movement of the mattress, small as it was, rattled Ali's skull. She closed her eyes.

A warm hand closed around her shoulder. "Are you okay?"

Ali blinked. Rob's face was inches from hers. Concern had turned his eyes a darker shade of brown.

"Do you have a twin?"

"Huh?"

"I can see two of you."

"I'll get a nurse."

"Just backing up will help."

He looked at her, confused for a second, then chuckled. "You must be getting better, if you are strong enough to pull my leg."

She didn't feel better at all.

He moved back, slightly, allowing the hand on her shoulder to stroke down her arm, until he could grab her hand and softly rub his fingers across her skin, just underneath her bruised knuckles. The gesture startled Ali. She tried to pull her hand away, but his fingers tightened on her.

"Now tell me," he said, effectively ending her struggles, as if he knew that her brain wasn't capable of multitasking at the moment. "Why were the two most dangerous Hybrid leaders in your training class last night?"

Ali shrugged her shoulders with care, moving their joined hands in the process. "Sam didn't say."

Rob's thumb stopped moving for a moment, before resuming the stroking rhythm. "He asked you to call him Sam? Not sir Sam? Not sir? Not even A001?"

"Sir Sam? Rob, are *you* feeling alright?"

"Just asking." He gave her a wry smile. "You don't do things halfway, do you?"

"I guess not," she conceded. "I've definitely gone all out pissing off the Chosen."

"You really shouldn't have done that."

"And what a gem of advice that is. Thanks, Rob." She pulled at her arm again, and this time he let go.

"My advice is that stupid, huh?"

"No. It's very smart. But I already know that. I'm not stupid either." She didn't know why she felt the sudden urge to lash out. Maybe a symptom of the concussion. Maybe her belated reaction to him taking liberties with her hand. Ali curled her fingers into her palm, ignoring the strange feeling of loss. The caring gesture had been disconcertingly nice.

"I know you aren't stupid." Rob frowned at her, as if even the thought was ridiculous. "I'm just worried about you."

"Why?" Ali asked, genuinely confused. "It's the first time I've gotten in trouble in months."

"One month. One."

This time it was Ali who frowned. Rob wasn't supposed to know about the confrontation at the Centre.

She blinked, cursing her brain for turning so much slower than normal.

How *did* he know? He hadn't been there. Just her and Trainer…and the human nurse writing the electronic incident report and logging it in Ali's medical record.

Ali looked at her friend with narrowed eyes.

Two red streaks appeared high on Rob's cheekbones, like two warning flags against his tanned skin.

Ali grit her teeth. "You had no right to hack my file."

He dragged the hand that had been holding hers over his face. "It was before I knew you better. It was practice." He sucked in a breath, as if he only now realized how bad it sounded. "I…I'm sorry, Ali."

Ali tried to hang onto the anger holding the pain in her body at bay a little bit longer, but the look on Rob's face made it impossible to stay mad at him. Soft-brown, apologetic puppy eyes. "Don't ever use me as one of your experiments again."

He lifted his head slowly. "I won't. I promise."

For once, no smile lurked in the corners of his mouth.

"And don't tell anybody else about the incident." It was hard enough to forget the bruising force of Trainer's metal-clad fists striking her body over and over again, without being pestered with questions by other Recruits.

Rob looked almost affronted. "I would never…"

Ali just glared at him.

"I promise that too."

***

At noon, Ali was sitting up in bed, when Beth came into the room.

The headache had finally subsided an hour before, and she felt almost hy-bred again. She mustn't look any better, though, Ali concluded when Beth's eyes filled with tears.

"Don't you dare cry," Ali immediately forestalled her friend's waterworks. "It wasn't your fault."

"Yes, it was," Beth sniffed. "It should be me in that bed."

"Heaven forbid, and have *me* watch beside *your* bed, all night?" Ali shivered in mock horror, relieved when Beth gave her a watery smile. "Thanks for doing that," Ali added more seriously. "Although, I wonder how you got the nurse to suspend your sleeping cycle?"

Beth's honey-coloured skin darkened a shade. "I told her you have singlehandedly taken on three Recruits."

"And?"

"I may have also implied that a human wouldn't stand a

chance, should you wake up in a violent mood."

Ali laughed. "She believed you?"

"She was new."

"I think I've underestimated you," Ali said grinning. "First you cosy up to an Assassin, hours later you threaten a nurse."

"I wasn't…," Beth said, her face suffused with colour. "I didn't cosy up to Sam."

"The full body hug could have fooled me."

"Must have been your concussion playing tricks on you then," Beth grumbled.

"And she lies, too."

A giggle escaped her friend's throat.

"How did Sam tackle Otis so quickly, anyway?" Ali asked, once Beth had regained her breath.

"It was quite amazing." Beth positively bounced with glee at the memory. "He came out of nowhere like a bullet, driving his shoulder into Otis's chest." She thumped her fist against her breast bone hard enough to make Ali flinch.

A pang shot through Ali's frontal lobe at the sudden sharp movement. She winced. "Without the theatrics, please."

Beth waved her off. "You should have seen it," she continued, her eyes sparkling. "The way Otis toppled over..." Another giggle escaped her. "And then Sam told Jay to let go of me. And Jay did. Just like that. You know what he said? Sam, I mean." She didn't wait for Ali's reply. "He said to let him know if they ever bother me again…uh…bother us again."

"Uh-huh."

"You know what I was thinking?"

"What?"

"The professor didn't really explain that whole compulsion thing very well. Something this important, one would have thought he'd give it a little bit more lecture time."

Ali looked at her friend and wondered how Beth had suddenly made the leap from a bald Hybrid Assassin to the exuberant human, whose hairdo rivalled that of Einstein.

"Take Sam, for example." Beth answered Ali's unspoken question moments later. "I know he ranks higher than any other Assassin. But who commands whom between leaders?" She looked at Ali questioningly, then continued when Ali just shrugged her shoulders. "Where do the Trainers, Marshals, and Medics fit into the system; where will I fit in once I'm inaugurated? Will I have the power to command the leader of the Assassins…for example?" She gnawed at her bottom lip

"Would you like to," Ali asked, "have your own pet Assassin, catering to your every whim?"

Beth flushed crimson.

Ali choked. "It was supposed to be a joke."

"Of course it was," Beth said, her gaze sliding away.

Ali just stared.

"You've seriously thought about it," she said finally, trying to wrap her mind around the unthinkable. "You've met him once and you're already contemplating a relationship with the leader of the Assassins."

It was…unbelievable.

Not the relationship part. Although Hybreeders were the

only members of the Program who were activated to be fertile, romantic relationships between other Hybrids weren't unheard of.

No, it was the combination of designations and personalities that made this pairing so unlikely.

"That's not what I said, at all," Beth defended herself.

"You didn't have to *Ms Psychiatrist*," Ali answered. "It's called nonverbal communication. That sunburn on your face is a dead giveaway."

Beth opened her mouth, no doubt to deny everything Ali had concluded, when a rumbling voice interrupted them from the doorway, making them flinch in unison.

"Rt2030."

"Yes, sir." Beth came to attention, even as an uneasy feeling settled in the pit of Ali's stomach. What was the Leader of the Protection Squad doing here?

"Go and get another dose of intravenous sunblock from the medical facilities."

Beth blinked in confusion for a second, before her training kicked in.

"Yes, sir. Right away." She turned back to the bed. "I was about to leave anyway."

No you weren't, Ali thought.

Beth shot a sidelong glance at Aiden. "Indeed, I was."

The uneasy feeling in Ali's stomach increased. She didn't want to be alone with the Protector. It was one thing to be saved in a training hall full of Recruits with an Assassin standing by her side; it was quite another being sought out by Aiden in the medical facilities, in a room with a door that closed quietly behind Beth.

Ali took a shuddering breath.

The rational part of her brain wondered what she was afraid of. Aiden was a Protector. He had even offered her his protection from the Chosen.

Still, the tremulous smile she plastered on her face tasted suspiciously like a plea for mercy. "Thanks for coming by."

There, that was nice and neutral. Now if she could just stop her hands from shaking.

Ali dug her fingers into her thighs.

Aiden regarded her dispassionately.

"Sam did quite a number on Otis," he finally said, completely ignoring both her statement and body language. "I hear Otis is still under observation for breathing problems."

Ali wasn't surprised. Sam was huge, almost as big as Aiden, and definitely bigger than the Chosen. As an Assassin, Sam would know exactly how to inflict maximum damage with every strike and how to hold back to keep from killing his opponent.

Ali wondered which one of the two tasks was more difficult for the Assassin. Was the killer instinct so deeply anchored in his genes that he had to fight the impulse constantly? Had he fought it when he had laid an arm around Ali to steady her?

The thought was troubling. But more disconcerting was the question, why Ali wasn't afraid of Sam, when he could have so easily snapped her neck, crushed her larynx or pummelled her heart until it stopped beating? Why was she afraid of Aiden instead? It didn't make sense.

Then the Protector took a step towards her, and she felt

it again. That primal fear. Prey in the eyes of a predator.

Ali forced her body to remain still, her heart rate to remain steady.

Aiden's gaze slid towards the Biomonitor next to her, before settling on her face.

He set a thumbnail-sized metal disk on the nightstand next to her bed. "A panic button," he explained, his eyes tracking her features, as if he was trying to figure out what she was thinking. As if he wanted to see into her mind. "I could have you injected with one. It would make things easier for both of us. It would notify me whenever you're experiencing high stress levels. But your level of Protection doesn't extend that far. Therefore, the manual option." He tapped the button once with his index finger. "Use it. Don't misuse it."

Ali swallowed hard. "Thanks."

For a moment, he studied her mutely. "I don't require gratitude. Protecting the weak is in my nature."

Ali sucked in a breath. Nobody had called her weak in a long time. Not since the day she had learned how to fight back.

Aiden didn't seem to care that he had offended her. His face stayed impassive, his expression shuttered. Still, Ali had the strange feeling that he had baited her on purpose. Had he intended to force a reaction? To what end?

She closed her hand around the panic button, still slightly warm from the heat of his skin. How long exactly had he held it in his hand? And what – she wondered – was he hiding behind his impenetrable mask of ice?

***

A few hours later, a middle-aged nurse came into the room to check on her recovery.

"Any more pain?"

Ali shook her head carefully. It still throbbed, but the sparks of pain she had felt with every movement were gone. Being bred to become a Hybrid had its advantages. Faster healing was one of them.

The nurse took a long look at the Biomonitor then used her authorized fingerprint to sign Ali out of the system.

"You may experience fluctuations in the severity of the symptoms over the next few days, especially once the level of intravenous painkillers in your bloodstream drops," she cautioned. "Resting your body and mind will be paramount. I have updated the database to show you're exempted from physical training until your inauguration. However, you will be required to attend mealtimes and lectures as usual. Do you understand these instructions?"

"I do." Ali gave her a docile nod, while inside she was cheering. No more Chosen waiting for her on her way to the training hall. No more lining up against the wall.

"Off you go." The nurse made a shooing motion with her hand, and Ali climbed off the bed.

Back in her room, Ali pulled the panic button from the pocket of her uniform. For some reason, being connected with the deadliest man in the Program in this fashion made her almost as nervous as being within his immediate vicinity.

What if she pressed the button by accident? What if she called him away from another important job?

Don't misuse it.

Ali carefully slid the button into the front pocket of the backpack she had found in her wardrobe. It was safer there. And she was safe too. The hallways leading to the lecture theatres and lunch hall were frequented by far too many Marshals to be dangerous. Or so Ali hoped, because she was not taking that button with her when she left her room tomorrow.

Chapter 6

"Electra, what time is it?" Ali asked the next morning, weaving out of the dimly lit bathroom in a drunken line, groaning when piercing light from the outside sliced through the transparent white curtains and into her brain.

Bad move.

"Blinds, close."

The small motor controlling the blinds came alive with a click and a whir. Seconds later, the light dimmed. Blessed darkness wrapped around her, reducing the splitting headache to a dull throb.

"Good morning, Ali. It is seven-thirty a.m."

The voice Ali had thought pleasant over the last few days reverberated in her skull.

"Talk a little bit louder, will you," she grumbled, immediately annoyed at her disproportionate frustration towards a device that didn't do anything but its job. She was a lousy patient.

"Sound volume control adjusted to higher level."

Ali slapped her hands over her ears as fireworks exploded in her head. "That's *not* what I meant."

"It is what you said," Electra pointed out, still yelling.

Ali ground her teeth. She couldn't win against the logic of a computer.

"Electra, lower your sound volume to ten percent."

She released her ears and heard a quiet rumble. Had the stupid device just told her off for not saying please?

Ali stared at the DID, but the screen remained black. No sound came from the speakers. She must have misheard. Maybe another crazy symptom of the concussion. Ali sighed.

Feeling as if the whole day loomed like an insurmountable obstacle ahead of her, she groped her way across the dark room back to the nightstand to find her sun lenses and heard the sound of a plastic tube hitting the floor.

"Painkillers." Her ears picked up what her mouth had said before her brain registered the meaning.

She bent to grab the tube. Blood rushed to her head until her eyes felt ready to pop out of their sockets. Ali swayed and grabbed blindly for the desk.

Goodness, what – and how much exactly – had they pumped into her veins in the medical facilities yesterday to make her feel so normal? She definitely could do with some more of it.

The pills tasted sweet as she popped two into her mouth and washed them down with some water from the bottle.

She finally found the container with her sun lenses and inserted the tinted disks into her eyes.

Ali braced. "Door, open."

Light from the hallway pierced through the protective barrier of the dark lenses.

"You don't look too good."

She jerked at the sound of Beth's voice outside her door.

"Sorry. I didn't mean to startle you. It's just – I haven't seen you at morning training and figured they probably exempted you. But after seeing you and Aiden yesterday, I just wanted to make sure—"

Ali held up her hand to stem the flow of words. Why was everyone talking so loudly today?

"Thanks Beth."

The other girl regarded her. "Bad headache, huh?" It was a whisper.

Ali braved a nod.

"Breakfast will fix you." Beth looped her arm through Ali's and joyfully steered them in the direction of the breakfast hall.

Ali wasn't sure how food would help to fix her head, but kept her mouth shut. It was the caring that counted, right?

Bright sunlight greeted them outside their building, forcing Ali to squint her eyes. When they entered the breakfast hall a few minutes later, she wished she could do the same with her ears.

Plates clattered against tables, cutlery clanged, glasses clinked and voices chattered in a merry cacophony of noise.

"Too loud," she groaned.

Beth reverted back to her normal voice to be heard above the din. "What's too loud?"

You. "Everything."

"We'll find a quiet corner."

Except there was none.

Ali plopped down on one of the chairs at a conveniently

empty table near the entrance of the hall. "This is good enough." She didn't have the energy to be dragged around the room.

"Are you sure?" Beth shot her a doubtful look, and Ali realized at once why everyone was staring at her. She was sitting in the middle of the *circle of death*, her feet planted firmly where the Hybrid's blood had formed a puddle around his head. Cold fingers squeezed her heart.

"Maybe over there, instead," Ali said, quickly moving to a table slightly further towards the back.

Beth looked relieved. "I'd prefer that. Stay here." She disappeared into the crowd.

When she came back a minute later, her hands were filled with fruits, coffee, and a scone.

"Have that."

She shoved a banana into Ali's hand. Peeled. Ali looked at it, then at Beth.

"My hands work fine."

"Your brain doesn't."

Ali sighed. She guessed she had just proved that to everyone here.

Ali took a careful bite of the banana and swept her gaze around the breakfast hall, feeling oddly removed from all the commotion.

The pills had finally started to kick in and sounds now came to her as if through a wall of cotton. Her eyes seemed to struggle picking up movements in real time, giving her a strange feeling of watching a recording in half slow motion. Her lenses completed the bizarre experience by tinting everything an unusual shade of dark. Above it all, her sense of touch seemed to have exploded until she couldn't help but focus on the velvety texture of the banana being crushed under her fingertips, its soft pulp ground to mush between her teeth.

"You may feel like you're in a fog for a while." Beth regarded her steadily. "That's normal after a concussion."

Yes, there was no doubt that Beth would make a good Psychiatrist after her inauguration.

Inauguration. Ali sat up in alarm. "My final assessment is today." How could she have forgotten something that important?

"Mine too. I'm really nervous. Look." Beth held out her trembling hands.

"Why are *you* nervous? You know the outcome."

Beth gnawed at her lower lip. "I *suspect* the outcome. That's what I tried to tell you the other day. According to the LiveNet, pre-assessments for Psychiatrists are never one-hundred percent reliable as most of us have a second – usually latent – ability which, in some cases, can take unexpected precedence. As far as I know, it has something to do with how this particular designation was derived from other designations. See," Beth elaborated, clearly overcompensating for her anxiousness with a lengthy discourse about her knowledge on the subject, "up until fifty years ago, the Program didn't think Hybrid Psychiatrists were necessary at all. Hybrids were supposed to be super-soldiers. As resilient as robots. The need for a therapist seemed out of place. However, what the Program had forgotten was why our race is better than robots in the first place: our human perception and reasoning. Although the microchip intervenes when a Hybrid breaches Program policy or tries to act against their designation, it doesn't generally tell us *how* to do things. It provides an end goal, but as long as we work towards this goal, there are few restrictions on the path we must take to achieve it. This allows us to handle our assignments a lot more delicately than robots could. It also means that we are sentient beings, and we understand the impact of our actions. Our genetic make-up ensures that we can withstand a large amount of emotional burden, but a lifetime of trauma can become overwhelming – even for us. Just think about a Hybreeder's endless pregnancies. The number of cold-blooded killings Assassins have to carry out. Trainers punishing Recruits on a daily basis. And yes, every now and then, Protectors can fail. Replacement of the affected Hybrids turned out to be uneconomic and so the idea of Hybrid Psychiatrists was born. Initially the aim was to simply create a new designation that could help our race deal with the psychological strain of enforcing New World law. But Hybrid Psychiatrists quickly proved valuable in a variety of situations, including crisis negotiations, human counselling, and criminal profiling. In other words, their work has become highly visible to the human population. Mistakes are impossible to cover up. That's why the Program takes great care about who they inaugurate as a Psychiatrist. They rather assign the latent designation, than risking a public outcry over a Hybrid who wasn't fit for the job." Beth fell silent, her stricken hazel eyes seeking Ali. "What if I'm not good enough? What if I end up as a Hybreeder instead?"

Ali sat in silence, unsure what to say. She wanted to

assure Beth, but they both knew that nothing was definite in the Program, until it was confirmed as an electronic record.

Maybe it was a blessing in disguise that Ali didn't know her designation. At least she couldn't be disappointed, if it didn't work out. Then again, Ali knew she would be disappointed anyway. Because the only designation *she* wanted – free Hybrid – wasn't even an option. "You'll be fine," she said at last, ignoring the feeling that might have just given voice to a lie. "*We* will be fine." A definite lie. Ali shut her mouth.

***

After breakfast, Ali and Beth walked to the lecture theatre together. Although they were still early, many seats were already taken. Several Recruits stood in smaller groups, discussing the upcoming assessment. Nervous excitement filled the room.

Ali felt her skin prickle in anxiety, despite the fog still clogging her brain.

"Shall we sit up there?" Beth pointed towards a couple of empty seats in a row halfway up the stairs.

Ali swept her gaze across the hall hoping to catch a glimpse of Rob. She hadn't seen him, since he admitted to hacking her medical record the day before. What was more surprising; she missed him.

Ali gave up on the third sweep and nodded at Beth, who was standing next to her, patiently waiting for her answer. "Up there it is."

Beth slid into the row first, her body weight automatically triggering the privacy screens that were hidden on both sides of the seat and activated only for assessment day. They glided into place like blinkers, with a quiet swish, effectively blocking Ali from seeing Beth or the screen of her DID, from where she sat down next to her.

There goes my last chance of fudging my results, Ali thought wryly, only half joking, just as the privacy screen on her other side latched into place.

She looked at the blank screen of the DID in front of her. This would be it, the ultimate test that would decide the rest of her life.

She would have preferred to be fully alert when she took the assessment, but an ad-hoc request after breakfast had revealed the Program was loath to let her postpone. She would have to make the best of it, today. There was no chance of re-taking, no pass or fail; there was only a result that would be translated into a lifetime commitment on the gold lining of a quarter-inch square microchip.

Ali looked at her mobi. Five minutes left.

The room slowly filled, the sounds of privacy screens sliding out almost continuous now that Recruits moved to take their seats.

Finally professor Tuft stepped into the room.

"All hail, Recruits." His trademark cheerful attitude did nothing to disperse the tension hanging thick and heavy in the air. "It's an exciting day today, the day of your final assessment." He paused for effect as he motioned for them to sit down. "In a minute your DIDs will provide you with a list of words, one word at a time. For every word you will have five seconds to write down another word that you associate with the first one. To do so, you will use the touch sensitive interface of the DID in front of you. After you finish, you will be automatically transferred to a virtual war games scenario." He looked around. "You may start the assessment now."

At his order the DID in front of Ali came to life.

The first word that flashed black on the white screen was *Blue*. Ali typed *Recruit.*

Fight. She typed Defend.

Human...Race.

The list went on and on. Whenever Ali entered an association, the next word lit up. She looked at the progress bar on the bottom. Halfway through. Her headache was coming back. Her concentration faltered.

Light...Dark.

How the Program could determine a designation from these answers was beyond her.

Friend...Beth.

She thought of Beth next to her. She really hoped the whole Psychiatrist thing would work out.

Black...Crack.

Where had that come from? Ali tried to amend her association to *Protection Squad*, but the device had already moved on to the next word.

Centre...Home.

Hybrid...Strong.

Ali stopped thinking about her answers and just typed the first thing that popped into her mind. There was no point second guessing what they wanted to hear anyway. Too many words. Too many possibilities.

Maybe that's what they were aiming for. Not intellect, just pure instinct. How better to determine the basic layout of an individual. But that still didn't explain how they gleaned anything from the convoluted mess of words.

After what felt like an eternity, the screen went dark.

A pair of wraparound goggles and noise cancelling earphones slid out from a hidden compartment underneath the desk.

Ali fitted the accessories and found herself thrown into a virtual world, where she stood on a rocky plateau at the edge of an abyss. The gorge fell away mere centimetres from her feet. Ali gulped and took a hasty step back from the precipice.

"What's your worst nightmare?"

She startled around at the rough voice behind her.

Aiden?

The black-clad Protector walked towards her, the intent look on his face so different from his previously shuttered expression it threw her for a moment.

"Sir?"

"Answer my question, Rt2120. What's your worst nightmare?"

He stopped a couple of steps in front of her, his flint grey eyes drilling into her, until she felt naked in front of him, despite her uniform.

With difficulty, Ali ignored his order pressing in on her like a physical being until the truth hovered readily on the tip of her tongue.

It was a sham. It had to be. *A virtual reality*, she reminded herself, pressing her lips together against the urge to confess her greatest weakness. This world wasn't real. *He* wasn't real, just an avatar programmed to resemble the leader of the

Protection Squad. A number of zeroes and ones on a hard drive on one of the Sanatorium's bioservers.

The thought helped only marginally. Someone must have studied Aiden at length to program such a believable, overwhelming representation of him. But a representation it was. A front for one of the Program's intelligent agents trying to collect information about her she would never normally divulge.

Ali shook her head in denial of the order.

The avatar's eyes narrowed, as if he truly was the most powerful Hybrid in the Program, not used to having someone defy his orders.

"A fighter," he said. "Not backing down in the face of a stronger opponent."

A memory of the Chosen attacking her flashed through Ali's mind before she realized the avatar couldn't know about the incident. He was probably talking about something much more recent, like her unwillingness to answer his question.

She kept her eyes fixated on his face, not sure what he would do next. She was uncomfortably aware of the rock falling away behind her, the gorge ready to swallow her whole, if she made a wrong move.

The avatar stepped closer still, dominating her with the sheer size of his body. "What happens if I take away your ability to fight?"

There words were spoken almost carelessly. Even so, the blood drained from Ali's face.

"Hit a sensitive spot there, have I?" A humourless smile curled the corner of the avatar's lips. "Kneel."

Ali's knees bent, hitting the hard ground. Broken shards of rock scraped her through the fabric of her uniform. Panic seized her. How had he managed that?

She tried to get back up, but her legs wouldn't move.

Her breath seesawed in and out of her lungs, as he continued to advance on her. The situation reminded her of Trainer at the Centre. Only this time she couldn't fight back. This time she was completely helpless.

How had he so quickly honed in on her greatest weakness?

"Look at me."

Her gaze lifted of its own accord, and Ali revised her impression. There was nothing about him that suggested a sadistic quality like the one that had driven Trainer. No fiery rage. If anything, he was purest ice. Utterly controlled. So much more dangerous, she realized, than a human with a flaring temper.

He reached out his hand, and Ali jerked back.

"Stay still."

The command rendered her utterly motionless. Defenceless. Panicked.

Strong fingers feathered over her head, her cheek. He cupped her chin, tilting her head back, until she felt completely at his mercy.

No, Ali reminded herself, trembling under his unwavering stare. It was her avatar that was at his mercy. Not the real her.

How had they done it? How had they made sure he could control her? A virus perhaps?

Focusing on the programming behind the scenes brought

back some measure of control.

Was this whole scenario premeditated to give Recruits a taste of compulsion?

That had to be it.

"So you crave freedom."

Her theory shattered.

No other Recruit craved freedom like she did. This line was tailored to her. How did they do it? How did he know?

How far advanced were the Program's intelligent agents playing out these scenarios?

Aiden traced her lip with his thumb.

For a second, Ali fought the insane urge to bite the digit in defiance. He would probably force her mouth shut, if she dared.

He could do much more than that, she realized with a shudder, taking in his considerable bulk. He could push her into the gorge, and she wouldn't be able to stop him.

Even worse, he could order her to jump.

Her eyes snapped back to the Protector's inscrutable face.

"I'll give you a choice."

He let go of her suddenly, motioning for her to get up and turn towards the abyss. Ali's heart hammered in her chest.

"Live your worst nightmare serving as my slave or jump into the gorge and be free in your death."

Ali stared back at him as if he had lost his mind. He gave her a choice between slavery and death?

He returned her gaze quietly. Intently.

The black void in front of her beckoned Ali. The part of her brain that still held onto reality told her that she couldn't truly die in a virtual war games scenario. It probably wouldn't even hurt too much with the painkillers still flowing strongly through her veins. Even if the program was linked to her mobi's pain controls.

She inched forward, until her toes curled over the edge of the abyss, and felt the looming shadow behind her tense. If she didn't know better, she would think there was as much at stake for him as there was for her.

"Which option will it be?" Aiden's breath wafted over her neck, making the little hairs at her nape rise. She hadn't even realized he had moved in so close behind her.

Ali tried to imagine what it would be like to live as his slave. Would it be Aiden, the avatar, or the intelligent agent representing the Program that she would serve? If it was the latter, nothing would change. She was already the Program's slave.

But she didn't have to be. Not in this alternate reality. She could jump and be free. Wasn't that what she had been dreaming about?

Ali fisted her hands until her nails bit into the flesh of her palm. Death wasn't the answer. It could never be.

"You," she said finally, pushing the words out between clenched teeth. "I choose you."

He made a surprised sound, something she doubted the real Aiden would ever stoop to. "Why?"

She contemplated her answer for a second. "I haven't been a coward in a long time."

He gripped her waist, turning her towards him so fast she would have fallen, had he not pulled her to safety with the ease of someone used to handling much heavier targets.

"You don't know what you're getting yourself into." He was right in her face. "You don't know what I'll ask of you. If you die, this is as bad as it gets."

Ali lifted her chin, returning Aiden's gaze with an unflinching stare of her own. "No," She had made her decision. "If I die, then this is as good as it gets. And it can never get better."

His fingers flexed convulsively on her waist.

"Choose me," he said, leaning in until he filled her world. "Choose me and I will never let you fall."

Ali gasped, surfacing from the program. She tore the glasses from her eyes and put them on the desk in front of her with trembling fingers.

She had no idea what had just happened. Aiden. The abyss. She couldn't even make sense of the scenario. And her head felt like someone had taken a hammer to it.

The privacy screens slid back.

Whatever she had done. It was over. Her fate was sealed. In three days she would be inaugurated and that would be it.

Ali got up, feeling nauseous, whether from the finality of her situation, the virtual scenario, or the concussion she wasn't sure.

"You are white as a ghost." Beth grabbed her arm, led her down the stairs and out of the theatre. "That war game scenario of yours must have been a nightmare."

Ali flinched. "The worst." She squinted into the spinning hallway.

Beth tilted her head. "Shall I get a Medic for you?"

"No. Just. Give me a second."

"At least have some fresh air." Beth pushed her into the

gardens through a set of double doors. Ali allowed the balmy breeze to wash over her.

Green acres. A group of trees. The river glinting in the sun.

The beautiful view chased away some of the darkness that seemed to linger in her mind. She took a deep breath, grateful for her sun lenses that kept the light sensitivity at bay.

"Thanks, Beth. It truly was a nightmare. How was your scenario?"

Beth studied her quietly, for a moment. "A hostage situation that required my profiling abilities," she said at last.

Ali stared into the distance. Definitely tailored to each individual, she thought. The knowledge made her insides squeeze with worry. What was the meaning of all this?

She followed Beth back indoors and almost collided with another Recruit.

"Careful."

Strong hands caught her arms.

"Rob?"

"I thought you had a concussion, not amnesia."

"Very funny." But something released inside of her at the familiar banter. She had been rather worried he was still cross with her after their last conversation.

Rob grinned at her. "Sorry I missed you for breakfast. Will you two lovely ladies join me for lunch?"

Ali felt her mouth twitch. Who *talked* like that?

"I can't," Beth said. "I'm attending a lunch-time workshop on the *Psychology of Assassinations*."

"Oh?" Rob asked only mildly interested while Ali was full-on curious.

Beth blushed.

Obviously Beth's future profession wasn't the only reason her friend was eager to attend this particular seminar. The other one, Ali bet, wore a red uniform with a yellow arrow on the chest.

"Ali?" Rob looked at her expectantly.

Ali's mobi chimed at that moment.

She stared at the little lounge icon on screen and felt her stomach clench.

"I just received an invitation for a Psychiatric assessment." Ali cleared her throat to take away the layer of fear that had snuck into it.

"When?" Rob asked, angling his head to look at her display.

"Tomorrow."

Beth tilted her head. "Why?"

"I have no idea," Ali said. She didn't think she wanted to know.

***

It was almost the end of the *Microchip Updates* lecture, when the painkillers wore off. At first, the change was so subtle that Ali didn't notice anything different until a blinding stab of pain made dark dots dance in front of her eyes. Fumbling clumsily for the pills in her pocket, Ali managed to drop the plastic tube a second time, watching helplessly as it rolled under her desk and dropped under the seat of the Recruit in front of Beth.

Beth shot her a questioning look. Ali gestured towards

the tube. "Painkill—" She snapped her mouth shut, an instant before the professor, an Ai Specialist, could pinpoint the location of their whispers. He frowned but continued the lecture.

Ali dropped her voice even further. "I'm not feeling too well." More like utterly awful, but from Beth's expression, she could see that for herself.

Beth sent a worried glance towards the front of the hall before levelling an even more worried one at Ali.

"I'll get them for you," she said, after a moment's hesitation.

"No. Don't."

But Beth had already disappeared under the desk.

Ali kept the professor in her line of vision, while praying for Beth to hurry up.

She grimaced when the thump of Beth's head against the underside of the desk preceded her hand extending towards Ali, clutching the tube like a trophy won at one of the Program's major competitions.

Ali grabbed the small container filled with white pills just as a roomful of eyes turned towards them, one pair burning into her in silent reproach; the eyes of the professor.

"I will see you both in front of me, after the lecture."

"Yes, sir." They answered in unison.

Damn.

"We will now focus on how to update your future microchip," the professor continued, as if there hadn't been any interruption at all. "As most of you will know from previous lectures, each microchip is first powered and updated by the bioservers at the Sanatorium, and later, once you are out on assignments, by satellites around the world. It is of paramount importance that you stay within range of at least one satellite at all times, as a failure in the power-feed will short circuit the chip within minutes. This will pose a grave danger to the vulnerable brain tissue next to your microchip and can result in brain damage, or death. To minimize the risk of a short circuit the power-feed is set up as a completely autonomous process and does not require user intervention. For the daily data update, on the other hand, you are required to actively connect to the bioservers or satellites. You can choose to do so at any time within a dedicated four-hour window each morning. If you fail to connect during this time – for example because you are in a critical phase of your assignment – the update will start automatically, the next time you establish a connection, or experience a sleeping cycle, whichever comes first. You will be unable to perform any non-essential physical or mental actions during the update. Your muscles and thought processes will effectively freeze. This condition is temporary. The update takes no more than thirty seconds and will provide you with the daily database of Program members and any changes to your assignments. The update is carried out wirelessly and we will cover at a later date how you can initiate it."

The door opened with a quiet swish and a young Marshal stepped into the lecture theatre.

Ali's eyes dropped to the chain mail gloves hooked to the Marshal's mud-brown trousers, and felt a cold sweat break out on her forehead.

He must have just come from an incident.

Responsible to deal with out of control Recruits and humans, when the occasion arose, Marshals faced a higher risk of injury than Guards, who simply looked after building and object security. Faraday gloves protected Marshals from the vicious warning shocks a Recruit's temper could incite and the knives some humans were still fond of as weapons.

But that wasn't their only use.

Ali's breath hitched as memories swamped her.

Trainer's fists hitting her body again and again, metal striking her face and torso with punishing blows. Her muscles had been twitching uncontrollably at that point, warning shocks slicing into her without pause. But she would have gladly borne all of that, if it hadn't been for the knowledge – the promise that she had read in Trainer's frenzied gaze. He had intended to break her completely that day. Even if it meant killing her in the process.

Ali dug her nails into her arm, before she could spiral completely out of control.

It was over. He would never hurt her again. She had made sure of it.

Now all she needed was to forget.

Ali lifted her gaze to the professor who was gesturing for the young Marshal to step forward.

"Derek will now show you a practical example of a live update."

The Marshal braced his stance. "I am now connecting to the satellite."

Derek's face and body froze, until he looked as if he was constipated. Suppressed giggles sounded around the room.

Ali willed herself to smile.

Ignoring the commotion, the professor calmly unhooked the gloves from the Marshal's trousers and backhanded him across the face, making Ali start with a vengeance. Red bloomed where Derek had been struck, but the Marshal didn't move.

"Timing your updates wisely is advisable," the professor said into the sudden silence. "Class dismissed."

Feeling sick to her stomach, Ali gathered her things and made her way to the front of the hall.

Derek's muscles had finally loosened, she saw, and his eyes re-focused. He looked confused when he touched his hand to his burning face.

Ali's stomach sank further. The exploitation of his vulnerable state had obviously not been agreed upon.

She stopped in front of the professor and felt Beth come up beside her.

"Recruits!" A slapping of the Marshall's chain mail against the professor's open palm punctuated the word. "I don't take kindly to disturbances."

Ali swallowed hard. "Sir, it wasn't Beth's fau—"

The glove hit his palm. Ali flinched.

"Don't speak Recruit, unless I ask you to."

"Yes, sir."

"You've recently had a concussion, and you're exempted from all training activities. Is that correct?" *Slap.*

"Yes, sir."

"In this case your friend here will take your punishment also."

Have Beth pay for something that was Ali's fault? Ali's heart tripped over in her chest.

"Sir, may I suggest a restriction of my idle time instead. Or any other disciplinary action that won't impact my exemption?"

"You may not." *Slap.* "Leave." *Slap.*

"But—"

"Leave, or I shall add a third punishment for your friend to endure."

Ali turned, feeling terrible. She had tried to do the right thing, saving Beth from the Chosen. It turned out her gesture of support was the very trigger of the punishment Beth now faced. Even worse – Trainer would have broken up the fight with the Chosen if it had gotten out of hand, but nobody would rescue Beth from a sanctioned punishment by the professor. How could her friend ever forgive her? How could Ali ever forgive herself?

Chapter 7

"Who is it, Electra?" Ali asked the next morning, when her brain finally registered the knocking sound that had woken her was coming from her door.

"Ms08," the DID answered instantly, showing an image of a young man in a mud-brown uniform. The camera captured his profile, and the angry red mark across the man's right cheekbone was clearly visible.

Derek?

He lifted his hand, and the rap on her door sounded again.

"Nightglow, start." Ali sat up in bed, suddenly wide awake. What was a Marshal doing at her door at four-thirty in the morning? "Electra. I'll be with him in a second."

The knocking sound ceased abruptly, and Ali knew that the DID had sent a message to the access indicator panel outside.

Ali grabbed her clothes and pulled them on over her pyjamas then stood at attention next to her bed.

"Door, open."

"Rt2120?" Derek's voice was rough with sleep.

"Yes, sir."

"Please follow me. Me105, Anthony, has requested to see you."

The Medic's name rang slightly familiar in her mind, but Ali couldn't come up with a face. She stepped into the brightly lit hallway, ignoring the momentary flare of pain behind her eyes. It settled to a dull ache moments later. Another day or two and the concussion symptoms should be gone completely. Just in time for her inauguration there would be no more fog to dull her senses. Wasn't it just splendid?

Ali heaved a silent sigh and followed the Marshal down the stairs and into the night. A small strip of grey lit the horizon where the sun would soon start its ascent, but for now the grounds lay dark and quiet, the silence only broken by the lonely chirp of a blackbird and the fall of their footsteps on the stone path leading to the medical facilities.

The air, for once devoid of the heavy heat and humidity of the Capital's summer, chased away the last of Ali's sleepiness.

Why would a Medic want to see her at this hour, she wondered, but knew better than to ask the Marshal walking quietly beside her. If he had permission to tell her, he would have done so, the minute she opened the door.

A Guard suddenly rounded the corner of an outhouse, his eyes narrowing briefly as he pointed his flashlight towards them. At the sight of the Marshal's uniform, he nodded in acknowledgement then disappeared back into the direction he had come from. Ali tried to discern how many Guards were milling around the grounds at night, but couldn't pinpoint their locations to count their numbers.

When they arrived at their destination, Derek motioned her into the building. "First door on the left."

This time, Ali was prepared for the flare of pain as her eyes adjusted to the light in the waiting room.

The receptionist's desk next to the entrance was empty, although a lonely cup of steaming coffee suggested that the night nurse would be back shortly. There was no one else in the room.

The first door to her left slid open as she approached.

"Good morning, Recruit." A Medic with wire-rimmed glasses looked at her from his position at the desk next to the door.

Ali tried hard not to stare at the outdated monstrosity perched on his nose. Why he would accentuate his weakness instead of having laser eye surgery to correct the obviously rare condition was beyond her.

"Rt2120."

Ali turned towards the gravelly voice at the back of the room and felt the air leave her lungs in a rush.

Lightly tanned skin set off the aristocratic features of a middle-aged man. His long brown hair was slicked back in a ponytail. But it was his piercing brown eyes that sucked her in. Compelling. *Dangerous*. Her gaze skittered away. She knew that face.

"Doctor." She felt stupid talking to his chest.

"Indeed."

The confirmation set her insides to trembling. Ali fought the urge to retreat.

"Recruit, look at me." The clipped command dragged her gaze back to his stern face. "Sit," he ordered, and she felt her knees give out.

He was commanding her as easily as a puppet on a string, she realized. Or a Hybrid with a chip. The thought steeled her spine. She wasn't going to make it *that* easy for him. Not until after her inauguration.

"Why am I here, Doctor?" she demanded, glad that her voice didn't quiver. Much.

The assessing look he gave her made it hard for Ali not to squirm.

"Anthony, explain."

The Medic's pupils dilated, as he launched into speech. "Your brain showed an unusual pattern when we diagnosed your concussion three days ago. We need to take a blood sample to carry out additional tests."

"Unusual, how?" Ali asked, her fingers digging into the soft padding of the chair. Unusual wasn't usually a good thing in the Program. She doubted her brain pattern would be an exception.

The snap of a latex glove sounded like a gunshot in the quiet room.

"We will confirm that after the tests," Doctor said decidedly. "Anthony, take the blood."

"Yes, sir."

Ali felt the stab of the needle at the inside of her elbow and the slow draw as red liquid started to trickle into the test tubes.

She was surprised that her blood still flowed, because as far as she could tell it had turned to ice in her veins.

"We will also insert a brain activity sensor," Anthony explained, pressing a power injector against her shoulder.

"After penetrating your skin, it will take ninety seconds until the sensor reaches your brain."

He pulled the trigger then disconnected the needle drawing blood. His pupils, Ali realized, had returned to their normal size.

"We have everything we need for now. The sensor will transfer data wirelessly for the next seven days before it will break down to molecular level and absorb into your body. He fed the test tubes one by one into the BioDetect device in the corner of the room. "Please stay seated while we have a look at your first test results in my office. I will be back to check on you shortly."

Ali watched, frozen, as the two men left the room through the back door. Moments later, the sensor attached to her brain with an uncomfortable tingle. She latched onto the sensation to pull herself out of her daze.

Ali stood, ignoring the wave of dizziness that swept over her. Anthony must have taken a fair amount of blood without her noticing. Or maybe it was a recurrence of her concussion symptoms that influenced her sense of balance. The floor finally stopped moving, and she tiptoed across the room.

"Door, unlatch," she whispered, hoping she would be able to move the heavy pane of glass manually, once it was unlocked.

The door's access indicator panel lit up.

Voice recognition invalid. Access denied.

Damn.

Ali pressed her ear against the frosted glass. The voices were faint, but she could make out some of the words.

"…dormant carrier of anima ātra…"

Anima ātra? She had heard the words before. It was a horror story nannies told hy-bred toddlers; of a malicious voice that lured Hybrids into darkness, so far they could never find their way back. But what did that have to do with Ali's brain activity pattern?

She listened harder.

"…her black soul will activate upon inauguration...course of illness two weeks…brain damage…death."

Ali gripped the wall as her brain made the connection.

The inaugurated Hybrid without a designation bleeding onto the lunch hall floor, the Medic frantically mumbling about Anthony and the dead Hybrid's black soul. Rob's dry tone as he wondered if there were more of them – and were they all doomed to die?

Ali's throat constricted, as panic slapped like water against the walls of her mind. *Anima ātra* was the black soul that had killed the Hybrid. Ali was a carrier. If they activated her through inauguration she would die a painful death.

A warning shock tore through her body with enough force to bring her to her knees. The pain steadied her like nothing else could have, dissolving the panic into a million drops of impending doom.

Ali heard footsteps approach the door and stumbled back to her chair.

"You look very pale." Anthony rushed forward to check Ali's pulse on her mobi's screen, and it took all her effort to stop her body from pulling back. Would he be the one inaugurating her? Bile rose in her throat.

Ali swallowed hard. "Just feeling faint from the blood test, sir," she lied.

"That's normal," Anthony assured her.

"The test results?" she asked.

"All clear."

Even watching for it, Ali saw no cue. It seemed the Medic had talents far beyond stitching Hybrids back together.

"Once you feel better, you are free to go."

"I am," she said, ignoring her rubbery legs.

"I shall see you for your inauguration in two days' time, then."

"Thank you, sir." She didn't think so.

***

The food in her mouth tasted like cardboard, but Ali forced herself to swallow. She had to make a plan. She had to get away. Far, far away. Starving her body of nutrients wasn't a good start to getting away and living through it.

She had used the time the other Recruits were training to search the LiveNet for information on the black soul. What she had found had almost turned her already upset stomach.

The black soul was the only illness the Program couldn't cure. It was a form of mental instability that activated upon inauguration and caused carriers to believe there was a living black Abyss lodged deep in their minds compelling them to commit mental suicide. According to rumours, the Abyss lay dormant as a small fissure from birth, but started to grow steadily after activation. Eventually it became so powerful that the carrier of the illness couldn't help but obey the dark beckoning to jump into the Abyss, triggering a chain-reaction of misfiring neurons that immediately started overloading the brain until cerebral haemorrhaging resulted in a one-hundred percent death rate. Doctor – various well-hidden articles rumoured – didn't only activate dormant carriers of the black soul, but sped up the course of the normally long-lasting illness. Although the manufactured time span of the black soul seemed to differ between individuals, research suggested Hybrids rarely lived beyond a few weeks after inauguration.

Now it seemed that Ali was next in line, the label 'tragic accident' waiting to be attached to her electronic record, before her deceased body had fully cooled.

"Something's wrong."

Ali looked up from her plate and straight into Beth's too perceptive eyes.

Why had she allowed self-reproach to pressure her into telling Rob that she needed some time alone with Beth? A soon-to-be-Psychiatrist was the last person Ali should be eating breakfast with right now, no matter how desperately she needed to apologize for the punishment Beth had taken on her behalf. Ali couldn't even look at the dark circles under Beth's eyes, without feeling awful.

She definitely couldn't tell Beth the truth about her condition. If Ali really managed to get away, the Program would look to get information from her friends first. Beth would probably be inaugurated by that point. One well-worded command and Beth would tell them everything she knew. Afterwards, she would likely be punished for failing to report Ali. *Punished again*, Ali thought guilt chasing through her. She couldn't bear knowing her friend would suffer once more for something Ali had done.

Ali shook her head. "What did he do?" she asked instead of answering, hoping Beth wouldn't fight the change of topic.

Beth tilted her head, but thankfully didn't press Ali further. "Forty-one hours of sleep deprivation."

"That's the second time you've lost sleep because of me, this week. First watching over me in the medical facilities, now as a punishment." Ali's guilt mounted.

Forty-one hours without sleep didn't sound like much for a Recruit, but their strenuous schedules sucked every last ounce of strength from their bodies. Ali had had to live through it once. It was an awful feeling, as if every limb was made out of lead and every slip into a dozing state punished by a warning shock from the mobi.

What made it worse was that Beth didn't deserve the punishment. It had been Ali's fault. It should have been Ali's punishment, but with her exemption...

"Wait. There was no physical punishment to go with the sleep deprivation?"

"None beyond the normal training times.

Which was more than enough, but still. "That wouldn't have impacted my convalescence." Not much anyway. "Why didn't he allow me to take my punishment?"

"Because you wanted it." Beth stabbed her food with the tip of her fork, too tired to lift the tool to her mouth. "It wouldn't be much of a punishment getting what you wanted, would it?"

"What do you mean?"

"The words 'may I suggest' should never leave your

mouth when negotiating a punishment. Reverse psychology would have worked better."

Ali frowned. Beth had a point. The irony of the situation was that, by not punishing Ali, the professor had managed to punish them both. He had just handed Ali's punishment to her in wrapping paper, all shiny and colourful, like a present she never wanted.

How had he known that watching her friend pay for something Ali did would be worse than any other punishment he could dish out?

***

Ali entered the Psychiatrist office at seven forty-five, wishing to be anywhere but here. She would even line up against the wall for Trainer if it meant she could escape the evaluation.

She didn't want to have her mind examined. She didn't believe in coincidences. To receive an invitation for a psychiatric assessment at this point... Anthony and Doctor must have suspected her black soul, even before the blood test confirmed it. Were they trying to get a before-and-after comparison? Sane versus insane.

"Ali, please."

The middle-aged female Hybrid sitting in a straight-backed chair in the middle of the sparsely furnished room motioned for Ali to come closer, tracking her every move with keen blue eyes.

Ali wondered if it had been a conscious decision to call her by her name instead of her identifier. She would almost bet on it. 'Building rapport' was what they had called it in the few *Psychology* lectures she had attended at the Centre.

It would make sense for a Psychiatrist to try and build rapport.

Ali sank slowly into the seat the woman indicated, trying not to feel like an insect under the microscope.

"Thank you for coming."

As if she had had a choice.

"Why was I invited?" What excuse did they tell you to use?

The woman smiled slightly. "This consultation is part of your assessment. You've recently had a concussion. Doctor wants to make sure it didn't have any impact on your cognitive abilities before inaugurating you."

"Of course." Ali barely held back a sneer.

The Psychiatrist's smile widened marginally. "If you have no further questions, I would like to begin the evaluation. Maybe we can start with you telling me about your virtual war games scenario."

Ali had suspected the question would come eventually. She just hadn't expected it so soon.

"I didn't understand it," she said honestly, having thought about and prepared the answer in advance. She doubted she could lie to the Psychiatrist. Years of dealing with Hybrids had sharpened more than her gaze.

"These scenarios aren't always straight forward. Don't fret." The woman gently patted Ali's arm.

So it was the good cop routine that was supposed to break her down, Ali thought, not pulling back from the Psychiatrist's touch. The less she reacted, the less she said, the better.

"Let me make it easier for you. How do you feel about

compulsion, Ali? The suppression of free will? Slavery, if you want." The woman withdrew her bony hand to gesture in the air, palms out and open, inviting Ali to speak.

Ali counted to three this time, to make it look like she was contemplating the question for the first time.

"I don't think anybody likes the thought of being so easily controlled." Rob's line from the hovercoach worked perfectly. Honest yet vague enough at the same time.

The Psychiatrist tilted her head and, for a moment, she reminded Ali of Beth. Then the sun lines around her eyes deepened and Ali saw the difference between the two women. Where Beth was inexperienced enough to let a question slide, the Hybrid in front of her had developed the tenacity of a bulldog a long time ago. "It is more than that for you, though. Isn't it?"

Ali didn't drop her gaze.

She wondered who on the hovercoach had talked. She had suspected that someone had reported their conversation since the inexplicable war games scenario. The Psychiatrist's questions confirmed her suspicion.

How much of what they had said was on record? Ali glanced at the sleek notepad sitting on the woman's lap, undoubtedly connected to the bioservers of the Sanatorium.

The woman sighed, misinterpreting her look.

"This is a confidential discussion."

Unquestionably, Ali thought. And gardening droids could fly.

She shook her head. She wasn't going to admit to anything.

Did they know that Rob could hack mobis, too? She

doubted it. Even if they suspected something, Rob was too smart to leave any electronic tracks behind. Beth's voice had been barely more than a whisper. And nobody had actually *seen* them.

Realising she wasn't getting anywhere, the Psychiatrist tried a different angle. "What is your definition of freedom?"

Ali didn't like this question any better than the last, but at least it wasn't directly related to her. Nobody could punish her for answering a hypothetical question wrong.

"The power to speak and act as one wants without fear of punishment."

"Do you think that this is possible?"

"It is for humans."

The woman contemplated her for a moment. "Is it? What happens to humans who break the law, acting like they want?"

"That's not the same."

"It is included in your definition of freedom."

"Obviously within reasonable boundaries."

"And who shall define these boundaries? You? Me? The Human Council?"

The question hung in the air for one endless moment, before the woman spoke again.

"Is your annoyance with the current governing body the reason you defy authority?"

"I don't—"

"You are right now."

Ali snapped her mouth shut.

"Why do you have a problem seeing others punished for

you, Ali?"

Ali stiffened. The woman was talking about Beth's punishment. What had that to do with anything?

"How is this related to my concussion?"

"It isn't. Not directly. I'd still like to talk to you about it. Tell me your thoughts."

Ali pressed her lips together. She had disliked the questions before. She outright hated this one. There were things better left untouched.

"Everyone would."

"Maybe. But this isn't about everyone. This is about you. Answer my question, Ali."

Ali grit her teeth. She was no match for the Hybrid, sitting there so calm and collected, firing question at her that had no answers. None that she was ready to give anyway.

"Because it's immoral?" the Psychiatrist prompted when the silence stretched between them. "Or is the problem a deeper one. Is it the loss of control? After all, if it is someone else getting punished, there is no way you can influence the situation."

She was skirting dangerously close to the truth, and Ali was getting more uncomfortable by the second.

Ali suppressed the urge to squirm. "I think you forget I'm a Recruit. Recruits don't have control."

"Unless they learn how to endure pain. You are very good at enduring pain, aren't you, Ali? Your mobi shows a warning shock at five-fifteen a.m. Your erratic brain activity balances out seconds later. It seems you're almost using the shocks as an anchor. Something to ground you."

The woman had access to the readings from Ali's brain

activity sensor? Was there anything about Ali she didn't know?

The thought angered Ali. And she used *that* to ground her. At least until the Psychiatrist spoke again.

"You realize that the same won't work after your inauguration? You won't be able to control anything if you are given an order. Not your own reaction. Not the situation around you. Why does that frighten you?"

"I'm not frightened."

"Of course you are. Frightened that someone might hurt you?"

That's what Ali had said to Rob. It was the truth, if not the full truth.

"Or maybe frightened that you will be forced to hurt someone else?"

Ali's eyes snapped up.

Just a lucky guess, she told herself. But if it had been, Ali's reaction had given her away.

"Who did you hurt without meaning to, Ali?"

"Beth." Let her believe that was all of it.

The woman shook her head. "Before that?"

"Nobody." Ali pressed her mouth shut.

The Psychiatrist's gaze dropped to the notepad, flipping through pages and pages of information. "Your mother died giving birth to you."

Ali ground her jaws together so hard she thought her teeth might break. "That has nothing to do with this." Her voice sounded as if she had swallowed gravel.

"You don't feel responsible?" The words came lightly. It didn't fool Ali for a second.

"How could I. It wasn't my fault."

"That's very sensible of you to say. Very rehearsed."

"I was a baby," Ali grated, pinning the Psychiatrist with a glare, only distantly aware that the woman's eyes were starkly dilated, now.

"A foetus, barely three months old. You wouldn't have cared if you lived or died. I'm sure your mother did."

"Don't—"

"Do you think she begged, Ali? Did she plead with the Medics to save her, instead of the mindless child?"

"Don't say that. Don't." Ali pushed her hands against her head. "It wasn't my fault."

"She lost her life so you could live. They didn't give her a choice at all."

"It wasn't my fault," Ali cried. But deep down she knew it was a lie.

Her breath hitched, her eyes watered.

"This assessment is over," she whispered, brokenly.

The Psychiatrist inclined her head once. "I got the answers I was looking for."

***

It was late at night, and the start of Ali's sleeping cycle was rapidly approaching. She had been scouring the LiveNet for hours, using her training exemption to work on her escape and forget about the upsetting events of the afternoon.

Both proved more difficult than she had anticipated.

She wanted to hate the Psychiatrist for what she had done, but found she could only hate herself. For being the reason her mother had died. For being unable to overcome the events.

Ali closed her eyes, taking a deep breath, and yanked her mind back to the task at hand.

At the Centre she had participated in a number of simulations where Recruits were asked to circumvent the Centre's security systems, as a means for the Program to find and patch the vulnerabilities. Like a lot of Recruits, Ali had delighted in finding ways to trick the simulation software, its virtual monitoring systems and avatars safeguarding the realistic online representation of the Centre's grounds.

Working on her actual escape from the Sanatorium, Ali quickly realized that with her life at stake, she was far less willing to take any risks. She was definitely not considering the heavily guarded gate at the front of the property as a suitable escape route. And a six-foot high, barbed wire fence running the length of the perimeter didn't leave many options.

Until now.

Ali stared at the outdated estate layout document in front of her. Why the plan was still on the LiveNet rather than the access-restricted electronic archive – the ArchiNet, she didn't know. But the mistake in the backup routine could very well be her ticket to freedom – if she could somehow ascertain that the elusive northern gate in the outdated plan actually existed. It was a two-day march from her quarters to the northern border; too far to risk her life for a potential draft, or incorrect design.

Ali looked at the pulsating red circle near the top of Electra's screen and wondered anew how a gate could disappear without a trace between one version of the plan and the next. According to the LiveNet there had been no construction works in the area for the past seven years.

"Electra, show me a LiveMap satellite view of the area in question."

The requested picture opened a second later, and Ali exhaled a frustrated breath. Where the gate or a fence was supposed to be, the canopy of a thick forest hid the ground.

She was about to check the most current estate layout again – there had to be *some* clue – when her mobi chimed a soft reminder. She had two minutes until her sleeping cycle started, and she still hadn't formulated a plan.

Chapter 8

Ali listened to the rhythmic *pitter-patter* of raindrops splattering against her balcony doors early the next morning and, for just a moment, allowed herself to believe in the illusion of safety. Then she swung her chair around and returned to a reality where a Psychiatrist had torn Ali's soul wide open just to see how she reacted and her inauguration had turned from a nightmare into a death sentence.

Ali closed her eyes against the painful reminder.

"Electra, open my most recent document collection."

She had been up for the last hour conducting more research and working on her escape plan. She was so worried someone could find out, she had encrypted all relevant information and closed all programs whenever she took a five minute break to stretch her tired muscles.

"Password required for speech recognition."

"Superman." The inherently human term she had once learned in *Human Culture* studies, had seemed perfect for security purposes.

"Access authorized. Opening S-Cape document collection, now."

Ali looked at the to-do list she had jotted down earlier. The need to confirm the existence of the northern gate was still at the top of the list. Second was the acquisition of a map and compass. Her mobi could serve as both, but the device had an inbuilt tracker and was controlling her sleep cycle, which meant she really had to get rid of it before she left. Items three and four dealt with two of her most worrisome tasks – transportation and ID outside the compound. She didn't even know where to start when it came to the human world outside. She had spent all of her life at the Centre and now here, at the Sanatorium. Except for the few day trips into the 'real world' and their lectures on *Human Culture*, she knew nothing about life outside of the confines of the Program. Most Hybrids didn't, until their chip updated with all the necessary information one day before their first assignment.

Ali heaved a sigh. She would have to deal with these issues once she actually cleared the gate.

Most of the remaining requirements revolved around equipment and timing.

Ali let her eyes drift to the last item on the list; her 'test run'.

She had been exempted from all physical exercise for a number of days and, although her concussion symptoms were mostly gone, she didn't know how far she could trust her body in a strenuous two-day hike. She certainly couldn't afford to faint.

Ali looked at the rain still battering the windowpane and considered using a treadmill in one of the training halls, then decided she could kill two birds with one stone. If she conducted her test run outside, she could prove that she was back to full health and determine the best route for her escape.

Just like the day before, Ali quickly obscured the tracks her research had left on the LiveNet as best she could. She had no doubt a dedicated Ai Specialist could tell what she had been up to and when, but Ali hoped to be far away before anybody even got suspicious enough to try.

She put on her waterproof jacket, closed down the incriminating document collection – praying Electra wasn't configured to report back on encrypted documents, and made her way to the side exit of the outhouse. Squeezing her eyes against the driving wind, she considered the beaten dirt track that led into the woods. Even in the eerie twilight of the summer storm, it afforded little cover. If she wanted to stay undetected, running that same path with a survival kit on her back and no mobi wrapped around her wrist, she would have to leave during the night. Tonight.

Not much time to finish a half-baked plan, she thought and felt fear squeeze her heart.

What if it didn't suffice?

It has to, she told herself sternly. A few hours was all the time she had. At this point, running was her only chance to stay alive.

***

Ali came to a stop at the edge of the forest. For close to an hour, she had pushed her body relentlessly, discovering the terrain on and off the beaten track. She was still standing. It was by no means a guarantee for her escape, but had at least served to alleviate the worst of her fears – whether her body could even endure the attempt.

Grateful for the protective canopy overhead that slowed the rain to a splatter of fat drops, Ali tried to catch her breath. Tendrils of steam curled from thousands of pine needles and leaves that cushioned the ground and mixed with the white puffs of air that burst from her mouth. Doubts and hurts had retreated to simmer in the back of her mind, and now it was only Ali...and a brown hare, hunkered down under a big fern. The animal quickly bolted when a small branch snapped underneath Ali's foot, the sudden movement startling a group of birds that had been huddling in the trees, too cold and wet to sing.

Ali knew exactly how they felt. Her own socks and insoles of her shoes were drenched. Her uniform was plastered to her body. Rivulets of water had found their way into the collar of her rain jacket and were now trailing down her spine.

She couldn't wait to take a hot shower, to warm her clammy skin.

Her mobi chimed softly, reminding her of her inauguration countdown. Less than twenty-four hours left and the detested device was still wrapped around her wrist, controlling her every move.

Ali sighed. She would need help taking it off. The good thing was, she knew exactly who to ask. The bad thing, by asking she would put him at risk of exposure with the Program. The worst, she didn't have an alternative.

Ali hurriedly crossed the distance to the outhouse and ducked back into the building through the side door. The shower would have to be a quick one. She needed to find

Rob.

***

Chip Communication Part 2. Ali stared at the bold black letters on the DID screen in front of her and worked hard to suppress the irritated sigh that was trying push its way past her lips.

It was late afternoon, and she still hadn't been able to speak to Rob. He hadn't attended breakfast, and, although she had finally managed to track him down just before the *Chip Communication Part 1* lecture in the morning, there had been no way to talk privately in a theatre full of Recruits – or in the hallway outside the theatre, for that matter. At lunch, a group of Ai Specialists had requested he ate with them, and now she could only watch the back of his head while she had to listen to another boring lecture from the professor. There was little chance that she would be able to catch up with him before evening training, or speak to him privately during dinner, which only left idle time.

Ali looked at her mobi. Only fifteen hours were left until her inauguration. And with every passing second, fate wove its net tighter around her.

She knew from the hovercoach that deactivating her mobi would take Rob a few minutes at most. Still, being seen entering his room hours before her disappearance couldn't bode well for Rob being questioned by Program officials, tomorrow.

Ali fisted her hands in her lap and squeezed her eyes shut.

Why did she always have to bring punishment and pain for the people who she cared for most?

***

Ali stood in front of Rob's door, nerves fluttering in her belly. This had seemed like a really good idea earlier, but doubt was an insidious companion. It gained strength with every passing second. Could she really do this to him? Put him at risk like that?

Before she could change her mind, the door slid open and Rob turned in his seat.

"What a nice surprise." His smile did little to loosen the tension in her muscles. "Come on in."

Their rooms looked almost identical, Ali realized as soon as she crossed the threshold. The same soft carpet covered the floor, two built-in wardrobes lined the doorway, and a big wooden desk gleamed dully in the soft evening light. Ali let her eyes pass over the slightly rumpled sheets of the queen-sized bed and to the familiar pair of white curtains that covered the balcony doors. Did they have the same view too?

Stop stalling. You haven't come here to compare furniture, have you?

Ali took a deep breath and finally dredged up the courage to look at Rob, who was regarding her with an amused expression. "One of my tricks for whatever goes on in that head of yours," he offered.

"That's exactly what I need," Ali said. "One of your special tricks."

"And which one would that be?" he asked, clearly puzzled by her serious tone of voice.

Ali nodded at the mobi that lay forgotten next to his DID. "I need you to deactivate my mobi again."

"What?" All amusement fled his face. "Why?"

"I have to leave."

"Leave?"

"Run away," she clarified.

"But…you can't."

"I must." She raised her hand to silence him. "Does the term black soul mean anything to you?"

His eyes widened in shock.

So he had looked up the definition after the incident in the lunch hall. She should have known. It was what she should have done, too. But back then she hadn't realized her world would shatter a few short days later. Tears suddenly pricked her eyes.

Ali bit her lip. "I'm a carrier." It was difficult to admit it out loud.

"How do you know?"

"Doctor ordered some tests—"

"You mean one of the Medics?" Rob asked.

"No. Doctor."

"You've met Doctor?"

"Yes."

"Hold on." He shook his head as if to clear it. "When did all of this happen?"

"Yesterday morning."

"Yesterday?" He sounded genuinely upset now. "Why didn't you come to me earlier?"

"There was nothing you could do."

"I could have talked to you. Held you. Hell, anything Ali."

"I'm sorry. I-I couldn't…I didn't want to put you in danger." I didn't want you to know I wasn't quite right in my head, either.

"Screw danger!" He dragged a rough hand over his face. "Maybe they won't inaugurate you?" he suggested hopefully.

Ali laughed humourlessly. "I know they will. They said so, and I've done some research on the LiveNet yesterday. They have inaugurated every known dormant carrier in the last twenty years."

"Why?"

Obviously his own searches hadn't been very detailed. And why should they? Rob had simply appeased his curiosity. Ali, on the other hand, was frantically trying to save her own life.

"Research, I guess." She shrugged her shoulders.

"How long does the illness last, before...you know...?"

"On average four years." Ali blew out an unsteady breath. "With me, they want to speed it up to two weeks." She dug her teeth into her lower lip to keep it from trembling.

"Two weeks?" Rob whispered. "So the rumours are true."

She nodded, trying to get her emotions under control. It was difficult when there was nothing but more bad news to talk about. "They seem to be at the drug testing stage. They call the drug *anialbus*."

"So there's hope." The relief in Rob's voice was almost palpable.

It took Ali a second to steady her voice enough to answer him. "I wouldn't call it that. For some reason Doctor always waits until the very last stage of the illness to test the serum.

At that point the test subjects are mentally severely unstable. So far, none of them has survived the administration of anialbus. The case files are hidden, but the evidence is there."

It was close to impossible to permanently get rid of Program related data. Although, whoever pulled the strings on this one – Doctor, most likely – had definitely tried their hardest to make sure the incriminating evidence stayed out of sight. To find it, someone either had to know what they were looking for or they had to be desperate.

"Do you understand now?" Ali asked, fisting her hands at her sides in helplessness. "If I don't run, I'll be next." The damn tears she refused to shed had found another way, down the inside of her nasal passage. Ali sniffed.

Rob gently rubbed her arms, until her fingers slowly unfurled. "We'll get you out of here. I'll help you with the mobi."

"Thanks." His kindness seemed to make it even more difficult to hold on to her control.

"What else do you need?"

She started shaking her head, but he merely waited until she looked back at him again.

"Tell me." He squeezed her wrists lightly.

Ali swallowed around the lump in her throat. "The Sanatorium is heavily guarded."

Rob nodded. It was common knowledge that the Program didn't take kindly to either intruders or escapees.

"One of the outdated estate layouts suggests that there's a gate, two days' walk north. I couldn't find any information on whether the layout is correct or not. I also don't know if it's guarded and how I can unlock it."

"If it's an outdated plan, then there may be some useful information on the ArchiNet."

Ali nodded. She had come to the same conclusion.

"I'll have a look at it."

"No." Hacking the ArchiNet was close to impossible. "If they find out—"

"They won't," Rob cut her off. "I know how to cover my tracks."

She didn't doubt it. Still, the feeling of dread she had been fighting since she realized that she had to drag Rob into this mess, remained.

"What if the gate turns out to be a dead-end option?"

Ali blew out a breath. "I'll deal with that only if I have to."

She could see Rob wasn't happy with the flaky plan. Neither was she.

"Anything else?"

"My inauguration is tomorrow, at seven a.m."

"Jeez, Ali. You're not making things easy." He looked at the clock. "Nine hours. I'll make it work. Somehow."

Ali felt as if a ton of bricks suddenly lifted off her chest. "Thank you," she whispered, wondering if he even knew how much his help meant to her.

"Thank me when we're out of here."

We? "No Rob. I leave alone. It's too dangerous."

"If you want my help, you'll get it on my terms. Besides, we may have to unlock the gate on site. Do you really think you'll be able to do that by yourself?"

No, she knew she couldn't. Ali bit her lips. He was

turning her whole arrangement on its head, defying her at every turn. Did he not realize that she was trying to protect him?

"I'll come with you," he said, his voice brooking no argument. "Even if I have to chase after you."

Ali exhaled a pent-up breath. He wouldn't change his mind, she knew. Deep down, she couldn't help but feel grateful that he insisted on accompanying her. How awfully selfish of her.

"Will you deactivate the mobi now?" she finally asked.

Rob shook his head. "They'll find out if it's inactive for too long. You'll have to wear it until we leave."

And wasn't that a surprise? Another piece of her carefully plotted scheme not quite working out the way she had planned?

Ali squeezed her eyes shut. Would anything at all go according to plan with this blasted escape?

Chapter 9

When night gave way to dawn the next day, Ali had long since answered her own question with a resounding 'no'. If her plan had been barely holding together yesterday, it was utterly in tatters today.

The date of her inauguration seemed to mock her as it displayed on top of Electra's screen. Her mobi, still firmly secured to her wrist, felt like a leaden weight pulling at her arm.

It was almost seven o'clock in the morning, and the sun was slowly crawling over the horizon, promising another hot day in the Capital.

The time for her night escape had passed, and Rob's brief *more difficult than I thought* message at five-thirty a.m. hadn't been comforting in the least.

Ali was ready to climb the walls.

"Electra. Message Rt2388."

"Good morning, Ali. What is the message you want to send?"

Have you freaking figured it out yet?

"Ready? Send."

A chime signalled the arrival of Rob's answer, moments later.

"Electra, read message."

"Message start. Not yet. Will take care of it. Catch you later. Message end."

Later? She didn't have later. Didn't he realize that she was running out of time?

As if on cue, a rap sounded at her door.

"Rt2120?" Derek asked when the heavy metal gave way.

Really? He couldn't remember her? "Yes, sir."

"Follow me."

Ali forced herself to walk past the backpack she had packed the night before in anticipation of their escape and out into the hallway. Now she was entirely dependent on Rob. A feeling of unease whispered through her body. Would he finish on time? How did he plan to get to her before she reached the inauguration room?

Goodness, she should have run, when she had the chance and to hell with the gate and the mobi. But it was too late now.

The short walk to the medical facilities did nothing to calm her nerves.

"Third door on the right." Derek gestured towards the back of the waiting room.

Ali's neck prickled and goose bumps covered her body.

She barely noticed the human receptionist who chatted animatedly to a colleague on her communication device, or the single Recruit who sat in one of the cushioned chairs to the side. Her feet dragged slowly over the polished linoleum floor as she approached the door.

This was it.

"Rt2120."

Ali flinched. She hadn't realized that Doctor would be there to supervise the inauguration.

"Doctor."

He was standing in the doorframe Derek had pointed her to. Behind Doctor, a reclining chair gleamed maliciously under the cold fluorescent lights. Her insides started to shake. *Right now* would be a good time for Rob to turn up. But the entrance at her back stayed closed.

She approached the inauguration room on trembling legs.

Five pairs of eyes stared back at her. The Medic with the wire-rimmed glasses, Anthony, was sitting in front of his DID. Doctor had retreated to just inside the door to let her pass, and two human nurses were waiting impatiently for her to stop dragging her feet. But it was the fifth pair of eyes that terrified Ali the most. The flat, lifeless stare of the steel-plated MediBot. MedicaFive.

Ali tore her gaze from the electronic name tag affixed to the MediBot's silver-gleaming chest and gulped a breath.

"Please lie face down."

Everything inside her wanted to balk.

And then what?

Did she really intend to take on a Hybrid and three humans all by herself?

The thought was tempting. But even with the element of surprise on her side she didn't doubt the outcome.

Ali felt her cheeks wedge into the small hole at the top of the chair as she followed Anthony's orders.

"Let's take off your mobi first." The electronic lock

opened with an audible click, and she felt deft fingers slide the device off her wrist. "You won't be needing this any longer."

Of course not. She would have something ten times as effective and a hundred times scarier inserted into her brain, in just a few minutes.

Fear clogged Ali's throat.

It was much too late for Rob to save her now. She hoped he realized that too. She wouldn't be able to live with herself if he was caught doing something stupidly heroic – like trying to break her out of the inauguration room. The things Program officials would do to him made a cold sweat break out on Ali's forehead.

The shackles around Ali's arms and legs snapped into place, pulling her back to her own predicament. The steel band around her head tightened. She instinctively tugged at the restraints and got nowhere. Ali's heart pounded in her chest.

Over. Her life was over.

A pair of polished shoes passed her line of sight that was restricted to a small oval on the floor. They stopped for one endless second.

Ali bit the inside of her cheek until she tasted blood. She wouldn't beg. *Never.*

"I'll watch from above." Doctor's steps receded towards the stairs at the back of the room then up to an observation box on the first floor that Ali had briefly glimpsed earlier.

Relief washed over her. Such a ridiculous thing: pride. And still; it was the one thing they hadn't taken from her. Yet.

"Let's get started." The wheels of Anthony's chair scraped over the floor as he returned to his desk. "Maeghan, connect her to the Biomonitor."

Ali felt a sensor being clipped to her right index finger. The familiar beeping of the Biomonitor announced the successful start of the feed a second later.

"MedicaFive, start the procedure."

Metallic fingers traced her skull, sending shivers down her back. Then the low hum of the laser cut into her brain. Ali squeezed her eyes shut against the impending panic curling through her blood.

She tore them open a second later at the sound of instruments clattering to the floor. She couldn't see anything from her position, but heard Anthony's surprised yelp to her left.

The steel band around her head released at the same time as her wrist shackles opened.

She pushed her body up as best she could, with her ankles still strapped to the chair. Rob was standing at the DID typing furiously at the fall-back touch screen keyboard. The Medic was lying on the floor next to him, his glasses shattered.

Ali swallowed.

"Is he—"

At the sound of her voice Rob turned. "Unconscious. It's not that easy to kill a Hybrid with one punch and we don't have time for more."

Thank goodness. Killing the Medic could have easily been Rob's death sentence.

Ali heard a movement in the corner and turned to find the

two human nurses huddling together. Their eyes were huge, panic evident in their faces.

Welcome to my world.

The thought was cut in two by the shill sound of an alarm. Ali looked up to where Doctor was standing calmly behind a pane of glass.

Her leg shackles released.

"We have to go. Now!"

Tearing her eyes from the dangerous depth of Doctor's gaze, Ali scrambled up from the chair and grabbed Rob's outstretched hand.

They were out of the door in a flash, speeding past the stunned receptionist and into the open.

Two Recruits against a compound full of Hybrids. They had to get away quickly, because their element of surprise was wearing thin fast, and in an out-and-out combat situation they didn't have the flicker of a chance.

Ali heard the footfalls of running feet and felt Rob push her towards an outhouse to their right.

"Get inside."

She ducked into the doorway an instant before a group of Guards rounded the corner. Rob was right behind her.

"To the back." He grabbed her hand again and dragged her down the corridor, then pulled her behind a spur in the wall when a number of Marshals from the building responded to the alarm.

Keeping her breathing shallow – quiet, Ali ignored the adrenaline hammering in her veins. She wouldn't be able to starve her body of oxygen for long. Her muscles burnt up the remains in her blood much faster than her tempered inhalations could accommodate for.

"Come."

The last Marshal had barely left the building before Rob ducked out of their hiding spot and pulled her down the hall towards the backdoor.

They burst out into the open, and Ali realized two things at once. The sun had fully cleared the horizon. And they had to be mad to try to escape in broad daylight.

"Disappear."

Rob's terse command was accompanied by a push between her shoulder blades that sent her stumbling into a group of Recruits out on their morning run. She collided with one of them and mumbled an apology.

Disappear.

Ali edged into the middle of the group. Not an easy task, considering that the Recruits were running in formation. She fought the urge to turn around and check on Rob, instead concentrating on the fast approaching tree line ahead of her.

Fifty meters... Thirty... Ten.

A movement to her left drew her attention. A couple of Guards were searching the area. But they weren't alone. In front of them two large Dobermans were sniffing the ground.

The woods closed behind her. Ali broke free from the group and ran into the trees. She had taken all of three steps when she heard the dogs bay.

Damn.

Pushing her body to full speed, she cut through the underbrush. For a minute, she only heard her own laboured breathing and the ever receding alarm while her thoughts spun a million miles an hour.

A hand gripped her shoulder. Slipped.

Ali reacted on instinct. Her body twisted, ducked. Her fingers curled to deliver a blow.

"Stop."

Her fist hovered an inch away from Rob's stomach.

Still breathing hard, Ali straightened. "Sorry. I thought you were one of them." She shot a worried glance towards the running track.

Rob followed her gaze. "They are on our trail. How's your head?"

She felt an unexpected flash of warmth at his concern for her welfare.

"Good enough for a hard and fast run."

He looked up from where he had hunched on the ground to rummage through a backpack similar to the one that Ali had left behind in her room. "Good. Because that's exactly what we'll do, as soon as I activate this." He extracted a tiny circular device.

"A sound and scent trap," Ali said surprised. "You really *did* take care of everything, didn't you?" And now she felt twice as bad for doubting him.

He pressed a button and threw the device into the bushes. The dogs baying turned into a pained yowl.

"Don't give me too much credit. It's your backpack I picked up, I just added a few bits and pieces I thought we'd need." He gave her a brief smile, then removed a handheld DID.

"This way."

She followed his lead as they took off at a dead run

through the woods.

Ali watched Rob jump over a fallen tree that blocked the narrow path a few feet in front of them and followed suit an instant later.

"They'll find the trap eventually," she panted, when a small clearing finally allowed her to catch up with him. "Then they'll sniff us out."

"The river will erase our scents."

Ali eyed the gleaming, meandering mass of water suspiciously. She had never considered it as an option for escape. She never had to. In her night-time scenario, nobody would have known she was gone until the next morning.

She considered it now. The currents were strong. Wading through it would be a nightmare, if not impossible. "It will cost us valuable time."

Rob shook his head, coming to a stop at the river shore. "No, it won't." He pulled a scrunched up object from the backpack. At a flick from his wrist, air rushed into it.

"A rubber boat?" No wonder it had taken him forever to get all this stuff together. "Where did you get that from?"

"The storage room has an electronic lock. Hop in."

He didn't have to tell her twice. The silence behind them was deafening. Not a good sign.

"Damn it's small." Ali scooted forward, for once glad she was considered to be a petite Recruit. Even so, there was almost no room left behind her in the tiny life raft.

"We'll fit. Don't worry." Rob gave the boat a push, then jumped in as soon as Ali felt the sandbank give way to water. The life raft reeled precariously.

"I think your definition of 'we'll fit' is different to mine."

But there was no denying his idea had been genius.

"Stop the boat!"

They both flinched at the deep command of a Marshal breaking through the woods. Water splashed around the Marshal's feet, soaking his uniform, as he followed them into the river.

"Too late," Rob said grimly, quickly hugging his arms around her to unfold a contractible paddle and using the current to manoeuvre them further into the middle of the stream, out of reach of the growing search party joining the Marshal.

Shouts and curses followed them.

Rob ignored the commotion, instead using the paddle with expert motions to steer them around rocks and floating branches. Squished inside the cage of his arms and legs, Ali couldn't do much more than sit still and pray.

After a few minutes, she forced herself to loosen the white-knuckled grip on the rope spanning the circumference of the boat's rim, and take a look over her shoulder. So far, nobody was chasing them in a watercraft.

Behind her, Rob was still tense.

"What?" Ali asked.

"There's only one reasonable point to get off the boat before the falls."

"Falls?" Ali sucked in a breath. Then the meaning of what Rob had said penetrated. "They'll wait for us there."

"They won't be fast enough, even if they take the hovercrafts, but it narrows the area they'll have to search considerably."

Ali gulped. "We'll have to get off after the falls?" It

wasn't really a question. They wouldn't have a chance to escape otherwise. "How bad are the falls?" She almost didn't dare ask.

"Survivable."

Ali tightened her hold on the handle-rope again. "Please tell me you have at least good news about the gate. Does it exist?"

"It does. According to sealed Program records, it was permanently closed six years ago and was subsequently removed from the estate layout documents. From what I've read, the Program now treats it the same way they treat any other part of the fence that runs the perimeter. There are no Guards patrolling the area, but the security camera is operational."

"Can you turn off the camera and open the gate?"

"I already have."

Ali swivelled her head to look at him. "You're a genius."

"Thanks." The smile on his face told her, how much her compliment meant to him, but the worry lines around his eyes didn't ease.

"Brace." Rob's voice sounded strained, and Ali realized that he was struggling to keep them afloat in the increasingly torrential river.

"Face forward, please," came another terse request.

Ali complied.

The sound of the water swelled until it drowned out the chirp from the birds at the river shore. Froth sprayed Ali's body, coating her hands and making them slippery on the rope.

She could feel Rob's chest expand into her back and

lifted her gaze.

All the air rushed out of her lungs.

Survivable.

She screamed.

The boat turned, the force of the current pulling Ali under, sucking her into an ever faster spinning downward spiral. Craggy boulders scraped her skin. Where was the surface? She couldn't see the light. Icy water crashed down on her, stirring up dirt and sand from the riverbed. Ali kicked her legs and got nowhere. The urge to inhale became stronger by the second. Panic threatened to overtake her. She needed to get out of this maelstrom.

A strong hand wrapped around her wrist and pulled. Ali broke the surface and sucked in a breath, coughing and sputtering.

"Rob?"

"Right here. I got you."

She could barely hear him over the roar of the river behind her.

"Thank you." Shivers wracked her body. She would have never made it out of there alone.

Rob draped one of her arms over the side of the boat, then boosted her up. Ali clutched at the life raft.

"I got you," he said again, settling once more behind her.

Ali nodded shakily. "You shouldn't have come after me. You could have died."

He lifted something out of the water. The rope she had held onto. Rob had tethered the boat to his waist, converting the rope into a lifeline.

"Sorry I took so long." He looked away, embarrassed.

"The damn rope was slippery as a fish."

Ali shook her head, dousing them both. "You're incredible."

His gaze shot back to hers. "Two compliments within the span of a few minutes. You're spoiling me."

Ali felt a smile tug at her lips. "Impossible."

The look he gave her warmed her insides, but did nothing to stop her teeth from chattering.

Rob pulled her more firmly against his body.

"We'll get off the boat soon. The hike will warm you up. Hopefully enough to dry your clothes for the night. Temperatures plunge after dark here. We can't afford to get sick sleeping in wet clothes."

Ali resisted the urge to snuggle further into his warmth. "I don't think we can afford to rest at night, either," she said.

"We have to. Unless you're willing to risk our legs *and* necks hiking through this uneven terrain at night."

He was right of course.

"I'm just worried they'll catch us. They have hovercrafts with nightlights that they can use on the access roads running through the forest. They have dogs that can track us through the thickest underbrush. They are Hybrids, for goodness sake. I don't know what I was thinking coming up with this crazy plan."

She felt Rob's lips against her temple. "Shh. I know."

"What if they catch us?" she asked, hating that her voice sounded so afraid.

She was crashing, she suddenly realized. She had been running on adrenaline since she got up in the morning and the unplanned dive had been the last straw. She fisted her hand and willed more adrenaline to be released into her blood. Rob's larger hand covered her own.

"Don't," he said. "Give yourself a break. You'll need your strength again, soon enough."

She slumped against him. "What if they catch us?" she asked once more.

"They'll punish us for running away. And it won't be pretty. But," Rob gave her head a soft kiss, "it won't be anything we haven't survived before. The Program may be known for a lot of unpleasant things, but they aren't known for killing or permanently damaging their members."

Except when they activated dormant carriers. The thought hung in the air between them.

"As I see it," Rob said, clearly trying his best to alleviate her fears, "the worst they can do is to go ahead with what they had planned anyway. Isn't it better to at least *try* to get away?"

Ali let out a shuddering breath. Of course, he was right. Again. "Thank you," she said. "I lost my composure there, for a second."

Rob chuckled. "It happens to the best of us. We're almost there." He pointed at a sandbank ahead and to their right.

The muscles in his arms bulged and squished her even further, as he stabbed at boulders anchored deeply in the riverbed, with a branch he had picked up to replace their lost paddle.

Ali held herself very still, quietly revelling in the feeling of being cocooned in his warmth. She felt almost…safe.

The crunch of rubber sliding over sand sounded loud in the little bayou.

"You get out first," Rob told her.

Ali pulled herself out of the boat. She heard splashing behind her and turned around.

"Let's hope it doesn't get stuck anytime soon." Rob watched the boat floating down the river with narrowed eyes.

"If they find this spot, they won't need the boat to know that we were here." Ali pointed at the ground, where brush marks and footprints told their own story of two Recruits on the run.

"Damn." Rob brushed fresh sand over the clearly visible tracks. "I doubt it will fool a trained Hybrid."

Ali agreed. Their best security measure was that they had passed at least two sandbanks before getting off. If the Hybrids investigated those first, Rob and Ali would have a head start. A head start they were losing more of with every second they stood still.

Obviously thinking along the same lines, Rob slung the dripping backpack over his shoulders. "Ready?" he asked, passing Ali's own question from this morning back to her.

"As I'll ever be."

***

It was just before midnight – and well past their allocated hiking time – when they finally crawled into a dark cave they had found on the slope of a hill. It gave Ali the creeps, but it would keep them dry in case the thunderclouds above delivered on their promise later on.

Ali sank to the stony ground, suppressing a groan. Her whole body hurt.

Determined to get what little comfort she could, she toed

off her wet boots and socks, wincing when the material pulled at the chafed and blistered skin of her feet.

At least they had made good time. Only a third of their journey remained.

"Have this."

She extended her hand in the direction of Rob's moving shadow and felt the spongy texture of a sandwich under her fingers. It seemed that at least the inside of the backpack had stayed reasonably dry.

Her stomach growled. She hadn't even realized how hungry she was.

Too tired to talk, they sat in silence while they ate their food and drank some water from the bottle they had shared during the hike.

The cave was eerily quiet, so different to the Sanatorium where Ali had gotten used to the sound of swishing doors, Guards mumbling outside her window as they patrolled the grounds, and the occasional bark of the dogs. Here, there was nothing. Not even the nocturnal animals disturbed the silence of the night. It was almost as if the forest was holding its breath.

A gust of cold air blew into the cave. Seconds later, the sound of raindrops hitting the soft forest floor drifted in through the entrance.

The pattering noise only increased Ali's feeling of isolation. She hugged her arms around her body, and stared forlorn at the dim nightlight that Rob had placed at their feet.

How could she miss something that had brought her nothing but pain and suffering? How could she long to be back with the people who had decided she was worth more dead than alive?

It didn't make sense.

Homesickness crashed in on her like a tidal wave.

"Come here."

Ali looked up and straight into Rob's watchful eyes. His arms were wide open.

She only hesitated a second before she scooted closer and leaned against his chest.

"Do you miss them, too?" she asked quietly, wondering when she had started to trust him so completely. "The only family we've ever known."

"Not as much as I'd miss you." He rubbed his cheek against her head and softly nuzzled her temple. "We'll get over losing them. It only takes time."

If only he knew that she couldn't even get over losing her mother. And the woman had been a stranger.

Ali sighed.

Rob's arms tightened instinctively, and something hard brushed against her side.

Ali sat up in alarm. "Your mobi—"

"It's hibernating and can't be traced." Rob pushed the long sleeve of his uniform up to expose the darkened display of the device. "I didn't want to deactivate it and take it off completely, in case someone stopped me on my way to the medical facilities."

Relaxing back against him, Ali touched the mobi's smooth surface. He had risked so much for her, this loyal, smart Recruit. She trailed her fingers from the cool metal to the warm skin of his forearm and felt his muscles twitch.

What she wouldn't give to lie in his arms like this all

night.

Unfortunately reality didn't care about her wishes, or her comfort.

Reluctantly Ali wriggled out of his embrace. "I'll take the first watch." Ali cut off Rob when he wanted to protest. "You've done a great job getting us out of there. It's time for me to contribute to this escape. I'll wake you up in three hours, and you can take over."

"Two hours," he said. "And take the thicker blanket with you. My bigger body will keep me warm."

She opened her mouth, but then nodded. His uniform felt mostly dry, unlike hers.

She moved to get up, but he snagged her wrist.

"Five more minutes," he said. "Please?"

She was defenceless against his request.

"Thank you," he mumbled, when she was once more wrapped up in his warmth.

She shook her head. "Thank *you*," she said, fully aware that she would have been utterly lost without him.

"Anytime." He hugged her against him, as if he needed to hold her as much as she needed to be held. "For you, Ali, anything. Anytime."

Chapter 10

"They're outside, heading straight for the cave." Rob's voice was so low Ali had to strain to hear him, but his urgency was clear as day. It was just before dawn, and they had been getting ready to leave when they had heard the noise and Rob had gone to investigate. "They must have found the boat and our tracks. We have less than a minute to get out of here."

Ali slipped the water bottle into the front pocket of the backpack. She had already packed the rest of their stuff.

"How many?"

"At least two. Maybe more."

She pulled on her boots as quickly as possible in the cave's utter darkness, gritting her teeth when one of the blisters opened, and pushed her socks into the pocket of her trousers. She could put them on later.

"I'm good to go." It was barely a whisper, but Rob must have heard her anyway. She felt him move past her and followed his shadow into the dimly lit forest outside.

They had just cleared the entrance when the first arrow hit Rob.

The Marshal breaking through the underbrush was as stunned at the shot as they were. Unsure what to do, he hesitated a second too long.

Rob, staggering under the effect of the fast-acting tranquilizer, pulled the dart from where it had penetrated the skin on his neck and plunged it into the Marshal's body before he collapsed to the ground.

Ali jumped forward, catching Rob an instant before his head could hit the jagged rocks in front of the cave. His body's deadweight took her down with him. Her tailbone hit the ground. Pain shot up her spine, but she barely noticed. Her focus was on the Marshal in front of her; a man with payback on his mind.

He looked dazed, but was strong enough to advance on them, the dart sticking out of his shoulder a lot less effective now that it had released most of the drug into Rob's system.

Ali struggled to her feet and shifted her body in front of Rob's unconscious form.

"Out of the way!" The Marshal's eyes were wild as they shifted between her and Rob.

"You'll have to go through me." She didn't budge.

The Marshal wavered.

Ali lowered her stance. Hand-to-hand combat with a drugged Hybrid was not something she would enjoy. He wouldn't feel a thing. This would be messy. And painful. *Unwinnable.*

She stood her ground.

The Marshal attacked.

"Freeze! Now."

The command locked the Marshal's muscles mid-lunge.

Out of balance, he toppled to the side.

Ali swung towards the voice and saw nothing but trees. Then a dark figure stepped into the clearing, tranquilizer gun in hand.

Aiden.

Her backpack suddenly weighed a ton. *Her* backpack. The one she had slipped the panic-button into. How could she have forgotten?

The small dart hit her neck. Her hand flew up to pull out the device, but never reached its destination as she started to fall into darkness.

***

Ali slowly drifted towards consciousness. She knew she did, because she could hear the quiet murmur of voices somewhere outside her head. *Not the cave*, she thought, taking in the cosy room temperature, the beeping of a Biomonitor next to her.

She tried to move her arms, and a small jolt of alarm shot through her at the feeling of metal digging into her wrists. She tried her feet instead.

Shackled.

The picture came together at once, and her eyes flew open as adrenaline overcame the last of the drug in her system.

She was back at the medical facilities, lying face down on the inauguration chair.

Ali lifted her head – the only thing that they hadn't strapped down.

All air rushed from her lungs.

Rob was sitting to her left, his head tilted back and

leaning heavily against the wall. His eyes were closed in a face that must have been struck brutally multiple times. Bruises were forming on his cheekbones, and he seemed to have trouble breathing through his nose. Metal cuffs were wrapped around his bare wrists and ankles, and were connected to the mobi that Ali had felt vibrate back to life when she had caught Rob's unconsciousness form in front of the cave.

Ali must have called his name, because his eyes suddenly opened, their usually vibrant colour clouded by pain.

"Seems like the little runaway is finally awake."

The voice from her nightmares had Ali jerking her head to the other side.

"We've been waiting for you, for a while now." Doctor clicked his tongue in admonishment.

Ali watched helplessly as he advanced on her restrained form.

She could barely make out his features – much less his expression – the way he loomed over her, a big, dark shadow against the overhead light. But she was almost certain she saw satisfaction gleaming in his eyes at the fear he saw in hers.

"Did you really think we wouldn't find you?" he asked, his eyebrows raised in calm enquiry.

Not anymore. Not now that she knew exactly how they had found them. Ali squeezed her eyes shut for a second. "The panic button, it included a tracker." They had never had a chance.

She turned her head back to where Rob was watching her with a pained expression. Guilt ate at her insides. She had done this to him.

"Yes," Doctor whispered next to her ear. "It is your fault." The words sliced into her body like daggers. How could she?

"Don't listen to him." Rob's voice sounded hoarse.

Ali shook her head. He didn't *know*.

"Have you still not learned your lesson, Recruit?" Doctor's footsteps trailed a path to Rob's chair. "Perhaps I should let Noah finish what he started?"

Rob clenched his teeth when Doctor's large thumb pressed the bruise on his cheek.

"But this time," he said, gripping Rob's jaw tightly. "I'll let him break your bones."

"No." The word was out, before she could stop it.

"How sweet. The girl wants to be a knight. Still trying to atone for killing your mother, are you?"

Ali's trembling increased under the full force of his stare. So he had read the Psychiatrist's notes. He knew how hard it was for her to see others punished, and he used the knowledge without remorse. She pushed herself to continue. "You're right," she said, lifting her chin. "It was my fault. I shouldn't have fought the inauguration, and I apologize. I'll take my punishment as you see fit." She almost choked on the last few words, but Rob had done enough for her. It was time she got the spotlight off him and back onto herself.

"Of course you will," Doctor said gently. "But first, we have an inauguration to care of."

Two Marshals and the Medic appeared at Doctor's side at his beckoning.

"Let's make sure it takes place without interruption this

time, shall we?"

Anthony saved her from answering by pushing her face into the seat. Ali felt the steel band snap closed around her head.

A sense of déjà vu overcame her. Just yesterday she had been in exactly the same position, except for the guilt now cursing through her body.

Ali felt the cold, lifeless fingers of MedicaFive tracing her skull, searching for the perfect spot to cut into her cranial bone. The low hum of the laser raised the hairs on her arms, and she held her breath, waiting for the pain. Instead she felt a dull pressure where the light beam cut into her flesh.

Ali's heart rate accelerated, causing the Biomonitor to issue a shrill warning.

Out of the corner of her eye, she saw Rob's legs strain against his shackles. A colourful bolt of discharge leapt from the shackles and electricity licked at his bare leg.

Ali jerked, and the hum cut off.

"I would be careful about fighting your bonds too much," Doctor told Rob in the sudden silence. "They are connected to your mobi's pain controls. If you trigger another warning shock and she moves a second time, MedicaFive may not be able to stop the laser in time. Restraints or not, she jerks and we may cut something important."

Ali focused on regulating her panic an instant too late. The Biomonitor screamed another warning. Rob's lower legs tensed, but otherwise didn't move.

"MedicaFive, continue."

The pressure resumed; then stopped.

"Screen two."

One of the floorboards below her slid away, revealing a screen embedded beneath. It flickered to life.

Ali gagged at the camera-feed of the open wound at the back of her head. Closing her eyes against the view, she forced herself to breathe slowly.

A crackling noise and Rob's hiss of pain had her eyes popping open a second later. But it was Doctor's face she saw, as he looked into the camera, positioned above the chair.

"You disappoint me, Recruit." He lifted his hand in front of his face, and Ali saw a remote control dangling from his fingers. "I can trigger the pain controls in his mobi manually too."

Her stomach churned. He had tasered Rob again, because she had closed her eyes. There had to be a second camera right next to the screen she was looking at, and it was probably feeding to one of the wall-mounted monitors. Bile rose in her throat. Who on earth had thought of a construction like that? And how evil did a man have to be to enjoy the spectacle? He was supposed to be human. There was nothing human about this monster.

She moved her eyes back to the screen, trying to ignore the satisfied smirk on his face as she struggled to comply with his wishes. He sat the remote back down on the instruments' table. *Within easy reach.*

She could do this. She could get through this without fainting. They were just pictures of her brain. The thought didn't help.

Ali watched the screen as MedicaFive extracted her microchip from a tiny plastic sleeve. Using its steel-tipped fingers, the MediBot sunk the device into the wound.

Ali swallowed hard, trying not to move. It was no use. She gagged again.

"Oh no, don't you ruin all this good effort now." Doctor's voice sounded almost…amused.

The screen went blessedly black then, and she felt the unmistakable pressure of MedicaFive closing the wound. The smell of burnt flesh threatened to snap the last of her control as the MediBot etched the Hybrid mark into her head. Taking slow, controlled breaths through her nose, Ali fought to hold the sickness at bay, when she felt her mind shift.

"We have entered stage one."

The shackles released, and Doctor's shoes pushed into her line of vision.

"Get up."

Ali complied before the chip could process the command. She wasn't ready to face the truth, didn't want to know if the chip could make her do things she didn't want to do. The room spun around her.

Doctor chuckled. "If everyone would be that eager, it could save us a lot of hassle inaugurating people."

Still perilously close to vomiting, fainting, or both, Ali couldn't do more than steady herself with a white-knuckled grip on the inauguration chair.

"Now to the punishment you were talking about taking earlier."

The room ground to an abrupt halt as adrenaline shot through her system. Had the inauguration not been punishment enough? Ali's eyes snagged on the small circular saw that was lying unused on the instruments' table. Had it really only been a few days since she had seen the recording? It felt like a lifetime.

Doctor reached for the remote.

The continuous discharge flashed white this time, making her scream in a voice that shook as violently as Rob's defenceless body. "Stop! Please, stop."

Doctor had obviously expected her reaction, because he rounded on her with astonishing swiftness. "There is one thing you will learn right now. I give orders. You *follow* them."

He lifted her hand and pressed the remote into her palm. "Your turn."

"No." But her fingers curled around the device of their own accord.

"Too low for your liking?" He turned the setting higher.

Ali bit her lip to keep her mouth shut and tasted blood.

"There's hope for you yet," Doctor said to Rob, who was trying to regain control over his muscles. "She's a fast learner." His focus swung back to her. "Now, flick the switch."

Ali could feel the compulsion in her brain gathering force as she struggled to keep her fingers off the trigger. She managed for a second. Two. She flicked the switch.

The sound of the discharge crackling turned her stomach anew. Rob's body shook.

"Keep your thumb on the trigger and turn up the intensity!"

Her index finger whispered over the touch dial, raising the intensity of the electrical current. Rob's body shook harder. Tears shot into her eyes. *She* was doing this to him.

"Higher."

She watched her body comply.

How long could Rob stand this before his heart gave out?

"Higher."

Her fingers hovered over the dial for a second, but the compulsion was too strong. Five more settings to go. The indicator started to glow a warning yellow. Was he going to ask her to turn it up higher until the dial ran out, until the indicator turned red?

Rob had said they didn't kill Recruits.

"Higher."

She whacked the dial on max. Rob jerked in his shackles, his eyes rolling back in his head.

"Stop."

She flicked the switch before he had finished speaking the single syllable. Her legs gave out, and she emptied her stomach right there on the floor.

"Smart after all." His voice didn't sound quite amused anymore.

Ali looked up at his face, wiping her mouth.

"So you figured I wouldn't let him die. You hurt him to help him. A valuable lesson that I hope you'll remember well, Hybrid. Sometimes we must hurt what we love the most."

He turned and left the room without another word.

Ali scrambled to her feet to check on Rob. He was slumped on the bench, his body continuing to spasm at irregular intervals.

She tapped his cheek lightly. "Rob?"

A moan escaped his lips.

"Rob...please..."

His eyes opened into slits.

Alive and conscious. Thank you.

She grabbed at his shackles. They were still locked, and she didn't have a key.

Her eyes darted frantically around the room. They were alone. Anthony and the Marshals must have left before she even got up, off the chair. There was an emergency button on the wall. She pressed it then took Rob's cheeks into her hands.

"Rob, look at me... No...no, don't pass out. The nurses will be here soon. I'm so sorry." She could feel tears running down her face, but she didn't care. "I'm so sorry. I...I couldn't control it."

It took him multiple attempts to speak.

"I know." His voice sounded like sandpaper. He licked his lips. "Glad it was me...not you... Not your fault."

"Of course it was my fault. I'm so sorry."

"He...made you."

The sob broke from her chest before she could hold it back. She had just tortured him, and he was still defending her.

The door slid open, and two nurses rushed in. They jerked back when they saw Ali.

"Help him," Ali winced, scrambling back against the counter when they continued to eye her warily. Goodness, she wasn't some beast. Then she caught sight of herself in the mirror. Her head was full of blood from the inauguration. Her lips were blue from shock and had a cut in the middle.

Her body shook as if *she* was the one who had almost been fried with electrical currents. She was a mess.

The nurses finally found their courage, rushing to help Rob. He roused further under the helping hands of the medical staff.

Time to leave, Ali decided before someone else gave her another order. She would stay as far away from Rob as possible. He was just not safe in her vicinity.

Pushing away from the counter, she stood for a few seconds to find her balance. Blood loss, shock... She really didn't want to faint. Rob needed help much more urgently than she did. She took a tentative step. The world stayed upright.

Ali took a last look at the friend who had almost gotten killed trying to save her life, and then left the room as quietly as possible.

***

Hours later, Ali cursed herself for her own inability to stay away.

She had thought she wandered aimlessly.

Staring at the number on the digital display next to the door in front of her, she had to admit that her roaming the hallways of the Sanatorium hadn't been so aimless after all. Ali ran a finger over the number. 2388. Her heart squeezed, and she let her hand fall back to her side.

What was she doing, standing in front of his door like this? Did she really think he would want to see her, after what she had done to him? Snowball's chance in hell, was probably the best phrase to describe *that* scenario. And what about her promise to stay away?

She was about to turn around, when she heard the quiet swish of the door.

"Ali?"

A wave of guilt slammed into her, when she saw his pale complexion in the soft light of the room. A fine tremor still shook his hands. He looked like hell.

Of course he does. You almost killed him.

She really should leave him alone. It would be the best for both of them. Ali took a tentative step back. Another one.

"Ali, come in. Please?"

Her steps faltered. How could she deny his wish? How couldn't she deny it?

The conflicting emotions tore at her. What was she supposed to do?

Ali glanced back at Rob. He was watching her. Waiting.

She stepped into the semi-darkness.

"Hi." His voice was rough. His normally brilliant smile barely clung to his lips. Ali felt like a villain. Her guilt increased.

"Don't look like that." He squeezed her hand. "I'm alive."

No thanks to her. Her gaze slid away.

He pulled on her hand until she looked at him again.

"I'm not blaming you, Ali. I know he made you do it. You didn't have a choice."

She heard the words, but they didn't help. It had been *her* thumb pulling that trigger, *her* finger raising the dial.

She looked at their joined hands in front of her. They both shook now. She swallowed hard.

"I-I tried." She couldn't manage more than a whisper. "I-

I tried so h-hard."

"I know."

"I'm sorry." She tore her hand from his and ran out of the room.

Chapter 11

The rain had come back. Thick grey clouds crowded the sky. Gale-force winds tore branches and leaves from the trees in the park and rattled the doors on her balcony.

The weather matched her mood. Grey, cold, ready to cry.

The night had only gotten worse after she had fled Rob's quarters and locked herself in her room on the off chance that he was trying to come after her. She didn't trust herself around him any longer.

She had trusted him, though. Trusted he wouldn't force his way inside, even though a tiny part of her had hoped he would.

Dark dreams had haunted her relentlessly, and the inauguration had entered its final stage in the early hours of the morning.

Ali knew, because the structure of her mind had cracked with enough force to send her mental-self reeling on a rocky plateau that looked shockingly familiar. Behind closed eyes, the fissure she had first discovered when she went to the medical facilities after her fight with the Chosen had torn open, hungrily swallowing avalanche after avalanche of broken boulders. As if that wasn't enough, the dark beckoning of the Abyss – an Abyss that Ali could feel with every fibre of her body – had risen from the developing gorge. A malicious hiss continued to taunt her, one monster to another.

You deserve to die for the betrayal of your friend and nobody will miss you.

The steady stream of spiteful remarks echoing off the walls of her mind had worn Ali down, until the Abyss's voice was everywhere. Her view was shifting between terrifying visuals from inside her head and the stark familiarity of the ceiling above her, and she couldn't help but wonder when Aiden would stroll into the room, calmly offering her death.

Ali crumpled the blanket in her fist.

That damned Protector. It was all his fault.

No it was yours, the Abyss hissed. You didn't remember the panic button. You almost killed your friend.

Ali shook her head, trying to dislodge the entity. Trying to fight it.

It was useless. The thing was in her mind.

For better, for worse. Until death do us part.

Ali clutched at her temples.

The quicker you accept it—

Ali clenched her back teeth until the pain in her head eclipsed the voice grating along her nerves.

The Abyss laughed. A rasping sound that made the hairs on Ali's nape rise.

I'll get you in the end.

Ali wanted to deny it, but the words rang true. She would

die. Two weeks and her brain would turn to mush.

Ali pushed her fist into her mouth to keep from wailing.

Why her?

She pressed her pillow to her chest, curled into a foetal position, and sobbed.

***

When Ali surfaced from her meltdown, the hiss was gone, but the Abyss still breathed and threatened inside her.

Outside, the rain had stopped and the wind had cleared most of the billowing clouds. Morning sunlight glinted around the edges of the thin white cover that remained, but instead of making her feel better, the beautiful sight just made her feel worse.

With effort, Ali finally dragged her body out of bed. She pulled the duffle bag with her possessions out of the wardrobe and dug to the bottom. A single chocolate bar fell into her hands. It was all that was left from the samples they had received during their *Human Culture* studies at the Centre. It was the only thing she could think of to lift her mood. A simple chemical reaction inside her brain.

She tore the wrapping.

"I'll have to take that off you."

Ali went utterly still at the deep rumble behind her. Forcing a calm expression onto her face, she turned to see the black-clad Hybrid who had saved her twice, betrayed her once, and looked as if he didn't care either way.

Standing just inside her door - a door she should have heard opening – he studied her with an inscrutable expression.

Live as my slave…

Ali shrugged off the memory. She doubted he even knew the Program was using his avatar for assessments.

She held out the chocolate bar to him. He would take it anyway.

Aiden's long fingers closed around the treat, brushing hers in the process. The soft tingle of electricity at her fingertips was unexpected, as was the sudden dilation of his pupils. He narrowed his eyes almost instantly, hiding the black discs.

"Wha—"

"Doctor is waiting for you in his Office," he interrupted her calmly then strode out of her room without another word.

Staring after his retreating back in confusion, Ali clenched and unclenched her hand to get rid of the sensation. Her day was just getting weirder and weirder.

***

The Office screamed wealth like all the official areas of the Sanatorium. An expensive hand-woven rug cushioned Ali's steps as she followed Aiden into the empty room. A large, naturally grown teak wood office desk was positioned strategically in the middle of the floor-to-ceiling windows that offered a jaw-dropping view of the surrounding gardens. Various state-of-the-art DID devices sat on top of the desk. In complete contrast, the bookshelves on the walls held rows and rows of old leather-bound books, each of which, Ali guessed, was probably worth more than the diamond-and-steel door leading into the building.

"You don't look impressed," Aiden remarked beside her, once more studying her face. It was the first thing he had said since she caught up with him halfway to the Office.

"I don't like pretence," she replied, stunning herself with her honesty.

Something had changed when they had inaugurated her the day before. Something in the power construct had shifted. It was almost as if she had lost her ability to bend to the Program's rules. How could she bend, when they had already broken her?

They had forced her to betray her friend, had taken away her life even though she was still breathing. What else could they do?

"Your honesty is admirable, if foolish, Hybrid."

Doctor's voice had Ali turning back to the door.

"Your black soul, even if somewhat daunting, does not exempt you from disciplinary action."

Daunting? Was he serious? He thought the *black soul* was daunting? How about deadly instead?

But Ali knew better than to voice her thoughts. A comment on interior decoration might go unpunished; sassing the Leader of the Program certainly would not. She may no longer be willing to play their games, but neither did she want to give them another reason to go after Rob. She wouldn't be able to bear it. She might as well give up and die. But contrary to what the chip in her brain dictated, her conscious self didn't have a death wish.

Doctor obviously read her silence as agreement, because he released her from his cold stare and took a seat behind the desk. He contemplated her for a few quiet seconds. "I assume you have entered the designation stage."

Except there was no designation for her, was there? Only

desperation. And death.

Rage and helplessness bubbled inside her.

Ali pushed her fingers into the ornate carvings running the length of the desk, grateful for the electronic equipment that hid her lower body from Doctor's eyes. As always the pain steadied her. "Yes, Doctor."

"Very well. In this case, you will be assigned a dedicated Protector with immediate effect. We wouldn't want you to die before you enter the testing phase for the anialbus serum."

Ali felt the woodwork bite into her skin.

"And who will this Protector be?" she asked, grinding timber against bone.

"Me."

Her eyes flew to the forbidding man standing beside her.

Instant denial hovered on the tip of her tongue, even as the logical part of her brain told her she should count herself lucky. Aiden was the best Protector the Program had. If anybody could keep her alive, it would be him. But he had also effectively signed her death sentence returning her to the compound.

His eyebrows lifted, daring her to speak.

"Aiden will be your Protector," Doctor confirmed, rendering any objections from her side useless.

Ali bit the inside of her cheek. The choice was made. She could agree reverently, or be forced into the union.

"Understood, Doctor."

Blood rushed back into her fingertips, as she let go of the desk.

Dealing with Aiden couldn't be harder than handling the

fact that her own mind was suddenly her enemy. Maybe she wouldn't even have to put up with him for the whole two weeks. Who knew when the Abyss would defeat her? She had come close enough to ending it all this morning. If the crack had been wider, the pull just a little bit stronger...

"To study the course of the illness without restrictions we will not limit your cognitive abilities at this point in time," Doctor continued. "However, our primary objective is to keep you alive until we can test the new batch of our anialbus serum. If, at any point in the process, we doubt that your actions are a direct result of the compulsion you experience due to your black soul, we won't hesitate to put a mindlock on you. Is that clear?"

Ali managed a nod, even though the threat had just added another layer of terror to her already messed up life. Fitting her with a mindlock would ensure that they could still test their serum, but she would be little more than a vegetating mass of cells. "Yes, Doctor."

They wouldn't let her go easily, she realized. Jumping into the Abyss for fun, or out of sheer desperation, was out of the question. And even if the chip won before the two weeks were over, even if she couldn't help but attempt diving head first into the black gorge, chances were that Aiden would be there in time to stop her. Obedient dog that he was.

Looking at him, Ali had trouble aligning the term with the powerful Protector standing next to her. Nevertheless, she had no doubt it was the truth. Aiden carried a chip like every other Hybrid, and his own wishes had little impact on his actions. He would do as Doctor dictated. And right now, what Doctor dictated was to keep her alive.

"To aid in your longevity…" The ridiculous comment brought her back to the present. "…we have scheduled daily meetings with Psy05, or as you will probably know her better, Rt2030."

Beth.

"She has been inaugurated as a Psychiatrist two days ago. You will be her first patient, and you will commence counselling after this meeting. Tomorrow morning, you will have an appointment with medical staff to calibrate the microchip to our instruments in the Lab. The Medics will make sure that we continue to receive information on your brain activity, after your current brain activity sensor dissolves." He looked straight into her eyes. "Your survival of the illness and the anialbus serum means as much to us as it does to you. I hope that you will make it. You are dismissed."

***

Ali stepped from the Office with Aiden by her side. Her stomach rumbled.

"You won't skip breakfast again, no matter how desperate you want to curl up in bed and die."

His guess was amazingly accurate.

Or a product of his dealings with other activated carriers that he had been asked to babysit over the years, Ali thought with a sinking heart. How many Hybrids had he accompanied on their way to insanity? Remorseless. Cold. Controlled.

"I don't need your advice." She flinched at the vehemence in her voice.

Aiden didn't even blink. "This wasn't advice. This was an order."

Sure enough she could feel the answering compulsion from the chip curl through her mind.

Who's the dog now?

She traced her fingers across the indentations the wood had left on the palm of her hand, finding an anchor in the little bolts of pain that transformed to colourful flashes behind her closed eyelids. It reminded her of fireworks. Searing but beautiful.

"Rt2120."

Ali reopened her eyes to find Aiden watching her with a blank expression.

"Why do you care?" she asked, her voice steadier than she would have anticipated. "I'm nothing to you. You didn't even know me a week ago. You've been ordered to keep me alive. My welfare beyond that is none of your concern."

"Who says I care?" he asked without inflection. "Do you *want* to jump?"

"Of course not. My black soul compels me—"

Ali shut her mouth as the meaning of his words suddenly penetrated.

He was P001. Protection was *his* compulsion, his designation. And she should have guessed that his skills extended much further than to simply keeping the target alive.

Somehow the possibility that her well-being was nothing more than a compulsion for him made things even worse. "I don't want your manufactured pity." She tossed the words at him with a spark of renewed anger.

"Well, you don't get a choice," he countered calmly, infuriating her even more. "Come. I'll take you to Beth."

And her legs started walking.

***

"Ali." Beth wrapped her in a tight hug the moment she stepped into the Psychiatrist's office.

Ali forced herself to stand still. She couldn't shake what had happened during her last psychiatric evaluation. It didn't make a difference that this time the Psychiatrist was Beth.

If anything, it was worse. What would Beth think of her now that she knew Ali wasn't quite right in the head? A mental illness, for goodness's sake. Ali squeezed her eyes shut in embarrassment.

"I'll see you after lunch."

At the reminder of the dark presence behind her, she pulled herself together and stepped out of Beth's embrace.

"Yes, sir."

"Uh-oh, what's going on with the two of you?"

Ali dragged her gaze from the closing door. "I have a nanny." And wasn't that just the icing on the cake of mortification.

"Him? Seriously? How're you getting along?"

We're not. "He just orders me around."

"For your own good, Ali, I'm sure. You should count yourself lucky. He's the best Protector the Program has. He'll keep you safe."

Ali shook her head. She didn't want to discuss the exasperating Hybrid or the fact that she couldn't even look out for herself anymore.

"Nice office," she said instead, latching onto the first

neutral topic that came to mind.

It was too. Compared to the Psychiatrist's office Ali had seen a few days ago, this room looked almost cosy with its overstuffed chairs, dark teak furniture and light-brown leather chaise lounge. Soft instrumental music floated from an inbuilt sound system, while smouldering incense sticks scented the air in an old-fashioned way that somehow worked.

"It is, isn't it?" Beth beamed at her, clearly in love with the setting. "It's designed to put Hybrids at ease."

It worked. Ali hated it. She didn't want to relax in the enemy's lair.

"Looks like you've hit the jackpot." Ali's attempt at a smile felt suspiciously like a grimace.

Beth pulled her down into one of the chairs. "And you haven't. I'm so sorry, Ali. How are you holding up?"

So this is when the psychoanalysis starts, Ali thought reluctantly impressed by her friend's smooth transition.

"I'm fine." And maybe if she said it often enough, she would believe it too.

"Any symptoms yet? Nightmares, mood swings, cracks in your mind?"

All of it. "Some."

"Which ones?"

"Goodness, Beth. Stop firing questions at me, will you? This isn't an interrogation."

"Of course it isn't. It's a psychiatric assessment, Ali. I'm *supposed* to ask you questions. Otherwise, I won't be able to help you."

"Then don't?"

"Don't help you? Why would you say that?"

Ali shrugged her shoulders. She had just arrived and already she needed to get out of here. Let Beth blame it on the mood swings if she wanted to.

But her friend wasn't finished yet. "You're going through a very tough time right now. You'll need all the help you can get."

"I'm telling you, I'm fine."

"Don't lie to me, Ali. You're scared."

"So you have finished your assessment now, huh? You have me all figured out."

"I don't have you all figured out. That's why I need you to tell me. I need honesty."

"From your patients?"

"From my *friends*!"

The words she had wanted to say suddenly stuck in her throat.

Ali swallowed around the lump. "I hate," she said quietly, "*hate* that everyone suddenly seems to know how I feel, what I will and won't, should and shouldn't do. It's still *my* life. Significantly reduced in length, but hey..."

Beth's face blurred in front of her.

Ali blinked, cursing when the first tear fell. She had known that this whole cosy setup was a trap.

"It's okay to cry." Beth touched her shoulder.

"No, it isn't." Ali sniffed. "It really isn't. I need to be strong."

"You need time to adjust."

"I don't *have* time."

"Not even a minute?" Beth shook her head. "Ali, you're

trying to skip ahead and get straight to the fighting part. Give yourself a break. Your whole life has been turned upside down."

"It's his fault. I hate him." Ali fisted her hands.

"Who do you hate?"

"Doctor. He didn't even c-care. He enjoyed that I was scared." The tears were flowing freely now. "I'm s-so scared, Beth."

"And that's okay too," her friend replied. "It's normal to be overwhelmed in the face of such a huge challenge. It's nothing to be embarrassed about, Ali. I'm scared too. For you and for me. You are my first patient. If I wasn't scared, that's when I would be worried. That's when you should be worried." She took Ali's hands and waited until Ali looked up. "I have the file from your previous evaluation."

Ali flinched, but Beth didn't let go. "I have downloaded every single bit of information from the servers to do with your activation. I have good guidance on how to treat you, how to prepare you for what lies ahead of you, now that I can use my microchip to access previous cases on the database. But, Ali, I need your help. Will you help me?"

Ali wiped at the tears still spilling over her cheeks and contemplated her friend's serious expression. Beth wasn't taking this responsibility lightly. Neither was she looking down on Ali, as if her illness suddenly made her a lesser being.

"I will help you," Ali said finally, hoarsely. "I will help me."

***

After lunch – time that Ali had spent hiding in her room

surprisingly without interruption through a Marshal – Aiden picked her up from her quarters to fill her in on her new daily routine.

As she followed him through the corridors of the outhouse and out into the gardens, Ali recalled Beth's parting words.

Remember, her friend had said, no matter how much you dislike being his protégé, for one reason or another, right now he's the only Hybrid standing between you and certain death.

It was a chilling realization, as was the reality that he would dictate her every move for the next two weeks, the way he did right now.

"Except for tomorrow when you will have your medical exam, you will continue your usual schedule of trainings and lectures with only a few minor changes that I will outline."

"Sir?" It wasn't what she had expected to hear. It didn't even make sense. "What good does the schedule do for someone who—" She couldn't say it.

Aiden didn't have the same problem. "Someone who is doomed to die?" he asked and Ali felt as if he had suckerpunched her in the gut.

"Yes." Her confirmation sounded way too thin.

"Occupational therapy. It will give you something to focus on besides your illness. It will keep you from dwelling on your fate." He swept his hand in a wide arch, encompassing the Sanatorium's buildings and grounds. "Unfortunately, there isn't much else available here that keeps a Hybrid busy." He looked back at her, his expression unreadable. "Unless you count chasing the occasional runaway."

Ali pressed her lips together. *Two-nil for the Protector.*

"You will train each morning before breakfast and in the evenings before dinner. Twice a day, in the morning after your Psychiatrist appointment and in the afternoon, you will attend study classes. You may choose the subjects yourself as you won't require specific education for your black soul."

No, Ali thought grimly, she guessed she didn't need specific education to die.

"After dinner, you'll have one hour of idle time and after that, you're required to be in your room by yourself until the sleeping cycle starts. During your idle time you are free to roam the buildings, read, train, or go and spend your time outdoors. Depending on my assessment of your state of mind I may decide to be present or absent at all times. This way." He suddenly grabbed her upper arm, jolting her system.

"As you didn't have time to sign up for any lectures yet, we will bring forward our evening training today. You will then have the rest of the afternoon free to look at the lecture schedule and sign up for the appropriate courses. Any questions so far?"

But Ali was no longer listening. The strength of his fingers digging into her skin suddenly drove home what he had just said.

"Our training, sir?"

"You and me."

One-to-one lessons with the most dangerous Hybrid in the entire Program? A Hybrid she had attempted to defy earlier?

Ali tried to dig her heels into the ground and found she couldn't. A sharp tug on her arm easily propelled her into the corridor of one of the more isolated outhouses.

Aiden pushed through the door of the empty martial arts room at the far end of the hallway and Ali's heart skipped a beat.

Was he planning to punish her?

Her eyes darted left and right, in search of a way out. There was only one door and Aiden stood in front of it.

His arms hung loosely at his sides, he looked relaxed, dangerous, and ready, all at the same time.

A wave of adrenaline flooded Ali's blood, her body's attempt to even the odds against a more powerful opponent. She didn't think it would be enough.

Almost without thought she assumed her defence position. Knees bent. Arms up. High alert.

Aiden didn't move. He was watching her with an intent look in his eyes.

Her breath came in rasping pants. Something she hadn't experienced since the first few lessons at the Centre, all those years ago. Not even when she had fought Otis had she felt this panicked.

Ali knew why. She wouldn't have the flicker of a chance against the Hybrid in front of her. She had never fought such a lethal opponent. He could kill her with one strike. Even worse, he could leave her bleeding on the floor. They wouldn't find her for hours.

"Look at me." Aiden's steady voice was the complete contrast to the turmoil in her head. It beckoned her to comply. "I'm here to protect you, not to kill you." The calm words snapped her focus away from the gory pictures in her head.

Of course he wouldn't kill her. He was her Protector.

Then why was she still terrified?

Aiden suddenly moved towards her. Before she could stop herself, Ali struck out. He easily deflected the blow, the muscles in his body shifting dangerously.

He gripped the nape of her neck and gently shook her. Tingles of awareness raced over her skin.

"You're having a panic attack," he said, "a symptom of the illness. Control your breathing, Hybrid. Two beats in, four beats out." He kept repeating the pattern until she breathed with him.

The slow rhythm helped. Her adrenaline level dropped. Moments later, she felt the connection with the chip snap into place. Her muscles froze, and a slow trickle of information downloaded from the bioservers into her brain.

The hall in front of her eyes darkened to a sheet of black, and all noise ceased to penetrate past her eardrums. Half a minute later the world snapped back into focus.

She hadn't even realized that she had forgotten to connect to the bioservers for the daily data update.

"From now on, you will update before morning training."

"Yes, sir." She felt the pressure from the chip against her vocal cords, to confirm the order. It was the first time she had felt the storm of compulsion gathering in her mind since lunch, Ali realized. But it had been the third command Aiden had given her since they had entered the hall.

Chapter 12

Ali looked at the dark figure reflecting on Electra's screen and wondered if there was anything the leader of the Protection Squad couldn't control. So far she had crossed *a tranquilizer dart at night* and *his own emotions* off the list. Now, it seemed that time itself was his slave, too.

"Ready?"

His voice sounded slightly rougher than the day before, and Ali felt a stirring of hope. Could it be that perfectly put together Aiden was at least struggling to get up in mornings, like most of the population?

"Yes, sir." She grabbed a bottle of water and walked towards the entrance that he blocked with his big body. He didn't move.

Ali stopped before she ran into him and tilted her head up to look at his face.

He was taller than she remembered. More powerful, too. Energy positively radiated from his body in waves.

She stepped back and thought she saw the ghost of a smile touch his lips at her cowardice.

"How're you feeling today?"

"Good." She was glad she could say it with conviction.

"No more panic attacks?"

"Nothing." Not a sound from the Abyss in the back of her mind.

Ali hoped the thing had died. Better it than Ali. If only she dared check on it.

Alone the thought gave her the creeps.

Aiden studied her face, zeroing in on her eyes. A second ticked by. Another. The urge to squirm was almost overwhelming. What was he doing?

"Have this," he released her gaze, and pushed something into her hand.

Ali looked at the cereal bar sticking out between her fingers.

So he *had* realized that her medical appointment made his order to attend breakfast impossible. She hoped he didn't expect gratitude for providing an alternative. Manipulative Hybrid.

Ali took a quick bite then hurried down the hall after Aiden's retreating back.

"Slow down…sir."

Aiden raised an eyebrow over his shoulder, but shortened his strides.

It seemed she wasn't the only one who didn't like taking orders.

But he can ignore you.

"I'll wait for you in the reception area," Aiden said minutes later, when they arrived at the medical facilities. "The examination room is over there."

Ali followed his gaze to a slightly open door and felt the

food in her stomach turn to lead.

"Go!"

Compulsion propelled her frozen body forward until she stood in the middle of her nightmare. Only MedicaFive was missing.

"They had to make them look alike," she said aloud, desperate to hear her own voice.

She sank into the Medic's chair.

Please let it be over soon, she prayed quietly and closed her eyes against a view she worried would hurtle her into another panic attack.

It will never be over. The insidious hiss bled from the fracture in her mind and dripped into her blood like black, putrid poison.

The Abyss was talking to her again.

A cry of desperation stuck in Ali's throat.

She tore her eyes open. They caught on the sparkling blade of a scalpel on the other side of the room, and her reality split.

With the soft material of the chair still pressed against her thighs, her feet firmly planted on the floor, Ali felt her body walk to the medical counter. She watched, entranced, as her right hand reached out to run her index finger along the sharp edge of the tool. A perfect masterpiece. Another finger joined the first.

At once, the unexpectedly heavy scalpel lay in her palm.

Ali turned the blade, its movement catching the fluorescent light from overhead.

She only hesitated a second before she pressed the cold metal against the small of her wrist. Ali traced her blue-black veins with the flat side of the blade, then tilted the tool slightly. The piercing tip felt almost like a caress. A droplet of black blood oozed onto the surface of her skin. She pressed down harder.

"Ali?"

The scalpel clattered to the floor.

"You look like you've seen a ghost."

Ali looked at her wrist. The blood was gone. The scalpel lay on the medical counter across the room, untouched. Ali was sitting in the chair.

She gripped the armrest and lifted her gaze to Anthony's.

"You have done this to me," she snarled, panic colouring her words as black as the blood in her veins had been.

"Ali—"

"Stay away from me." She pushed the chair backwards. Her shoes screamed against the linoleum floor. The backrest hit the counter with force, sending an array of gauze packages flying. Ali didn't care. "This is *your* fault," she spat, waving her wrist at him.

He held out his hand, shaking his head. "You were a dormant carrier from birth. I had nothing to do with your genetic assembly."

"Is that what you tell yourself, when you can't sleep at nights? You're a monster."

"A monster who's trying to help you, right now. Let me help you, Ali. Calm down."

She didn't feel like calming down. She felt like screaming.

So she did.

The door sliced open.

"Silence!"

The command fired through her body. Her vocal cords gave out. She was nothing. A shell without free will. A gathering of cells controlled by a foreign force. Sobs shook her, although no sound left her lips.

Aiden loomed large at the entrance of the room, his gaze fixated on the Medic.

"Why the hell did you let her freak out like that?"

Anthony blanched. "She was already..." He swallowed. "I couldn't—"

"Excuses," Aiden cut him off. "You have a rank. Learn how to use it." He pierced Ali with a glare. "Get yourself under control, Hybrid."

Ali stared back at him through burning eyes, fighting the compulsion until it seared a path into her brain. Painful. Anchoring.

"Yes, sir."

His departure left her feeling oddly bereft.

She dragged her gaze to Anthony who was clearly struggling to regain his composure. Why was he so afraid of Aiden? As a Medic, he should rank higher than the Protector and still Anthony had cowered in front of the other man. It didn't make sense. Nothing made sense anymore.

"I will need to take a small amount of blood." Anthony pointed at her hand still gripping the armrest. He eyed her warily, clearly expecting her to jump at him any second. Or start screaming again.

Ali did neither. Instead she held out her arm.

He finally dredged up the courage to stab her finger with the laser and collect the blood.

Red blood, Ali realized. She doubted she would have had the energy to care either way. Right now, she just felt numb.

Ali watched with little interest as Anthony configured the instruments to work with the chip.

"The Biomonitor confirms that your illness is progressing as planned."

She wasn't surprised. She could feel it inside of her.

"That's all for today," Anthony said, looking relieved. "You're free to go."

Ali left the examination room as if in trance. She didn't even notice Aiden still waiting for her until he touched her arm sending tingles through her body.

"Alana."

His voice was sharp as the tip of the scalpel had been when it had pierced her skin. Ali lifted her eyes to his with difficulty. He looked different somehow. Almost as if he was in pain. Why did he know her full name?

"Are you alright?" Her voice sounded strange. The question more so. He wasn't the one who had just had the most bone chilling vision of his entire life. But there was something about his eyes that she couldn't ignore.

"Fine. What happened in there?"

"I—" She didn't know.

He grabbed her elbow a little too fierce and gave her a shake. Ali could feel her body flop with the movement. Her teeth rattled.

"Alana, look at me."

She *was* looking at him. She was falling into his eyes.

"Focus!"

Compulsion adjusted her vision to focus on the flint grey

irises surrounding his pupils. His eyes, she realized, weren't completely grey. White veins shot out from the centre like lightning, giving her the impression of the sky on a stormy day. The grey clouds suddenly darkened, and he gave her another slight shake.

"Tell me what happened in there."

The compulsion was almost familiar now, the way it slid through her brain, prompting her to answer.

"I had a daydream," she said slowly. "I was cutting my artery with a scalpel."

His eyes flicked to her hand, and Ali realized she was stroking her fingers over her wrist in an almost obsessive fashion. She forced herself to stop.

"I thought I was supposed to jump into an Abyss, not slit my wrists." She looked at him, lost.

"That's why it's called a dream," he said. "We substitute things. But that's not why you screamed. Why did you scream?"

How did he know? "Seeing Anthony again..." Ali trailed off, swallowing hard. "I just lost it."

"Don't do that again."

"Is that an order?"

His lips twitched. "A state of panic cannot be controlled. Not even through compulsion."

"What does that mean?" Her brain still had trouble catching up with the real world.

"I can't order you not to panic. It was a polite request."

Polite? She didn't think so. Aiden wouldn't know polite if it stepped on his toes.

"I'll try."

"Don't try. Just do it," he said and slid back into his usual dispassionate self.

Ali blinked. Had she imagined the thin crack in his thick layer of control?

She followed willingly as he guided her out of the medical facilities. Sunshine wrapped her in its warm embrace, and Ali took a deep breath.

This was only day two of the illness. What would she feel like on day seven? Day eight?

She was so immersed in her worries that she didn't realize Aiden had steered her in the direction of the training rooms until they stepped into the hall and the familiar scent of wood, sweat, and leather tickled her nose.

She looked up at him. He wanted to train with her *now*?

"It will take your mind off what happened." He waited calmly until she followed him over the threshold.

Good dog, Ali. Good dog.

***

Three hours later, Ali entered the lunch hall with mixed feelings. As Aiden had promised, she had forgotten all about the incident during the training with him, but it had come crashing back the minute she had entered the Psychiatrist's office. Talking to Beth about it had proved to be more difficult than Ali had imagined.

Admitting a weakness had never been her strength.

It bore testament to Beth's skills as a Psychiatrist that she had managed to pry most of it out of Ali anyway. In the end, Beth had been pleased with the way their session had gone. Ali, on the other hand, was still trying to figure out how she felt about her friend's interrogation techniques.

"Ali."

The remembered horror of that deep, beautiful voice sounding hoarse and broken shattered her contemplations and unleashed another of the too many monsters in her mind.

"Rob." She tried to smile through the vision of his body hanging lifeless in its shackles, and failed.

"Oh, no. Don't you dare." His voice was firm. "We've been through this. I've forgiven you." He grabbed her hand. "I've stayed away from you, Ali. I've tried to give you space to get over it. But I can't wait any longer." He laid his free hand against her cheek. "For the last time, Ali. I'm still your friend. Unless you don't want me to be. Which will hurt more than anything you could have done with that bloody remote."

"It's not only the remote, though," Ali said, swallowing hard and blinking away tears. "I forgot the panic button, Rob. That's how they tracked us."

He shook his head. "I thought I told you. I found the thing when I packed the sound and scent trap for the dogs. I put it back to where it came from. The storage room."

"But Doctor—"

"…is very good at messing with people's minds." She felt his thumb rub gently over her cheek. "It wasn't your fault, Ali. We were just too slow." He tilted up her chin, the corner of his mouth kicking up. "Now do you want to try that smile again?"

"How touching."

Ali's head whipped around, an almost feral growl gathering in her throat. There was only so much she could endure in one day. A tête-à-tête with the Chosen went well beyond that scope.

Ali tried to extract her hand from Rob's grip, but Rob held her fast.

"Piss off, Otis."

"Don't give me orders, *Recruit*."

Surprise halted her struggles.

"What's the matter, Otis? Jealous you can't order me around like the rest of your crew?"

"I don't need to order you, I can just pound you into the dirt." Otis threw a left hand punch so fast his hand blurred.

Ali reacted on instinct, twisting Rob behind her, using the hand he was holding as leverage and blocking the punch with her own left arm.

"Bitch."

"Cease your fight." A Marshal pushed through the throng of spectators in hurried strides.

Ali felt the compulsion from the chip curling through her mind. At the same time she saw Otis's pupils dilate. His arms dropped to his sides. "I'll get you."

She pulled her lips back into a snarl. "Unless the chip gets me first. Stand in line, moron."

Otis's face turned purpled with rage. "If I could—"

But his muscles wouldn't cooperate.

"To your seats. All of you." The Marshal's voice caused another thread of compulsion to spike through Ali's brain.

"Are you okay?" she asked Rob as he sank into the chair to her right.

"Yes. Thanks for saving me. Although," he leaned closer until his lips brushed her ear, "it's not very manly to be defended by a woman."

"Oh, please!"

A low chuckle vibrated against her skin.

Ali moved back to look at him. "Why aren't you inaugurated?"

The light in his eyes dimmed immediately. "It's my punishment, for helping you."

Another one, she thought. "Why the inauguration?"

"Obviously," Rob said, choosing his words carefully, "emotions are largely repressed in Ai Specialists."

"And?" Ali prompted.

Rob winced. "They figured it would be worse for me to…see you wilt away and die before they turn me into an Ai whizz."

Ali felt the blood drain from her face. "That's what they said?" she whispered.

"I'm so sorry, Ali."

She shook her head, trying to swallow around the lump in her throat. "It's not your fault."

"I shouldn't have told you."

"I asked."

"I should have made it sound... nicer," he insisted.

A humourless laugh escaped her constricted throat. "There's nothing nice about death."

***

"Missed your calling?"

Ali started at the deep voice behind her.

She had felt out of sorts since lunch, but the mortification that set her cheeks aflame as she followed Aiden's gaze to the screen indicator on the wall brought her back to reality at once.

Why couldn't she choose to wait five metres to the left, for him to pick her up for their evening training session? Maybe then he wouldn't have realized which lecture she had been attending all afternoon. And maybe Earth didn't revolve around the sun after all.

"I don't think I would have become a member of your squad, even if things had turned out differently."

His lips twitched. "Did it help, then?" he asked gravely, chasing another heat wave over her skin.

"No, sir," she admitted. Hours of *Protection Studies* hadn't made an iota of difference. Aiden was still as much of a riddle to her now as he had been before.

Ali stalked in the direction of the exit.

"Good. I have a reputation to uphold."

She whirled around. Was the big, bad Leader of the Protection Squad actually teasing her?

She couldn't tell for sure, and the thought was almost as disconcerting as the possibility that there was another side to Aiden's personality she didn't know how to deal with.

"When did you know you would become a Protector?" she asked, scrambling to get them back on solid ground.

"I was inaugurated when I was ten."

She halted, surprised. "Ten? But that's...impossible. Nobody is inaugurated before the age of twenty-one."

Only at that age was a Recruit's brain able to deal with the added layer of complexity that the microchip represented.

Ali sought to make sense of the unbelievable. "Why so early?"

Aiden raised a mocking brow. "I thought it was

impossible?"

Ali ground her teeth. He was being deliberately difficult. "You have no reason to lie," she told him.

To her surprise, she saw his features soften. For a second, his eyes warmed and the muscles around his mouth relaxed slightly. There was something else in his gaze too. Something she couldn't quite place. "Tell me," she implored, spurred by the shift in awareness.

Aiden suddenly turned away. "There was a need for a Protector," he answered coolly, and Ali instinctively knew that she had lost him, although she didn't know how.

"You could have died," she said tonelessly, wishing he would look back at her. Wishing she could re-establish whatever it was that had been between them a moment ago.

"That would have been unfortunate." His eyes, when he finally looked back at her, were hard as stone. "But that is none of your concern."

Ali pushed her nails into her skin.

She had known he was unpredictable. Then why did his words hurt like a physical blow?

She was glad when they finally reached the training hall.

"We'll have to share the space with some other Hybrids today."

Aiden motioned her to an empty set of exercise mats and unclipped a set of coiled skipping ropes from his belt. His expression was shuttered when he handed her the shorter one.

"Start warming up."

Ali felt the familiar thread of compulsion run through her and gave in without a fight.

She quickly found her rhythm skipping and watched as Aiden uncoiled the second length of rope. He started moving with fluid grace.

Although Ali had trained with him before, she had never had the chance to actually watch him this closely. The muscles beneath his black workout gear shifted with each rotation of his wrists; the tendons in his forearms stood out in stark relief.

Everything he did, Ali realized, he did with maximum efficiency. His feet cleared the floor by mere centimetres, his arms and legs worked in perfect coordination. The rest of his body was, for all intents and purposes, motionless.

Caught up in her fascination, Ali felt her own foot snag on the rope. She tripped.

A hard arm gripped her waist.

A familiar tingle seeped into her skin where Aiden's muscular chest pressed against her back, while he held her half-sitting on his thighs. Thoroughly embarrassed for the second time in an hour, Ali struggled to find her feet and pushed up through the steel band of his arm.

"Thanks." Her voice sounded oddly breathless.

Aiden suddenly let go.

Taking a small step to restore her balance, Ali turned to face him.

"Your eyes," she said, staring at his dilated pupils. "You felt...compelled to catch me."

"Yes."

Ali ignored the stab of disappointment. So what if it had been his designation taking care of her...again.

She watched as his pupils slowly contracted to their

original size, then let her gaze roam the rest of his features. His face looked drawn – almost as if he was in pain, she realized.

Had he fought the compulsion?

It couldn't be. The incident had been over too quickly for him to resist and for the pain to kick in.

Maybe the strange current she felt whenever he touched her was affecting him as well.

"Did—"

"No more questions," he interrupted firmly. "Start stretching."

He grabbed their discarded ropes from the floor and, without another word, crossed the hall to speak to one of the Trainers.

When Aiden walked back to her ten minutes later, no trace of the incident remained on his face.

"Attack," he said when she got up from the floor, where she had practiced her splits. "Three point kick punch combination."

He was obviously picking up where they had left off this morning.

Just like before, he blocked her attack easily then asked her for a different combination. No matter how hard she tried, Ali couldn't get past his defences. He corrected her patiently.

After an hour, sweat coated her body while he still looked as fresh as he was at the start of the training.

"Stop."

She sank to the floor.

"You are too slow. Your aim is frightful." He shook his

head. "Your Trainer should have picked up on this a long time ago."

Trainer at the Centre had been much too busy humiliating her to correct her fighting style.

She shrugged her shoulders. "What difference does it make, now? I'll take my shortcomings to my early grave."

"Not if I can help it."

She wondered if he was talking about the grave, or her fighting.

***

"I really don't think you should be here."

It was nine o'clock and idle time had just started. Rob had shown up exactly on the hour, strolling into her softly-lit room, as if he wasn't anxious at all that Ali might snap and threaten his life again.

"I really think I should." He sat down on the bed next to her, pulling her against his side before she could protest. "What are you worried about, Ali? You're not going to suddenly try and kill me."

"I did once."

"Because Doctor gave you an order."

She could hear the exasperation in his voice at having to go over the same argument again. Well, he wouldn't have to if he would just keep his distance.

"I'm not going to let you face this alone, Ali. I'm here for you."

The promise broke down her resistance as easily as if it was nothing. How did he do that? How could he warm her with a few simple words, when just a few seconds ago lingering doubts of what she could do to him had chilled her to the core?

He pulled her tighter against his body, his fingers digging into the muscles of her shoulder.

Ali winced.

He let go of her at once. "Are you hurt?" His eyes roamed her body the way they had that long-ago day in the medical facilities.

"Just sore."

He relaxed at her words. "Tough training, huh?"

"You have no idea."

The training with Aiden had taken a turn for the worse after she had regained her breath. They had gone through every single technique again and again, until he was satisfied. Something he wasn't very often, as she had found out. By the time he had asked her to stop a second time, her arms and legs had felt like lead, and she had barely managed to cool down before collapsing onto the floor.

Rob ran his palm lightly up her arm. His hand started kneading the muscles in increasing circles, loosening knots and kinks. A groan of delight escaped Ali's throat. "Could you keep doing this forever?"

Rob chuckled quietly and adjusted his position so she was leaning against his front and he could massage both sides of her neck simultaneously.

Ali felt her body melt into the mattress.

Back at the Centre she and her roommate had often taken turns massaging each other after a long day of physical exercises. Somehow Ali couldn't remember it ever feeling this good.

"I could do better with some oil." Rob said after a while,

tearing her from her blissed-out state.

Ali thought of the healing solution for strained and torn muscles that every Recruit was issued by the Program. Adding it to Rob's magical hands would double the effectiveness of this impromptu massage. But oil would also mean her uniform would have to go.

Rob found another knot next to her shoulder blade, and Ali felt her eyes roll back in her head.

"In the bedside table drawer."

She felt an unfamiliar flutter in her belly when the words left her mouth. She heard Rob rummage around her drawer and pulled her shirt over her head with trembling fingers.

When it cleared her eyes she saw Rob staring at her chest that was covered only by a small black sports bra.

Ali pulled at the stretchy fabric. "This too?" She hadn't really thought this through.

Neither had he, if his glowing red ears were any indication. Rob cleared his throat. "Maybe you could lie face down on the bed, so I don't…so you aren't…" He exhaled a frustrated breath. "The oil was a stupid idea. I'll put it back." He leaned over to put the bottle on her nightstand, but Ali grabbed his wrist.

She wanted his hands on her naked skin, she realized. She wanted him stroking along her body.

"I would…" She swallowed against the butterflies trying to crawl out of her stomach. "My muscles are really sore."

She slowly released her hold on him.

He averted his eyes, but made no move to put the oil away. He was giving her privacy to take off her bra. The thought sent heat over Ali's skin. She whipped her bra over her head before she could chicken out then buried her face in the cool covers. She covered her naked sides with her arms.

"Ready."

Although face down, she felt it the instant Rob turned his eyes on her. Her skin prickled, and the butterflies in her stomach flapped their wings even harder.

"Alright." Rob's breath tickled the small hairs at the back of her neck as he blew out a stream of breath. "I'll start at the top and work to the bottom...your lower back...if that's alright?"

"Okay."

Ali felt something trickling onto her shoulders, then Rob's warm hand at her nape as he caught a runaway rivulet of the scented oil. He smoothed the oil into her back.

The soothing sounds of a violin drifted from Electra's speakers.

Ali jerked. "Electra what are you doing?" She had completely forgotten that she had booted up the DID earlier.

"My database says that a romantic setting requires soothing music in eighty-nine percent of the cases."

Ali felt her face flame. "This isn't a romantic setting, Electra."

"This setting has all the required markers. I catalogued them. My database confirms."

Ali felt her jaw drop. "You're watching us?" She couldn't believe it. The audacity.

"I am always watching you, Ali. However, you need not worry. I am very discreet."

Ali just stared. Next to her, Rob's body shook with

suppressed laughter.

"You knew that?" she asked incredulously.

He extended his hands, shaking so hard she thought he might fall off the bed.

Ali felt her own lips twitch. "You could have warned me."

"I didn't know she would take initiative," he gasped.

"The two of you…" Her attempt to sound stern failed miserably. She glowered at the DID. "Electra, *sleep*."

A little chime announced the initiation of Electra's powering-down routine.

Just before the screen flashed to black she heard Rob say, "But leave the music on for us."

Chapter 13

Ali looked up at the high rise building and almost missed the electrical pulse rushing towards her like a hovercar in the fast lane. The pulse swerved at the last instant, avoiding an accident by mere millimetres as it brushed past her, startling her out of her trance.

Ali jumped onto the sidewalk trying to calm her racing heart.

The city was a dangerous place for strangers, but there was something in this city that she needed to see. She didn't know what it was, but she knew it was there in the chip that appeared as a diamond-and-steel construction, just around the corner of her emotional centre.

Feeling the pull towards the alien structure, Ali gathered her courage and crossed the short distance to the entrance.

Inside, cold air welcomed her. The atmosphere felt eerie. Dead. Something so different to the warmth in the rest of her mind, it was impossible to mistake it for anything else than what it was – a foreign body trying to fit in; a peculiarity in the cavern of her brain, barely integrated – contrary to what the Medics wanted other Hybrids to believe.

Ali stepped further into the hall. The sound of her feet hitting the marble floor echoed loudly in the empty space. Elevators chimed their welcome at the back of the entrance hall, and Ali slipped into the next available car.

The ascent was slow.

Ali stared at the wall-mounted diamond buttons that indicated the floors.

The doors opened with a chime at level ten, revealing a carpeted foyer. Spacious and bright, it tried hard to be welcoming, but only managed to feel oddly repelling. A strange metallic tang hung in the air.

Ali stepped out of the car and realized that the air was even colder than downstairs. Goose bumps covered her skin. She shivered.

A large clock on the wall was counting down the time. There wasn't much time left. Tension gripped her. She had to be quick.

Ali turned from the timepiece to walk into the room and the hallway beyond.

The temperature dropped further as she approached a bend in the wall. Sounds of fighting drifted along the corridor, the slapping of flesh against flesh as unmistakable as the intermittent yelps of pain. Someone was getting hurt badly on the other side. She had to help them.

Breaking into a run Ali rounded the corner and saw two figures fighting in the middle of a room. Both of them were bleeding from multiple wounds.

Ali stopped dead when she recognized their faces. There in her mind, in a corner of the chip, she was locked in mortal combat with herself.

"Shh, Ali. It's just a nightmare."

A nightmare.

Ali dragged in a breath.

Just a nightmare. Another one.

She made a conscious effort to relax back against Rob's chest then startled forward.

Rob? In her room?

She looked up at him.

"Hi." His teeth flashed white in the darkness.

"What are you doing here?" Her voice came out sharper than she had intended.

The white disappeared.

"You...uh...fell asleep during the massage. I was about to leave, when you started thrashing around. I touched your arm, and you quieted down. I thought I'd let you sleep and stay for a while. But then you had the nightmare..." He shrugged his shoulders apologetically. "In any case, you're awake now...so I better get going." He was out of her bed in a flash. Still fully clothed.

Ali looked at him. "What's the time?" she asked, stalling.

"Past midnight."

He grabbed the bottle of massage oil from where it sat next to Electra on the desk and put it back into her drawer. Ali knew he would be out of her room in less than thirty seconds if she didn't say something fast.

"Rob?"

"Yes?"

"I-I'm sorry I fell asleep."

He gave her a wry smile. "I'm glad it was relaxing."

Ali felt her fingers dig into the mattress. "You know what

else would be relaxing?"

"What?"

Her heart picked up a frantic beat. "If you would stay with me tonight."

Silence greeted her words.

"It would help me sleep," she added quietly when Rob continued to stare at her with an unreadable expression.

"Will I be able to hold you?" he asked finally, a thread of longing in his voice that she recognized too well.

Ali nodded mutely.

"Good," he whispered, slipping under the covers and curling around her protectively. "Because knowing you're safely in my arms, at least for tonight, will help me sleep better too."

***

Ali was awake long before the soft chime of Electra's alarm rang through the quiet room.

She wondered if she had even gone to sleep. To her, it seemed as if she had spent the night revelling in the closeness of Rob behind her, his arm draped next to hers over her waist, his clothes-covered chest pressed to her back and their legs tangled under the covers. It was one of the few advantages of being a Hybrid – the fact that her biorhythm was no longer governed by time. No more enforced sleeping cycles. No more dedicated lunch times. Everything in a Hybrids life was determined by their assignment. Ali had no assignment. She was free to do as she pleased, as long as she adhered to her daily schedule.

Ali kept her breathing even and tried to figure out a way to shut off the alarm without waking Rob.

"Good morning, sunshine." Rob's breath tickled her ear.

The butterflies in Ali's stomach fluttered their wings. "Electra, alarm off." She looked over her shoulder. "Good morning." So much for trying not to wake him. Ali turned onto her back. "Did you sleep alright?"

"Better than ever." Rob's still drowsy eyes were full of warmth as he held her gaze.

Ali felt herself blush.

"Why didn't your mobi issue a warning shock when you stayed past idle time?" she asked.

He waved his empty wrist in front of her eyes. "I took it off when I started the massage. Also…" He gave her a wry grin. "I worked hard on deactivating the warning shocks after the incident in the inauguration room. Hey!" He softly tilted her face towards his.

Ali sighed. "I'm working on getting over it. I am! Just give me some time. Okay?"

Rob nodded and picked up the mobi from the bedside table to put it back on his wrist. He activated it using the small mobile DID that Ali had seen him bring along the day before. "When do you normally start your morning training?"

Ali looked at the clock.

"Damn." How could she have forgotten? She was about to jump out of bed when the door to her room slid open.

Ali dove under the covers.

She heard Rob's chuckle, then Aiden's deep voice. "Explain, Recruit."

Even without a chip, Ali doubted that Rob could withstand the authority of the command. But if she had thought Rob would crumble under the superiority of the other man, she had been wrong.

"I came by to teach Ali how to set up the security on a mobile DID, sir," came the muffled reply through the comforter.

Ali forced her head back out from under the covers and saw Rob gesturing towards the device in his lap.

She took a relieved breath. He was deliberately drawing Aiden's gaze to his arm…and the mobi around his wrist.

"And that's why she's in bed with you. Naked."

Ali gasped, yanking the covers up to her neck. She had completely forgotten she wasn't wearing a bra.

"I'm sure that was unnecessary, sir." Rob's voice changed from pleasant to barely civil in a matter of seconds.

Aiden's jaw hardened. "Your bruises are healing nicely," he remarked calmly.

"Rob, don't," Ali pleaded, grabbing his arm.

Aiden's eyes dropped to her hand before they pinned her to the bed. "I'll meet you in the great training hall in exactly eight minutes. Don't be late."

Before Ali could reply, he turned on his heels and left the room.

"Why did you do that?" Rob demanded when the door slid closed behind the Protector. His muscles were rigid underneath her fingers.

"Do what?" Ali asked, still clutching the sheet to her naked chest.

"Stop me."

"I was worried for you," Ali said, taken aback by his reaction.

"You think I can't handle the man on my own?"

"I *know* you can't handle him," she replied, her own anger stirring. "He's a Hybrid, for goodness sake. You're a Recruit. Never mind the fact that he's also P001, the Leader of the Protection Squad."

Rob ground his teeth, but couldn't refute the facts laid out before him. "How long does it take to get to the training hall?" he asked finally.

"Five minutes. Three minutes to get ready." Ali looked at the clock again. "Two minutes, now."

Rob grasped her shoulder. "Let him wait."

"Are you mad?"

"He's not going to punish you."

"What?"

"He's your Protector. He can't punish you."

"And I can't disobey him," Ali replied. "Don't you understand? It hurts."

Rob let go of her at once. "I'm sorry." He dragged a hand over his face. "I don't know what's wrong with me. I'd better out of your way." He rolled out of bed. "I'll see you at breakfast." And in a flash he was gone.

***

"Prepare."

Ali's body automatically relaxed into fight mode at Aiden's command.

He had been firing instructions at her since the minute she stepped into the training hall, teaching her more about blocking her pain receptors in the last five minutes than she had learned in a full two-hour lecture of *Chip Communications*. The biofeedback command that used a certain portion of the chip to make her immune to pain in combat situations was highly complex, and Ali knew that it would take her days to bring it to perfection. Days that Aiden was obviously unwilling to give her.

Ali looked at the Protector's stern face and prayed that she would survive the next two hours.

"Fight."

She didn't have time to process the word before Jacob's first blow hit her arm.

The sting jolted her into action, and she managed to block the next hit from the newly inaugurated Assassin who had been as surprised by Aiden's order to join them as Ali had been.

Ali immediately tried to follow up her block with a three-punch combination, but Jacob was just too fast. He easily deflected her first punch then turned the tables to attack her again, driving her back across the hall.

Ali held on to her defence for about thirty seconds, until a kick to her thigh made her leg buckle under her. Switching into floor mode, she managed to scissor her legs around Jacob's and took him down to the floor with her.

Within seconds, the Assassin had her pinned to the ground. Face pressed flat into the floor, his weight fully on her, Ali felt like she was buried under a rock.

"Get up."

She hadn't even realized Jacob's weight had lifted off her, until she heard Aiden's expressionless voice from above.

Eyeing both men warily, Ali rolled to her feet and felt the shooting pain in her thigh where Jacob had kicked her. The

Assassin looked miserable as he noticed her limp, but Ali knew the chip wouldn't let him slack.

"Use the command to block your pain receptors," Aiden ordered from the side-line.

Ali shot him a murderous look. At least she now knew why he had involved Jacob today. Rob had been right. Even standing at the edge of the fighting area had to be killing Aiden.

Ali found it hard to dredge up any sympathy.

"Implemented," she ground out between clenched teeth.

"Show me."

Ali shifted her full weight onto her injured leg and received a terse nod.

"Again."

A punch hit her ribs. Air exploded from her mouth, and she almost doubled over. Ali tried to wheeze in a breath, but her lungs wouldn't work. She stumbled backwards, black dots dancing in front of her eyes.

"Breathe."

Idiot. I'm trying.

She would have shouted it, but there was no air. Water filled her eyes, as she strained to suck in a breath. It didn't work. Her throat felt as if it had closed up. Jacob hadn't even touched her throat. The black dots in her vision started to connect, and she could feel herself go under, as if she was diving into a black sea.

She was falling and expected to hit the floor at any second, but there was no pain, only nothing.

When she came to, she was lying on her back.

Ali hauled in a big breath, and tears of relief sprang to

her eyes when it travelled to her lungs. She tried to shift, but something was holding her down.

She opened her eyes and stormy grey filled her vision. Then the rest of Aiden's face swam into focus.

"Chip status?" he ordered tightly.

"Bruises only," she replied.

And then he said what she had expected next. "Again."

***

Ali was still fuming from her training with Aiden when she met Rob in the breakfast hall, after a quick warm shower to soothe her aching muscles. She hated that the Protector could so easily control her through compulsion. She hated it particularly today.

"I wish I at least had a real designation." Ali stabbed at her food, the only thing in her life she could poke and prod, without it fighting back. "Assassin would be good." Never mind the fact that she abhorred killing people. At least she would have enough chip-induced combat skills to take down the leader of the Protection Squad a peg or two. Right now that sounded like a perfect capability to have.

Rob looked at her over his fork, before pushing the last bite of scrambled eggs into his mouth.

"Hmm," he said, a frown marring the perfection of his forehead.

Ali sighed. She shouldn't have said that. After what had happened in her room earlier this morning, she—.

Rob suddenly froze.

"What?"

"I've just had an idea." He dropped the remaining slice of his buttered toast onto her plate. "Have that."

"Where are you going?"

But he was already out of earshot.

***

Ali knocked on the Psychiatrist's office door. "Beth?"

"One second...come on in, Ali."

"You have hair." The sight was so unusual in a compound full of Recruits and Hybrids with smoothly shaved heads, Ali did a double-take.

"I have fuzz," Beth laughed and ran her hand over the tiny curls. "It's amazing. I can't stop touching it."

And Ali couldn't stop staring. Yesterday she had been too distraught to pay attention to Beth's appearance during their counselling session. Not so today. "How come you're allowed to have hair all of a sudden?" As far as Ali knew the Program was adamant that their Hybrid-mark had to be clearly visible at all times. For human protection, as they said.

"I made the application as soon as I was inaugurated." Beth sank into one of the overstuffed chairs and motioned for Ali to sit on the lounge. "The confirmation came back three days ago. I still can't believe they granted my request. I think I only got away with it, because I am the dedicated on-site Psychiatrist and won't be leaving the Sanatorium. Ever." Beth sighed. "If only it wouldn't take so long to grow. And I have curls too."

Ali bit her lip. "Good thing you have time then." She could have hit herself for the statement a second later. Why did she have to say that? Why make them both feel bad?

But the words were out and there was no taking them back.

Beth regarded her thoughtfully for a second. "You should do it, too."

Ali looked at her friend. "Do what?"

"Grow your hair, silly. They're not going to object, I'm almost certain."

Ali touched her own, slightly scratchy head. Aiden really hadn't give her much time to shave in the morning. "Maybe," she said. "But it won't grow long."

"It doesn't matter." Beth waved her off. "It's about doing it. Do it."

"Okay." *Why not.* It wasn't like she had a whole heap of other things to look forward to. "What are you doing?" Ali watched as Beth skipped around her desk to sit down in front of her DID.

"Filling out an application form for you. What else?" Beth grinned at her.

"Now?"

"Of course now. When did you want to do it?"

Ali shrugged. Beth was right. And her excitement was contagious.

"Okay. Let's do it together then," Ali said an unexpected grin tugging at her lips. She wouldn't trade Beth for any other Psychiatrist. Not in a million years and not for one with a million years of experience. She just couldn't imagine anybody else doing what Beth had managed within the first few minutes of Ali stepping into her office. Make her forget why she was here.

***

"Ready?"

Ali slipped into her shoes and nodded. "Where are we

going?"

It was their idle time once more, and Rob was picking her up for a stroll. Or so his earlier message had suggested.

"We'll research your breakfast proposal." He led her out of the room.

"You want to turn me into an Assassin?" She hadn't *really* meant what she had said in the heat of the moment over a plate of toast.

Rob laughed. "I mean this in the nicest possible way, Ali. You would suck as an Assassin."

Ali gave him a wry grin. He read her far too easily.

"Then what?" she asked.

"The fact that a Hybrid with a black soul could have a designation too," Rob said. "I had never thought of it before."

"But you do now?"

"Traces of information on the LiveNet suggest dormant carriers have been inaugurated with all kinds of designations, until Doctor decided to speed up the illness."

"And that is helpful, how?" Ali asked, trying to understand.

Rob waited until they were out of the building before he answered in a low voice.

"I've been trying to find a way to reprogram your chip, over the last few days."

Ali stopped and blinked hard to get rid of the excess moisture suddenly gathering in her eyes. "You've worked on helping me all this time?" He just kept stunning her, this strong Recruit next to her with a heart as big as his body. "What did you find?"

Rob nudged her back into a walk. "A lot of problems, mostly. Front and centre, the fact that I don't know what the code of a microchip looks like. Only inaugurated Ai Specialists know, because that's what they do. They develop microchips. And to develop something better, they need to know what's currently on the market." He took a deep breath. "Now imagine an Ai Specialist with a black soul. What would you do?"

"Use my knowledge to reprogram the chip?"

"Exactly. And what's the only way to access the chip?"

Ali frowned. "There isn't one. The only time the chip receives new information is during the daily data update from the bioservers."

"Correct. But what if it isn't a data update you receive? What if it is a virus instead? One that reprograms your chip."

A sliver of excitement stole through Ali's body as they passed the outhouse that they had fled through so long ago. Rob steered her onto the stone path leading away from the woods. "You think someone tried that?" Ali asked. "Wouldn't there at least be rumours?"

"Not if he failed."

Her excitement fled. "Which wouldn't help us at all."

"I wouldn't say that. If I have the program, I may find out where he went wrong. Then we can do it differently. Provided the underlying coding structure of the chip hasn't changed too much."

A lot of ifs. But they were better than nothing. "Thank you." The simple words didn't seem to be enough to express her gratitude for his continued efforts.

Rob grabbed her hand and waited until she lifted her eyes

to his. "Together we'll find a way," he promised. There wasn't a shred of doubt in his voice. "Okay?"

Ali nodded, praying he would be right. "Will you tell me now where we are going?"

Rob laced their fingers together and Ali felt warmth seeping into her body. Without meaning to she found herself holding onto him harder.

The corners of his mouth kicked up in a smile.

"The incident – if it happened – must have happened a long time ago," he explained, his voice low to keep it from carrying in the quiet of the night. "The data artefacts we are looking for couldn't be on the LiveNet or even the ArchiNet any longer. We'll have to check the long-time offline data storage."

"Can't you check that from your room?" Ali asked surprised.

"You mean hack into it? No. I'll need physical access to the servers. Offline means the data storage is a standalone system. Even I can't hack a connection that isn't there. The good thing is, the storage is here, at the Sanatorium." He pointed into the darkness, where a glass-and-steel structure stuck out of the landscape like a sore thumb. A steady blue light above the door of the modern building indicated an activated security system.

"In the data warehouse?"

"Yes. I will need you to stand guard."

He tugged her behind a group of trees when a Guard rounded the corner, a small portable nightlight in his hands.

Rob let go of her to pull his mobile DID out of his pocket and Ali instantly missed the connection.

He nodded towards the Guard. "It takes him ten minutes to make his round." Rob's whisper travelled no further than her ears. "I'll leave as soon as he's out of sight. You'll stand here and whistle if you see someone coming. I shouldn't be more than five minutes."

They waited in silence as the Guard went to check the locks on the front door of the building, then continued on his designated route. Just before he rounded the second corner, he looked in their direction. Ali shrank deeper into the cover.

"Don't worry," Rob whispered. "It's too dark for him to see us."

Indeed, the Guard disappeared a second later.

Ali felt the ghost of a movement beside her. Then nothing.

Seconds ticked by before she saw Rob casually stroll towards the front door. He looked around. A quiet click sounded, and the door opened. *How did he do that?*

Ali hunched down behind a bush and waited as seconds turned into minutes.

Suddenly, her neck prickled in warning. She saw a dark figure walk along the pathway towards the data warehouse. A smaller, four-legged form had its nose pressed firmly to the ground in front of it.

A dog. Ali went rigid.

She stepped out of the shadows, whistling an old tune at the top of her lungs.

Acting as if she was just out for a late-night stroll, Ali ambled down the path towards the unfamiliar pair. She was almost in front of them, when the Guard stopped.

"Roger, sit." The puppy – she realized, relieved – planted

its butt on the ground without hesitation. A very well-trained puppy. Her relief died. Was it trained enough to detect intruders?

"How cute." The Guard reeled back at her excited squeak. "And it's so well behaved. How old is it?" She prayed that the pup wouldn't bite her as she hunched down to pat its head.

"Please don't touch him without permission."

Only to distract you. She pulled back her hand.

"He has just turned three."

"Three years?" she asked stunned.

He looked at her suspiciously. "Months."

Ali racked her brain for something else to say when she heard Rob's voice behind her. "There you are. I was looking for you. You suddenly disappeared."

Ali gave him a smile she hoped looked apologetic. "I saw the puppy and just *had to* see it."

"She worked with the puppies at the Centre," Rob said to the Guard.

Ali cringed, but the Guard just grumbled. "Roger, come."

They watched the pair walk away, the puppy sticking his head on the ground to sniff the door of the data warehouse as they walked past. Ali held her breath, but the pup didn't bark.

She turned to look at Rob. "Dog trainers never give excited attention to a puppy in training," she said pointedly.

"Oops." He gave her a sheepish look then waved his DID in front of her nose. "But you'll forgive me."

"Oh my!" Ali breathed, forgetting everything about the puppy. "You managed to get what we were looking for?"

He grinned. "I did."

"Tell me."

"First, let's get back, before a real dog comes along.

Chapter 14

The visit to the data warehouse was still on her mind when Ali made her way to the training hall the next morning. Über-punctual Aiden had for once failed to show up in front of her door, and Ali wondered if he was still angry about walking in on her and Rob, or embarrassed.

Embarrassed? Aiden? Ali snorted. She doubted the stoic Protector even knew the definition of the word.

Whatever it was, she had bigger dilemmas to contemplate than Aiden's unpredictable moods. Things like the message Rob had sent her in the morning via an encrypted channel he had set up between Electra and his own mobile DID.

According to the data analysis Rob had run overnight, the Ai Specialist with the black soul had made a number of programming errors that kept the virus from executing correctly. The difficulty was not only to fix the errors, but to find them in the first place. *After all*, Rob's message had explained, *there are thousands of lines of code to search. And that's not the only problem. I'll also have to upgrade the code to work with the new chip. I don't have a sample,*

but can probably get enough information from the daily data
update now that I have the Ai Specialist's virus to compare
it to. Realistically, it will take a number of days to solve all
the issues.

Ali pushed open the doors to the gardens and once more
contemplated the implications. Her time was running out in
little over a week. An uncomfortably close call. And that
was assuming she didn't give in to the darkness of the Abyss
earlier.

The malicious being stirred in the back of her mind at the
thought. It always seemed to know when Ali was thinking
about it.

Ali felt it languidly stretching, as if after a long sleep.
Then a lazy hiss bled from the fracture.

Come closer, it beckoned.

Ali closed her eyes, clapped her hands over her ears, and
started humming.

The creature laughed. That won't work. I'm inside your
head. Come look at me, at least.

"No." She had avoided it since the day of her
inauguration. Listening to it had been bad enough.

Don't you want to see?

Ali shook her head and pressed her lips together.

Liar. You are craving to know what lies in my depth.
Come closer, and I will show you.

The intoxicating whisper was impossible to resist.

Against her will, Ali's eyes fluttered open to the foreign
landscape of her mind.

She looked around. She was standing alone on the stony
ledge, a lonely tree beside her. Shards of broken rock bit into

the soles of her naked feet.

In front of her, the Abyss curled like a black snake through the eerie twilight. A dark cloud billowed from its depth and rode towards her on currents of cool air.

There you are. Wads of smoke twined seductively around her body, tearing at her clothes and shoving from behind.

Ali realized in horror that her feet were shuffling closer towards the cliff.

"No," she breathed, averting her eyes from the steam-breathing gorge, her body straining against the malicious force. "I'm not ready to jump. Let go!"

I know you're not, the Abyss whispered darkly. But look, Ali. Look. Gaze into me, fully…and I shall finally gaze into you.

Ali stumbled against the wall of the corridor outside the training hall, blood pumping in her ears.

"Alana, look at me." The tingle that spread along her jaw where Aiden had hooked a finger under her chin pulled her back from the brink. "You must fight it," he said, and Ali laughed, the sound echoing hollowly from the walls of her mind.

"You are using compulsion to fight my compulsion?" she asked, torn by so many forces pulling her in different directions.

Aiden's face remained expressionless. "If it works."

"It's ridiculous," she replied, her eyes catching on the blade strapped to his belt. "Like me telling you 'take your knife and cut me'."

He moved so fast she could barely see his hand before

fire bloomed on her shoulder. Blood soaked into the material of her workout top.

Aiden held out the knife in his hand for her to see. His starkly dilated eyes clashed with hers. "Do you still think it's ridiculous?"

He wiped the blade on his uniform, the droplets of blood invisible on the black material.

"Go get the wound cleaned at the medical facilities. Tell them the blade was sterilized but caustic. And Ali," he sheathed the knife with expert motions, "fight the compulsion."

Ali stared, unable to move, as he walked out of the outhouse and disappeared around the corner.

He had cut her just to make a point. He had cut her, when she thought he couldn't hurt her.

Ali pulled apart the torn material of her uniform, where the blade had penetrated. The cut was superficial. No deeper than a paper-cut. Even so, the caustic agent bit like fire fangs into her skin.

Compulsion finally overruled her shock, and her feet started moving in the direction of the medical facilities.

***

The waiting room had been filled to capacity with early morning emergencies. By the time Ali had made it back to her room and changed into a new uniform, breakfast had started.

As expected, she found Rob at their table.

"Where have you been," he asked in lieu of a greeting.

"Training overran." Not quite the truth, but as close as she could get without sending him on a crusade he couldn't win.

He looked at her suspiciously, then frowned. "Ali, your eyes."

"Are blue?" she asked only half listening, for – after hours of trying – her mind was still unable to make sense of Aiden's puzzling behaviour. Any attempt to harm her should have been crushed by his compulsion to protect her.

"No. Yes. I mean, they look darker than normal. Are you even listening to me?"

"Huh?"

"That's a no, then." Rob heaved a sigh. "Where's your head?"

Ali stared at her friend. No, that wasn't the right term. Not after what had happened two nights ago. Still, she couldn't come up with a better one.

"The Abyss," she said finally, plucking a grape from its stem. "I saw it in my mind."

"When? Where? Are you alright?"

Ali tilted her head. "You don't think I'm crazy?"

"Why would I?"

"Others do." She had heard the whispers, had tried to ignore them. It was hard.

Rob glared at the room in general. "That's because they're idiots. Don't listen to them. You're no crazier than I am. It's the chip that's messing with your mind. We'll prove it to them soon."

Ali sat forward. "Did you find the errors then?"

"Not all of them. Not yet." He gathered her hand in his larger one. "I won't stop until I have."

Ali squeezed his fingers. "Thank you. Again." She gently

touched the faded bruise mark on his cheek. "I can't believe you're doing this. I can't believe you're still helping me, now that you know." She pulled her hand away. "I know it's late to say this, Rob, but – goodness, – I couldn't bear them torturing you again, if they found us out. The memories alone are giving me nightmares. If you don't want to—"

"Don't," Rob interrupted her gently. "I will do everything in my power to save you. And nothing – you hear me? – nothing, will change my mind." He pulled her hand back towards him and kissed her palm. "Because no punishment can compare to a life without you."

***

"They have granted permission for you to grow your hair." Beth turned the DID screen to show Ali the message.

Ali sucked in a breath. "That's awesome." After an awful morning, her day was finally looking up.

"I could barely wait to tell you." Beth's gaze dropped to Ali's eyebrows. "Honey-gold and grey. What an unusual combination."

"What's grey?" Ali asked.

"Your eyes."

Ali shook her head. "Blue. I have blue eyes."

Beth leaned forward to take a closer look. "No, they are definitely grey. DID, mirror."

Ali gasped. "But..." She wasn't going mad. Not in this regard. Ali blinked. The greyish tinge remained. "Impossible," she breathed, her heart hammering in her chest.

"DID, search LiveNet entries for grey coloured eyes," Beth instructed, sounding as worried as Ali felt. "You should get that checked in the medical facilities."

"I was just there this morning. They didn't find anything during their routine body scan."

Ali dug her nails into her skin to keep from freaking out. It seemed lately the conditioning she had undergone at the Centre was dissolving along with her sanity. Biofeedback she had used successfully for years to calm her body's panicked responses, seemed to get harder to implement whenever she felt off-balance. A catch-22.

Beth's DID chimed at that moment.

"What does it say?"

"Hold on." Beth scanned the search results. "Oh my! How could I have missed that?"

"Beth?"

"It's a symptom." Beth turned the screen. "Third line from the top."

Ali read aloud. "…the change of pigmentation in an activated carrier's eye from any colour to grey, and later black, can be ascribed to the progression of the illness known as anima ātra or the black soul." She looked at her suddenly trembling hands. "I will have black eyes?"

No wonder Aiden had studied her so closely, every morning.

Look at me.

She had thought he had just demanded her attention, when in fact he was gauging her sanity.

"It's the only visible sign of the illness," Beth confirmed, still reading.

Ali's breath hitched. It was more than that. It was the irrefutable evidence that her mind was changing and there was nothing she could do.

Her hands trembled harder. "It can't be," she whispered frantically. "It *can't* be. I won't let it be. You hear me?"

"Ali, you're hyperventilating. Control yourself, Hybrid."

"No." Ali jumped out of her seat and paced across the room, too far gone to listen to reason. "They're blue," she protested. "They have to be blue. You're wrong. Rob is wrong. You are all *wrong*." She pushed her fingers into her eyes and rocked back and forth.

"Stop, Rt2120."

A thread of compulsion whispered through her mind.

"I can't," she wailed.

"You must," Beth ordered. "Sit down."

"Argh!" Ali's right fist hit the wall with a dull thud, leaving a bloody streak behind. "I'll have black eyes. Black eyes." Her knees gave out, and she crumpled to the floor.

***

Meet me at the training circuit.

Ali couldn't help the groan escaping her mouth when she saw Aiden's message flash on Electra's screen after dinner. She had asked him earlier to postpone their training, to allow the flexible, watertight plaster on her hand to set. Secretly, however, she had hoped he would cancel their session altogether. She didn't want to face him. Not now. Maybe never again.

He had cut her, had lied to her, at least by omission, and Ali still felt too raw from her *episode* during the counselling session with Beth to deal with any more of his games.

Ali moved her fingers experimentally inside the bandage and winced when the abraded skin on her knuckles pushed against the biodegradable material.

Driving her fist into the wall had been a singularly stupid idea. It had also been the only thing likely to provide enough of a jolt to push back the panic attack. Especially since Aiden hadn't been there to pull her back from the brink, the way he had so successfully done twice already, no pain necessary. Except for the pain he dished out himself.

Ali shook her head. How could he still profess he was protecting her when his designation so clearly didn't keep him from harming her?

Reaching the ground floor of the outhouse, Ali stepped into the dim evening light and followed the directions the chip fed directly into her brain. Solar-powered lamps guided her away from the mansion and towards a small grouping of trees. The start/finish line of the outside training circuit was marked by a single black-and-white pillar. An interactive map was propped into the earth close-by. Ali activated the display.

"Lovely," she grumbled, when she took in the huge areal the circuit covered. "That's at least twice as much slithering through the mud as I would require to check off this particular 'must do before you die' box."

She looked around. Her torture master was nowhere to be seen. Yet.

Behind her, another late-night training group approached the circuit with unusual haste. One of the Hybrids turned to speak to another, allowing the light from the lamps to play over his profile. It was only a second that Ali could make out his features. It was enough time for her to recognize the puckered scar on his cheek.

Chosen.

Ali melted into the shadow of a large oak tree.

Had they seen her? Were they here for her?

She ducked further into the shrubbery. For a minute she heard only her own regulated breathing. Then a branch cracked gun-shot loud to her right. A distinct rustle followed.

Definitely here for her.

Ali leashed her pain receptors just as the first Chosen, a Guard, broke through the thicket. He was almost upon her when he tripped in the twilight. Flailing his arms, he stumbled towards her. Ali struck at his neck. The Guard slumped to the ground.

One down. Three to go. Ali swung around and felt her breath strangling in her throat. Three lethal Assassins stood against a backdrop of tree trunks, their faces familiar even shrouded in darkness.

Jay attacked first. Ali struck at his knee. The Chosen blocked then countered. He was much faster than her, but the sheer will to survive gave Ali the edge she needed.

She saw a flash of movement to her right and barely dodged a blow with a branch from Mace. The piece of wood missed her head by a fraction. Ali yanked at the stick, sending Mace to the ground. She heard a pained yelp but didn't turn as Jay attacked again.

Ali blocked then counterattacked, punching his nose. Blood spurted, and he staggered for just a moment. Still, he was standing, while Otis closed in.

Ali retreated, passing Mace in the process. His face was contorted in fury and pain. A trickle of blood oozed from a wound on his thigh where he had fallen onto the branch in his hand.

Jay had recovered and came at her again. Ali dodged, sending his fist into the tree trunk behind her. Jay howled.

Mace swore.

Ali turned to Otis. She struck at his neck with the side of her palm.

Otis choked. Staggered. Then came at her again. A paralyzing blow hit Ali's bruised thigh.

All three Assassins were back on their feet now and slowly closing in on her.

Ali's shoulders bumped into the tree behind her as Otis's hand wrapped around her throat. Jay and Mace sprang forward at once, grabbing her arms in a punishing hold.

"I told you, we'd come for you. We don't fear the Protection Squad." Otis's voice was hoarse from the strike she had landed. "Now you suffer, bitch. Slowly." He choked her harder and delivered a powerful punch to her gut.

Ali's breath wheezed in and out of her lungs.

"Let her go, or die."

Ali sobbed in relief as all three of the Chosen released her at once. She sank to the ground, gulping big breaths of air. A second longer and she would have begged.

"Can you stand?" Aiden asked, his eyes never leaving the Chosen.

Ali awkwardly pushed to her feet. "Yes, sir. I can."

"Are you able to make it to the complex alone?"

"I can," she said again, her voice steadier this time.

"Go," Aiden ordered. Then he turned to the Chosen. "Release the hold on your pain receptors."

※ ※ ※

Ali didn't stop until she stood in front of Rob's room. She didn't want to go to the medical facilities again. She hated the stench of metal and disinfectant, the memories that crashed in on her each time she entered. The chip said that nothing was broken, so she didn't need treatment. What she really needed was a good hug.

"Goodness, Ali. Is that your blood?" Rob started towards her, as soon as the door slid open.

Ali looked at her clothes. "It's Jay's," she croaked.

"The bastard choked you."

"No. Otis choked me."

Rob's expression turned thunderous. "I'll kill them both."

"I think Aiden might be doing that right now," she said.

If anything, his expression darkened even more. "He just swept in before you suffocated, did he?"

Ali gaped at her friend. "Rt2388, you're being unreasonable."

"Me unreasonable? Look at your throat, Ali. You could've died. He's supposed to *protect* you."

"And you're supposed to hug me, dammit." Tears suddenly filled her eyes. It had been one hell of a long day.

Rob looked at her stunned. "What do you mean?"

"What do you think I mean?" she shot back. "I just told you."

"You came here because you wanted a hug?"

Ali barely held back the *Duh!*

For a moment, he looked as if he was searching for a hidden meaning, when she so clearly spelled it all out for him. Then he walked towards her.

"Come here," he said, extending his hand. All anger was gone from his voice.

"It's too late," Ali grumbled. "Now that you've told me my clothes are all bloody."

Rob pulled her carefully towards his body. "I don't care about your clothes." He nuzzled her temple. "Unless you're suggesting you want to get naked with me again."

Although she knew he was just trying to distract her from what had happened, Ali couldn't help but glare. "I'm hurt."

"And I'm very good at applying salves. I thought I'd proved that the other night."

That finally elicited a small, reluctant chuckle from her. "Maybe another time," she said, feeling a lot better now that his arms were firmly around her. She snuggled further into his embrace. "But next time I want to see you naked too." Ali pushed a hand under his pullover and ran her fingers over his hard stomach

Rob groaned. "I thought you didn't enjoy torture."

Ali smiled into his neck. "Is that how it feels?"

"You tell me," he whispered, pushing his own hand under her uniform.

Ali's breath hitched.

He traced his fingertips up and down her spine. "Sorry for freaking out on you. It drives me crazy to see you hurt."

Ali pushed back until she could look into his eyes. "I understand," she said, lightly touching his cheek.

Rob captured her hand against his face.

"Let me kiss you, Ali," he said, his eyes like molten caramel. "Let me make it better."

"Yes."

Rob cupped her cheek, running the pad of his thumb over her lips. "So soft." He brushed over her mouth in a feather-light kiss. "So sweet."

Ali tilted her head into his palm.

"More?" he asked, his thumb soothing the line of her jaw in slow strokes.

"Please," Ali whispered. She felt as if she was floating on clouds.

This time, his warm lips pressed more firmly against hers. His hands pulled her tightly against his chest.

Sensations spread through Ali's body, gathering in her bruised belly. She wrapped her hands around his neck.

Rob groaned and sucked at her lip, then dipped his tongue inside her mouth. "This is dangerous." He pulled back slightly.

"Why?"

"Because I want to do so much more to you. I want to rain kisses all over your body. I want to…" His eyes darted to the bed at her back.

Sexual intercourse. Ali didn't feign ignorance. Although the practical aspects of reproduction in the Program were only relevant to Hybreeders – who were usually artificially inseminated, all Recruits were given basic information about *the human act*. Explained from a scientific point of view, the process hadn't sounded enjoyable, at all.

Ali's expression must have reflected her thoughts, because Rob hushed her with another caress. "We don't have to do this now. You're hurt, and I didn't mean to pressure you. I'm counting myself lucky to just hold you."

"And kiss me?" She was desperate to feel the glory of his mouth on hers again.

"And kiss you," he said lowering his head until their lips fused together and she lost herself once more to his tender touch.

Chapter 15

Memories of the latest nightmare were almost gone by the time Ali caught herself with the razor in her hand the next morning.

She stared at the sharpened blade the way she had every morning since the incident in the medical facilities, with equal parts fascination and dread.

Just like the days before, she felt nothing. No compulsion to slash her wrists. Not even the smallest inclination to hurt herself.

"It was a day dream. Get over it." Annoyed, Ali tossed the razor into the waste disposal unit. "It didn't mean anything."

It means you're going well and truly insane. The hissing sound caused Ali's muscles to tense, even before realized where it was coming from.

"Go away," Ali said to the dark expanse in her mind, baring her teeth. "I didn't ask for your opinion."

Why are you here then? Standing on the ledge, looking at me, the Abyss hissed.

"Because I can't stay away from you." The words were

out so fast, Ali had no chance of holding them back.

With dread she realized that they were true.

Her sanity was fraying around the edges; her cravings to visit the ledge becoming more and more frequent. Moments ago, she hadn't even realized that she had shifted from the physical to her mental plane until the Abyss pointed out that she was standing on the ledge. The malicious being was gaining strength, draining her conscious choices until she felt her control slowly slipping away. How long, she wondered, until the creature managed to entice her to look into its depths and leap? How long until she was doomed? Because whatever she found at the bottom of the gorge – she knew with frightening certainty – would be worth dying for.

Disturbed by her own thoughts, Ali stepped out of her mind and up to the balcony doors. She pulled the curtains to one side. The complex was slowly waking up, the first Hybrids making their way to the training grounds. The sun was up in the sky again. The world continued to turn.

Soon Aiden would pick her up for her morning training and slowly – routinely – another day would go by.

Was this really all she was destined to be? A small cog in the wheel, spinning mindlessly until she broke. Was there no more to life than this?

Ali heard the door open behind her and spoke before she could second guess her words.

"I don't care about your stupid routine."

**

Aiden was heartless.

Her attempt to tell him she wanted to take a 'day off' to do as she pleased hadn't gone the way she had hoped, and now they were locked in a shouting match. At least Ali was. Aiden was as calm as always, which infuriated her even more. She hated that she couldn't elicit a reaction in him.

"It's for your own good," he pointed out reasonably.

"Bullshit." Ali sliced her hand through the air with force. She didn't care that she was out of control again. This was one argument she intended to win. "It's *my* life. It should be *my* choice."

"It doesn't work this way in the Program. I daresay you know that."

The small part of her brain, the one that still held on to logic, wondered why he even bothered to reason with her when he could so easily shut her up and make her comply with a single command. The bigger part, however, told her that it didn't matter, because as long as he kept talking there was still hope.

"I'm trying to keep you safe, Alana."

"Well, don't. Not today. You did a shit job of it anyway."

Aiden's jaw hardened. His face lost all emotion. She hadn't even realized how much he had opened up in her presence.

"You're right," he said icily, after a moment of deafening silence. "It's your life. It should be your choice to die."

He left her room, and Ali stared after him. What a stupid, *stupid* thing to accuse him off.

What if he didn't come back to her now? She hadn't wanted him to leave her forever. Just for one day. Was that too much to ask?

She frantically searched for some way to apologize, but his rigid back made it clear that even begging wouldn't change his mind at this point.

As if that wasn't enough, the Abyss stirred in the back of her mind. Its trademark hiss sounded inordinately pleased. *There is nobody who can stop me from killing you now.*

The verbal blow hit Ali's chest with force, making her stumble against the wall. "What about me?"

Chilling laughter rolled through the cavern of her mind. *You are not strong enough to defy me on your own.*

Ali opened her mouth to protest, but self-doubts spread inside her like a lethal disease. What if the Abyss was speaking the truth? She could already feel their fight wearing on her.

She slowly slid down the wall, and buried her head in her hands.

She wouldn't cry, she told herself. She was stronger than this. She had to be.

Yet, tears started rolling down her cheeks.

***

At lunch time, Ali still felt deflated from the argument in the morning, but the razor-sharp desperation was gone. And she was hungry.

When she entered the lunch hall, she saw the reflection of her rumpled uniform in one of the windows and mentally shrugged her shoulders. Let them look at her funny. She didn't have the intention to stay for very long anyway.

She had just grabbed one of the travel packs of food from the buffet when she saw a head of stubby brown curls move at the back of the room.

Oh no, she had completely forgotten to cancel her morning appointment with Beth.

Ali weaved her way to her friend's side.

"There you are. Aiden told me you wouldn't attend your session today. I was worried."

Ali felt a stab of guilt at hearing the relief in Beth's voice. Her illness was starting to impact her friends.

"Sorry, Beth. I… What do you mean, Aiden *told* you?"

Beth tilted her head. "He ordered me to leave you be. Why?"

"Shouldn't you outrank him?"

"I thought so, too." A crease appeared in Beth's forehead. "I definitely felt compelled to obey. I was wondering… It's strange, right?"

Indeed, Ali thought. Medical staff of all kind generally outranked other Hybrids. It was necessary in case of an emergency.

"I do outrank Sam," Beth mused, her glowing cheeks positively screaming *interesting story*.

Ali pushed the newest piece of information that didn't fit into the puzzle that was Aiden to the back of her mind to hear Beth's news. "How do you know?"

Beth steered her towards a quiet table. "Sam was with Aiden when he told me about you. Aiden left, but Sam ended up staying at my office, to help me kill the time. We talked." Beth's voice dropped to a whisper. "I told him how frightening his designation was, and how I was worried he could turn assassin at any moment if someone gave him the order. He called me a smart girl to consider the threat, but said I didn't have anything to fear from him because I ranked higher and he would have to do everything I said. I wanted to believe him, but Aiden had just given me an order." She sighed. "Sam must have realized I wasn't convinced, because he asked me to command him to do something he would never normally do." Beth shrugged her shoulders, as if something like that happened to her on a daily basis. Then she fell quiet.

"So? What did you order him to do?" Ali asked. "Bark like a dog?"

Beth giggled. "I would never do such a heinous thing."

"What then?"

"I asked him – no, *told* him – to kiss me."

"You didn't."

Beth bobbed her head.

"And?"

Beth's cheeks rivalled with the tomatoes on her plate.

"I think that's answer enough," Ali laughed, thinking of her own kiss with Rob and how she had never wanted it to end. "Did you enjoy it?"

"More than I would have ever imagined. But I couldn't believe what he said afterwards."

"What?"

"He said he would have kissed me anyway."

Ali grinned. "And *that* was when you asked him to bark like a dog."

***

After leaving a giggling Beth behind in the lunch hall, Ali swung by Rob's room to find him busy trying to debug the code to reprogram her chip. He gave her a fleeting smile and another not-so-fleeting, toe-curling kiss. He offered for her to stay with him, but Ali knew he couldn't really afford the distraction.

It irritated her to no end that a distraction was all she was at this point. She wanted to help in this quest to save her life, not sit idle while he was doing all the work. Of course that wasn't how Rob saw it.

You're helping by staying alive, he said every time she brought it up.

Ali didn't think something everyone else did with ease should be considered a big achievement on her part.

She finally decided to wander outside. Whatever happened tomorrow with Aiden, she had gained this day for herself. She was determined to make the best of it.

Walking along the training courts to the forest at the back of the mansion, Ali followed the path to the river that she and Rob had taken on that fateful day, when they had tried to run away. It seemed like an eternity ago.

Ali wondered what her life would have been like if they had actually managed to escape.

It was difficult to imagine. She barely knew anything about the 'real world', apart from how to enforce New World laws. Had she been a normal Hybrid, she would have eventually learned all the ins and outs of human society when her chip updated for her first assignment. As a bearer of the black soul, Ali would never get the chance.

She quickly pushed the thought out of her mind before the Abyss could latch onto it. If nothing else, Ali was almost certain the malicious being fed off her dark emotions like a leech fed on blood.

She crawled onto a boulder overlooking the river shore and unpacked her lunch.

The atmosphere in the forest was soothing. The absence

of Hybrids and electronics allowed her overactive mind to finally unwind.

She set the wrapping down beside her and pinned it with a pebble to hold it against the wind.

The sandwich she had taken from the lunch hall reminded her again of their escape, the water that lapped at the river shore reminded her of their wild ride down the falls.

Ali felt a smile tugging at her lips. In hindsight, she was glad for the adventure. The way Rob had pressed against her in the tiny boat. His arm around her in the cave. She had lived more in a few short hours than she had in twenty-one years, and it was all because of the one Recruit who, right now, worked like crazy to save her life.

Ali wondered how she had gotten so lucky. What did he see in her that spurred him to defy everything they had been taught for over two decades? Was it purely his appetite for risk? Or was there more?

Could it possibly be that she was as precious to him, as he was to her?

***

When Ali arrived back at her quarters just before dinner, she felt ready to take on the world. She had ended her afternoon with a long stroll over meadows and fields, soaking up the sun while the worries of her life slowly drained away.

Take this, Aiden, she thought with grim satisfaction as she skipped into the bathroom to wash the grit from the boulder off her hands. She hadn't felt this good since her inauguration, maybe never.

Definitely not when he had forced her into his routine.

From now on she would do what *she* thought was best, and to hell with the Protector. For all she cared he could leave her alone forever.

Smiling, Ali looked into the mirror above the sink and shrank back with a gasp.

Flat grey eyes stared back at her. The bluish hue, that had given her at least a small measure of comfort since her episode in the Psychiatrist office, was gone completely. Thin white lines covered the grey disks like a spider's web, giving her iris a shattered look. At the centre surrounding her pupils, a darker ring had begun to form.

Ali's insides started to shake as she touched her fingers to the alien reflection.

"Why are you doing this to me?" she asked the Abyss in a trembling voice.

Because I can, came the hiss from its depth. Because you challenged me.

A twirl of smoke rose from the crack, fanning out into a silvery veil.

Had she changed planes again without thinking? Ali looked around, feeling her breath come in choppy spurts. She was standing on the ledge. Smoke billowed around her.

Don't you think it's a pretty colour? Much prettier than blue for sure.

"It's not my eye colour." Ali tore the thin veil apart with her hands.

It is now.

The hiss reassembled its particles until it loomed like a wavering shadow over her.

It makes more sense too, don't you think? Shattered eyes

for a shattered soul.

Chapter 16

More than her soul felt shattered when Ali woke the next morning. She had skipped dinner and instead crawled back into bed, the night before. Hugging her pillow, she had alternated between fear, rage, and desperation until she had finally fallen into another nightmare, in the early hours of the morning.

At least she had withstood the craving to return to the ledge.

Dark twirls of smoke shifted lazily in the perpetual twilight of her mind, at the thought. Ali ignored them, the way she had ignored all other attempts of the alluring being to garner her attention, throughout the night.

She clicked her tongue. "Good morning, Electra. Did I receive any messages?"

"No messages," the DID confirmed. "But I have a question for you, if I may."

"What is it?"

"Why do you still use voice commands, now that you have been inaugurated?"

Ali watched the smoke slowly gathering closer. "I've too

many things in my mind already. I'd rather you aren't one of them."

A chime sounded from Electra's speakers as darkness slithered over Ali's skin and gripped. Goose bumps rose all over her body. "Let go." She flapped her arms to disperse the grey mass. The wafts clung to her like cockleburs.

Not this time. I can taste your desire to look into me. I'm gorging on it. The creature chuckled.

"You're crazy, Abyss."

Then I am in good company. I hear you are going slowly insane.

"Not insane enough to succumb to your pleading. I'll never look at your blackened heart."

Then why are you walking towards me, Ali? Another step and...

Ali gasped, her toes curling over the edge of the cliff. One more step and she would have fallen into the nothingness beyond.

She tried to retreat and found she couldn't.

Now you will look into me, the Abyss purred into her ear.

No. Ali dropped to her knees, her face buried deep in the palms of her hands.

Such determination. I will enjoy making you beg.

"I'll never beg."

Of course you will. Nobody can beat time.

"Whatever you're offering," Ali said stubbornly, "it couldn't be possibly worth my life."

If you are so certain, why don't you look at it? You can judge the price yourself. I promise it will get rid of the craving you have been fighting all these days.

Ali's eyes popped open. She stared at the smoke, trying to judge its sincerity.

It was madness to believe the malicious being. Or maybe it was insanity.

Whatever it was, it made her eyes drop, her gaze snagging on the darkness below. "I can't see anything. You offer me nothing?"

A chuckle grated along her nerves. *Blessed nothingness, Ali. No guilt, no fear. I offer you what you crave the most.*

The strangled sound that escaped her throat echoed from the walls of her mind.

"Freedom," she breathed, her throat dry as the desert. It was the one thing worth dying for. "You're offering freedom."

Indeed, I do. One step and you can have it all.

"Alana, don't do it. It's telling you lies." A tingle spread along her shoulder.

"Aiden?" Her eyes stayed focused on the treasure she had thought was forever out of her reach. She could almost touch it. Just a little bit further.

"Yes, it's me. Your Protector. Come back to me."

Nerve endings fired all over her body, as tingles raced across her skin.

Her vision wavered. She lost sight of the offering.

Ali tore her eyes open to the world.

The Abyss had been honest was her first conscious thought. The craving to see its depth was gone. In its place was the burgeoning obsession to obtain the offered prize instead. Why would she even want to resist?

Because they would put a mindlock on you, Ali answered

her own question. Leashed, dead, or a vegetating mass of cells. Her options were dire or worse, at best. Desperation filled her, as reality hit her with all the subtlety of an uppercut.

Her knees gave out, and she expected to fall, but Aiden's arms tightened on her waist. She held onto his body, as the world spun around her then started dissolving in front of her eyes.

She slowly became aware of her surroundings. His heart beating steady underneath her hands. Tingles still raced across her thighs, where she was sitting on his lap.

"Are you back with me?" Aiden's voice rumbled softly.

Pressed against his body, his arms around her, Ali could almost pretend that he cared. She looked at his face, and her pretence vanished. His pupils were heavily dilated, once more.

Ali pushed at his chest for him to let go. It was as effective as moving a mountain.

"I need to go to the bathroom," she said, surreptitiously wiping her nose.

Aiden slowly released her. "Five minutes."

The chip in her brain started counting down seconds.

The mirror in the bathroom recoiled at her sight.

She looked like a mess with her bloodshot eyes. She was a mess. Her whole life was a mess.

No. Ali stopped the negative spiral of thoughts. She turned on the tap and determinedly washed the tears off her face.

When she came back out after four minutes and thirty-two seconds, Aiden rose to his feet in one smooth motion.

He immediately zeroed in on her eyes. This time, Ali knew why. She also knew what he saw. Her irises had changed their colour once more and were now almost as dark as his.

She averted her gaze, feeling oddly ashamed. As if it was her fault.

Maybe it was.

"Breakfast will start in eight minutes," he said, his own pupils back to their normal size. "I'm cancelling our morning training."

So he still intended to train her, even after the disastrous insult she had flung at him the day before. He was still her Protector. Relief flooded her.

"Aiden." It was the first time she had spoken his name to his face. "About yesterday—"

"You will make up for it in your evening session."

***

"He made you cry."

Rob's comment caught her at the wrong time, her emotions still raw from her near miss. Ali bristled. "Why do you always assume the worst of him?" she asked, remembering Rob's reaction after her run-in with the Chosen. He had slandered Aiden then, too. And Ali had used his comments to insult the Protector. Shame sharpened her voice to a cutting edge. "Just because you don't understand him—"

"I don't *trust* him."

"Why not?"

"Because you're always closemouthed after you come back from your training with him."

"Rubbish," Ali huffed.

"True," Rob countered. "Do you think I don't notice, when you're not telling me everything?"

"You don't need to know *everything* about me, Rob."

Rob's jaw tightened with suppressed anger. "I see. I only get to know the things I need to fix your head.

Ali's breath caught in her throat. "That was unnecessary." For the first time she was truly put out with him. "I almost died half an hour ago. Aiden saved me. Again."

She saw shock move over Rob's face, but didn't wait for him to speak. If he apologized, she would have to forgive him. She wanted to be mad for a while.

She grabbed an apple from the buffet and left the breakfast hall without looking back.

Twenty minutes later, Rob sat down next to her under an ironbark tree in the garden, his arms dangling over his knees. "I'm sorry." He bumped her shoulder. "I shouldn't have said that."

Ali shook her head. Her anger had long since diminished. "It wasn't your fault. I handled it badly. I should have told you right away what had happened, instead of leading you on."

"Is that what you've been doing?" Rob asked, the side of his lip curling up in a smile.

This time it was Ali bumping *his* shoulder.

Rob chuckled and pulled her against his body.

For a moment, Ali marvelled in the feeling of his chest under her hand, his arm around her, then she pushed back to look into his eyes. "The thought that you feel exploited by me," she picked a piece of imaginary fluff from his shirt, "it makes me feel awful." She forced herself to look at him. "Please stop trying to reprogram the chip."

"No."

"But—"

"No, Ali. Don't even say it." Rob framed her face in his large hands. "I said that only in anger. I told you before that I would do anything to save your life. A little disagreement about a certain Hybrid isn't going to change my mind. *Nothing* is going to change my mind. Whatever happens, I stand by my word."

***

"Oh, good. You're here." Beth motioned her into the Psychiatrist office, and Ali felt some of her tension drain away. She hadn't even realized how much she had missed their counselling session, the day before.

When had her aversion to share details of her illness morphed into relief that she could talk to someone without fear of being judged? She couldn't recall. It didn't make her feelings any less true.

Ali sank into one of the overstuffed chairs. "I'm glad to be back. I have much to tell." She gave a little self-deprecating laugh. "Some of it might sound insane."

***

The evening training with Aiden was harder than ever, but Ali didn't complain.

She finally understood why the routine was so important. It was, exactly as Aiden had said, a form of occupational therapy. The strict schedule drained the vast amounts of physical and mental energy Ali had at her disposal as a Hybrid; energy that, if left to accumulate, found another outlet in a craving she couldn't resist.

Aiden came at her again with a punch combination that drove the air from her lungs, but astonishingly didn't set off a single pain receptor in her body. Ali countered with a strike to his lower leg that he managed to block easily. He wrapped his arm around her neck.

Ali shook her head to clear it, as she tried to sit up. "What happened?" Hadn't she just been standing up? Fighting…"You strangled me?"

"So I did."

Was that amusement in his voice?

"Why?"

The noise he made sounded suspiciously like a laugh. He rolled back onto his feet. "You are too slow. Get faster, or I'll strangle you again."

Nobody could ever accuse him of lacking ideas on how to motivate Hybrids. Ali pushed off the floor, wiping her face on her arm. *What had put him in such a good mood?* she wondered. And how could he still look calm and collected after an hour of working out? He hadn't even broken a sweat. He wasn't breathing hard either.

"Again." His fist flew towards her then past her face as she dodged the blow. Her other hand drove forward in an uppercut, that he deflected with his quick defence. The impact of flesh against bone sounded loud in her ears as he kicked at her with his left foot. Ali blocked with her lower leg then drove her fist into his side. She pulled the punch at the last second bruising instead of breaking his rib cage.

"Freeze."

Her muscles locked in position, her hand trapped against

his body.

"Chip, use tactile and visual impressions for three dimensional point of view."

A perfect replica of their current combat situation appeared in Ali's mind at his command. Only the lock he had compelled on her body kept her jaw from dropping open.

She had known that Protectors could access a variety of combat related functions on their microchips, but why was *she* able to see the mental image?

"Focus on point of contact."

Ali's focus shifted to accommodate Aiden's order.

She saw her fist connected to his ribs in her first ever successful strike. Although she had felt the impact moments earlier, the visual confirmation made pride swell inside her.

Then he rotated the image to show her a different angle, and her elation drained away. There, a hair's breadth from her neck hovered the side of Aiden's hand in a swipe that would have ended the fight in the next instant.

"Unfreeze."

Aiden stepped back, as her muscles started responding to neural impulses, once more.

"You are getting better," he said.

"I lost the fight."

"Some fights you can't win." He lifted his uniform to show her where a bruise the size of her fist was already forming on his ribs. "All you can do is hope to leave a lasting impression."

***

"It won't work."

The last of Ali's hope shattered at the certainty in Rob's statement. He had asked her earlier to come to his room to test the now 'healthy virus' as he had jokingly called the corrected code. But five minutes into their first trial run they had encountered a problem – a newly implemented Biosignature that protected her chip's programming from unauthorized alterations.

Rob had worked furiously for the last two hours trying to find a backdoor into the chip. It seemed there was none.

Ali sat slouched in her seat trying to process the finality of her situation. "Could you short-circuit it instead?" she asked in a last ditch attempt to avoid the inevitable.

"You'd have a less than one percent survival chance," was the only thing Rob said.

Ali didn't like the idea either. Then again, between the most certainly lethal anialbus serum and the definitely lethal Abyss, any alternative was better than death. "Could you?"

"Yes," he said finally. Reluctantly. "I could feed an infinite loop into your chip through your normal data update channels. The loop could overload the chip until it's too busy to maintain the power-feed."

Clearly he had thought about the idea before.

"What about the Biosignature?" Ali asked.

"It wouldn't come in to play. The feed wouldn't touch on the chip's original programming."

It was a real possibility then. Somehow Ali didn't feel quite relieved. "How long would it take to program the feed?" she asked, focusing on the facts.

"A day, maybe two."

She still had a week until her predestined end. Enough

time.

"Will you do it?" She fought the urge to vomit. She was asking him to kill her. *Less than one percent...*

Rob's hand tightened around the touch screen stylus he had used to manipulate the narrow-spaced code on his mobile DID. "You once told me not to use you as an experiment ever again."

"You were willing to reprogram," she pointed out.

"That was a calculated risk. What you're proposing is a death sentence." The knuckles on his hand turned white.

Ali swallowed. "You promised," she said, her voice little more than a whisper. "Anything. Anytime. Did you lie?"

She saw the pain clouding his eyes and hated herself. How could she do this to him, when she knew how a person could suffer over the guilt of killing another? "Did you?"

The stylus shattered. "I didn't," he answered her tonelessly.

Chapter 17

The room was dark.

"Electra, what's the time?"

"Four-fifteen a.m."

Too early to get up. Not even Rob would appreciate a visit at this time in the night. Not after the way she had coerced him into helping her yesterday.

Ali pushed the heels of her hands against her temples and fought the guilt churning in her gut.

You are a coward, Ali, the Abyss hissed darkly, at once latching on to her troubling thoughts. Too gutless to end it all yourself. Instead you're ruining a good Recruit. You'll get your freedom one way or the other, but what about him? Have you thought of that? It will break him to kill you.

Ali glared at the creature, realizing her mistake a second too late.

Blessed nothingness beckoned in its depth. Its allure stronger than ever before.

Ali swayed towards the edge of the cliff.

That's right. Come closer. Sacrifice yourself. The insidious hiss twined around her body and whispered seductively in her ear. The world is better off without you. Remember?

She did remember. She didn't deserve to live.

She had killed her mother, she had hurt her friends. The memories were like gaping wounds.

Ali bit down hard on her lip as she stared into the gorge dropping away at her feet. "I…I should do it. I should jump." Her voice sounded hollow.

Why draw out the inevitable?

A tear rolled down Ali's cheek and she swiped it away with trembling fingers. "I could be free in an instant. Free of the endless desperation. Free of my greatest fears. If I'm just brave enough to let go of life."

"And what about us?" asked a familiar voice outside Ali's head.

"What about you, Electra?"

"Do you not care what your freedom will do to us?"

Ali picked up a pebble, turned it a few times between her fingers then hurled it into the black Abyss. She listened to the silence that followed.

"What do you mean?" she asked the DID, when she finally decided there would be no sound of impact.

"Do you not care that we will ask ourselves *why* for the rest of our lives? Why were we not able to save you? Where did we go wrong? What could we have done differently? Do you not care about our feelings at all? Our desperation? Our anguish?"

"You're a computer, Electra. You don't know what desperation is."

"Are you so sure about that, Ali? And what about Beth?

Rob? Aiden? Do they not feel desperation either? Are you selfish enough to disregard them and what they have done for you, all this time? You take what you need from them, but you are unwilling to give anything back."

"I'm willing to die for them," Ali shouted, her voice breaking. "What else do you want from me?"

"Live for them, instead," Electra said simply. "Freedom is priceless, but so is life. Show that you care, too. Step away from the edge, take responsibility for your actions and fight."

"And what if I lose?" It was Ali's greatest fear.

"Then at least you can die knowing that you have tried."

***

Ali's chest still felt too tight, when she entered Rob's room ten minutes later. She didn't know why Electra had taken it upon herself to speak to Ali the way she had, but she sure had saved Ali's life – and given her a whole lot to think about.

Trust the logic of a computer to put it all in perspective.

But it wasn't Electra's insight into a Hybrid's emotional world that had made Ali decide to bother Rob at this early hour, after all. It was the truth the Abyss had spoken.

At least she didn't have to feel bad about waking him, Ali thought when she saw Rob was working on his DID. His mobi lay dead on the desk beside him.

"I can't believe they never realized you can do that." She said as he turned his chair to face her, more to stall for time than because she was truly surprised the Program had never noticed. "How did you make sure it reactivated, before we were captured?"

Rob followed her gaze to the device in question. "When I programmed the mobi to hibernate, I disabled all the components, except for the monitoring of my vital signs. Once the measurements fell beneath a certain threshold, indicating I was unconscious rather than asleep, all functionality enabled automatically. I thought it prudent that they could find us, should something happen to us out there."

Ali gave him a tentative smile. Even during their escape he had put their safety before their success. He was always trying to look out for her. Even when she made it close to impossible for him.

The thought gave her pause and she shifted uncomfortably. After their last conversation, she felt like she owed him an apology. But saying the words would be meaningless, unless she retracted her request at the same time. And *that* she couldn't do. She would, however, do her best to take the guilt from him that Ali had lived with for the last two decades. "How is the infinite loop coming along?"

"The loop itself isn't the problem. It's uploading it into your chip that I'm working on." He dragged a hand over his face. Deep shadows were visible under his eyes.

"Ali, are you sure you want to go through with this? I really don't want to fry your brain."

Ali swallowed. He had a way of putting things bluntly. On the other hand, he had just given her the perfect opportunity to say what she came here to say.

She sank down on his bed and took his hands. "Rob." She struggled for words. "Whatever happens, I want you to remember that the blame is on me. I've decided to go through with this. I take full responsibility."

"It's not that easy."

She knew it wasn't, but she had to make sure he understood. Electra was right. Rob would be devastated if Ali died. Ali couldn't allow for him to feel responsible, too.

Ali squeezed Rob's hand tighter. "I won't lie to you. I'm absolutely terrified of what will happen." Even the thought of what they would attempt made her break out into a cold sweat. "But I know, no matter what, I'd rather die because I made the wrong decision, than because someone else made the wrong decision for me."

Rob looked at her with anguish in his eyes. Ali hated to have put it there. Especially there, where she normally looked for light and laughter.

"Come to my room before your morning training, the day after tomorrow," Rob said, his voice rough with emotion. "Don't update your microchip, we'll do that here. As soon as you connect to the bioservers, I'll breach the wireless transmission, get a lock on where your data update is stored, replace it with the code, and feed the loop into your brain to overload the chip. Once the power-feed is lost, it should take approximately five minutes before the chip's emergency energy storage is depleted."

At which point she'd either drop dead, damage her brain, or – with a tiny chance of less than one percent – would keep living happily ever after.

"Thank you," she whispered, banishing the thought that she might very well be thanking him for killing her.

***

When Ali left Rob's room, she heard the insistent sound

of the electronic clock across the hall strike five forty-five.

Damn. She was supposed to meet Aiden for training.

Even as she broke into a run, she cringed at the thought of being late. She briefly considered going directly to the gym then discarded the thought immediately. When sparring with Aiden, she needed all the help she could get. That included proper workout shoes and clothes.

Ali panted, when she finally entered the training hall at five fifty-two.

"You are late."

As if she didn't know.

"One hundred push-ups."

The man was insane. But obviously serious, she realized as he swept her feet out from under her body, forcing her arms to catch her weight.

He counted for her. Way too fast. Ali tried to keep up and felt the strain in her arms get worse.

"... ninety-eight, ninety-nine, one hundred. Up! And block."

The punch came so fast Ali didn't have the ghost of a chance, with her arms limp like noodles. And what about warm up anyway?

"You had your warm-up running here."

She hadn't even realized that she had spoken aloud.

Ali dodged a punch that would have pushed her ribs out of her back and wondered how it was that Aiden had never sent her to the medical facilities with broken bones. Was he really that good? Could he always pull his punches on the spot when he saw she wasn't fast enough?

"Focus."

The command snapped her back to the present in a flurry of compulsion, just in time to block a straight fist to the face. Ouch. She had almost been able to feel her nasal bone shattering there for a moment.

The next attack was just as vicious. Sweat starting pouring down her body. The way the session went, she would have to go back and pick up a new set of workout clothes before their evening training.

***

Ali made her way back to her quarters during her lunch break, to pick up the clothes she needed. Entering her room, her eyes automatically checked Electra's clock.

She would have to rush to get back to the lunch hall in time to grab some food before everything was gone. Her stomach growled. She definitely didn't want to miss out.

Ali slipped her clothes into her gym bag and was about to leave when her eyes caught on the tube of painkillers she had received after her concussion. The container was on her bedside table where she had left it, but there was something about it… Ali stepped closer and felt the bag drop from her numb hands.

With her heart in her throat, Ali stormed into the Office's reception area minutes later, carrying the tube in front of her body like a poisonous snake.

"Open the door."

The supermodel aka receptionist flinched at her harsh tone, but regained her composure fast. "I can't—"

"Of course you can." She stared the blonde down.

"Office door, open."

"Rt2120." Doctor looked collected, if somewhat

surprised by her appearance.

Ali ignored his frown, as she slammed the bottle down on his desk. "I thought you wanted to keep me alive for as long as possible, not send me into oblivion with a tube of atracillin."

She knew her staged entry was somehow diminished by the edge of panic in her voice, but the discovery that someone had re-filled her painkillers with the black, egg-shaped pills she had come across during her research of the black soul, had blown the calm she so desperately needed to stay alive.

Days ago, she had taken the painkillers in the dark. Had her concussion symptoms not considerably eased since her inauguration, she may have done the same today – and could have ended up taking one of the atracillin pills instead. Produced to temporarily block any conscious thought, atracillin would have prevented everyone and everything from stopping Ali's mind from hurling itself into the Abyss.

"And why would you think it was me placing the pills?" Doctor asked in a dangerous voice.

Because only Medics had access to atracillin, and only he ranked higher than a Medic. But, pinned to her spot by his piercing brown eyes, Ali couldn't voice her thoughts. "Are you saying Anthony did this without your permission, sir?" she asked, aware she was losing ground fast.

"I'm saying you shouldn't have come here without an appointment, nor should you *ever* insult me again." His words, though deceptively calm, still ripped through her like a hurricane. Forceful. Compelling.

Ali pushed her nails into the soft skin on her palm and

lifted her chin. It wouldn't do her any good to show weakness to this monster.

The ghost of a smile touched his face. "I believe I may have underestimated you, Hybrid." He picked up the bottle. The pills rattled loudly in the quiet room. "I will keep this," he said. "I'm sure it will come in handy when we find the perpetrators."

Ali felt uneasiness sliding down her spine, at the cold calculation in his voice.

"I will have access to your room restricted to you and Aiden only." He lifted a single brow, his eyes drilling into her.

"Thank you, sir" …she guessed was the adequate response.

"You're welcome. We are looking out for our kind." …said the human to the Hybrid who he had implanted with a suicide chip.

Ali sighed. It had to make sense in this human's twisted mind, because it sure didn't make any sense to her.

Chapter 18

"Ali."

It was the next day – her last day, before they would try to short circuit the chip – and the magnitude of what they were going to attempt was finally starting to sink in.

She could be dead in less than twenty-four hours, gone from this world without a trace.

Suppressing the urge to rant at the unfairness of life, Ali turned around to see Sam strolling down the corridor in the direction of the training halls. "Ready for your training?"

She did the only thing that was left to do: hold up appearances. "Yes, sir. Where's Aiden?"

"Aiden can't make it and has asked me to supervise your morning session. He said he'll catch up with you double, this afternoon."

Great. Aiden was going to make her life difficult, until the last minute. What a befitting end to an uncomfortable alliance.

She heaved a deep sigh and saw the corner of Sam's mouth curl upwards.

"Don't worry. He told me not to hurt you...too much."

She was inclined to dispute the statement, when she collapsed onto the floor an hour and a half later. Sam had driven her relentlessly the whole time. He had focused more on building her core strength and endurance rather than her fighting skills, but she didn't hurt less because of it.

"You are evil." The words were out before she could stop them, and she slapped her hand in front of her mouth.

Sam laughed. "And proud of it." His blue eyes sparkled as he winked at her.

Once again, Ali was stunned that such an easy-going Hybrid could be one of the most dangerous Assassins the Program had ever bred. She guessed his demeanour was part of his armoury. His victims would never see death coming, until it was too late.

"Up with you. I'll take you to the breakfast hall."

Ali shot him a sideways glance. That was unexpected.

"You're meeting Beth there, right?"

Maybe not so unexpected, after all. "Yes, sir." Ali took a big gulp of water from her bottle. "Are you going to ask her for some idle time, sir?"

"Are you familiar with the term 'curiosity killed the cat', Hybrid?"

"Curiosity. Insanity." Ali shrugged her shoulders. "What's the difference?"

***

Breakfast went by fast. Sam decided to eat at their table, drawing long looks from the other young Hybrids and longer looks from the woman sitting across from him.

He gave as good as he got though, Ali thought with a secret smile.

She could have almost felt like a third wheel, except watching the unlikely couple dance around each other in words and gestures, was entirely too entertaining.

Ali just prayed that their public display of interest wouldn't get them into trouble. After all, a partner was a weakness that could be easily exploited to enforce compliance.

The image of Rob hanging in his chains after she had tortured him flashed through her mind. They had certainly exploited Ali's weakness.

After food – at least Ali had eaten in the hall for once – she and Beth made their way down the winding access road to the green meadow beyond.

"They don't mind if you hold your appointments outside?" she asked Beth, as they left the building.

"No. As long as I stay on site, they don't interfere much with what I do. The benefits are too significant to be overlooked. Hybrids are demonstrably more focused after an hour outside than they are after a counselling session in the confines of my office. Why? Do you mind?"

"I'm not complaining." Ali looked at her friend. "I actually find the outdoors soothing. Almost as if nature keeps the darkness at bay."

"I've read that, too, in a number of case studies that I've found on the LiveNet. That was another reason why I wanted to come out here with you."

Ali felt a smile spread across her face. Beth had become a true friend, who was going way beyond the call of duty to help her. Now Ali should be a real friend too. "About, Sam..."

A tell-tale flush spread across Beth's cheeks.

"What's going on with the two of you?"

"I...I'm not sure," Beth admitted. "I think we're taking things slowly."

"Really? Like kissing-in-your-office and having-breakfast-in-public-together slowly?"

Beth giggled embarrassed.

"It's his designation," she said, sobering. "It's still quite scary. I know I outrank him, but if he wanted to kill me – if he was told to – I doubt I'd ever see it coming. I'd be dead before I could utter a word."

"Life's a risk," Ali agreed. She knew that better than most Hybrids. "I guess you could run scared all your life and try to stay away from everyone and everything, just to be safe. But that wouldn't be much of a life, would it?"

"Hey," Beth jabbed a finger into her ribs. "I'm the Psychiatrist. I'm supposed to say all the meaningful things."

They were still laughing when a hovertruck roared around the bend, its rear fishtailing from one side of the road to the other. It was driving way too fast, speeding directly at them. Ali was about to jump to safety when she realized that Beth was staring at the hovercraft like a deer in the headlights. Her eyes wide open, she seemed frozen to the spot; not a single muscle was moving in her body.

"Beth," Ali shouted to no avail.

The engine revved up. Another two seconds and...

Ali tackled Beth, taking them both to the ground on the other side of the road. The impact jarred her teeth.

"Wha—" Beth shook her head. "What happened?"

"You tell me." Ali tried to calm her racing heart. Even

using her standard biofeedback exercise, it proved difficult. She had almost watched her friend die.

"I-I don't know." Beth was clearly shaken, her hands icy cold. "I-I couldn't move." She looked at her body as if it belonged to someone else. "I knew I was in danger, but I couldn't jump to safety."

"I think you should get checked out by a Medic. Immediately." Ali pulled her friend up from the ground, steadying her, when Beth wobbled precariously. "Come. I'll take you to the medical facilities."

Beth didn't budge. "What if it happens again," she whispered, staring wide-eyed at the access road

Ali looked at her usually level-headed friend and felt her heart squeeze. "It won't. I promise." She positioned herself between Beth and the road then tugged at her friend's arm to get her to move.

Beth was still shaking when they walked past the hovertruck sitting in the parking lot, with its engine turned off. An Ai Specialist was meddling with the computer built into the front panel.

"What's the problem with the vehicle?" Beth asked, her voice too thin but still carrying the weight of a Hybrid in a medical profession.

The Ai Specialist's pupils dilated, and he responded without pause. "The board computer tripped, taking out some of the safety measures. A crash into the building was only prevented by the electronic tokens under the street further down the road that triggered an automatic brake."

The electronic tokens had to have taken effect after the hovertruck had sped past them.

"Does this happen often?" Ali asked.

The Hybrid looked at her with a blank face.

"Answer her," Beth ordered.

"Maybe once or twice a year."

"And nobody ever thought of doing something about it?" Ali couldn't believe it.

"They installed the street tokens."

Obviously the mansion was more important than any unsuspecting Hybrids walking on the access road. Then again, Hybrids didn't normally freeze when they saw danger.

Ali felt an icy hand grip her arm.

"I'm feeling dizzy."

Ali turned to see her friend's normally tanned skin turn ashen. She gripped Beth's elbow and pulled her in the direction of the medical facilities, away from the offending vehicle.

"I think I hit my head when you tackled me."

"What does your chip say?"

"Lots of bruises. No brain injury."

"We'll get you checked out, anyway. If the connection with the chip is affected, the results may be incorrect."

Ali flagged down one of the nurses as soon as they stepped into the waiting room. "We require a full brain and body scan."

The nurse looked at their dirty clothes and scratched hands.

"Take a seat over there, and I'll get one of the Medics for you."

Less than two minutes later, Ali heard a familiar voice

that set her teeth on edge.

"Psy05, you need a body scan?" Anthony came to a halt in front of them.

"I do." Beth rose unsteadily to her feet. "And a brain scan, if possible."

"Certainly. Please come along." He led the way to the examination room.

Ali took a seat in the corner, as Beth recounted the events.

Anthony frowned. "You said you couldn't walk away, although you knew you were in danger?"

"Yes."

The Medic nodded at a nurse, who had followed them into the room. The staff member inclined her head almost imperceptibly and left. Cold settled in the pit of Ali's stomach. Something was going on here. Something bad.

Beth must have noticed it too, because her hands balled into fists at her sides.

"We'll start with the brain scan," Anthony said, lowering the backrest of Beth's chair. The Biomonitor in the corner of the room came to life a second later.

Anthony's eyes flickered to the screen. "It works," he mumbled surprised, studying the schematic images that didn't make any sense to Ali.

"What works, sir?" Ali felt more dread curling in her belly. Something working wasn't necessarily a good thing when it was inside a Hybrid's brain.

Anthony looked at her, momentarily startled out of the intense scrutiny of the screen.

"The chip."

"What do you mean, the chip works?" Beth's voice sounded strained.

"Everything in due course." Anthony patted Beth's fist, then turned around to grab the handheld body scan device. A second picture appeared on screen.

Ali saw Beth clench her teeth against the urge to shake the answers out of the Medic. She knew the feeling well.

"Your body scan looks fine. You have low blood sugar, therefore the dizziness. No broken or fractured bones. A few bruises probably from hitting the street. The bruises should go away within a day or two."

He pointed out the area of the bruises, which Ali thought was completely unnecessary. Surely Beth could feel where she had bruised.

It seemed like the Medic was stalling for time.

Moments later, Ali realized why.

"Good morning, Hybrids. I hear we have cause to celebrate." Doctor was unusually jovial as he stepped into the room.

The bad feeling in Ali's stomach increased.

She could see Beth squeezing the side of the chair even harder. "How so, sir?" she asked.

Doctor looked down at her the way a gardening droid would study a rare specimen of orchid. A small smile tilted his lips. "Me, because you are living proof that we can override a Hybrid's natural fight or flight instinct with the chip. You, because you are *living* proof."

"Why override such basic instincts, sir," Ali asked, against her better judgment.

"Suicide missions," Doctor said succinctly.

Silence followed his statement.

"I'm not suicidal," Beth said finally, in a trembling voice.

"You wouldn't have sufficed as a test subject if you were. We needed someone who had the opposite tendencies before inauguration, to make sure that the results were caused by the chip. Your personality fit the profile perfectly, and your profession binds you to the Sanatorium – a place where you should have been safe." Doctor's eyes shifted to Ali. "It seems you cannot be safe anywhere these days."

Ali wanted to claw the indifference off his face so badly her whole body shook.

Doctor turned to Anthony. "I trust you will inform the Ai Specialists for the programming of the next chips. A hovertruck shouldn't have triggered the compulsion."

"Yes, Doctor."

"And what about me?" Beth asked.

Doctor turned around, already halfway to the door. "I would suggest, keeping out of harm's way," he said. "After all, we may need you one day." With that, he walked out of the room, leaving behind two devastated women and a Medic who looked entirely too excited by the findings that had shattered their lives.

***

Ali and Beth left the medical facilities an hour later, after Anthony had run a separate body scan on Ali to confirm that she too was fine, as far as physical health went. He had also shown Ali the state of her irises on the Biomonitor. Magnified to ten times their size, the slate grey disks looked like prisoners behind the mesh of white veins.

The last thing Anthony had confirmed, before sending

them on their way, had been the progression of Ali's illness. According to the Biomonitor, she was way past the fifty percent mark in regard to her symptoms.

More than half dead, Ali thought with a grim sense of humour.

She couldn't decide who was worse off. Her with her cravings to commit suicide, or Beth with her inability to walk away.

"How am I ever going to stay alive?" Beth's huge eyes glittered with tears. "I don't even know what type of danger triggers the compulsion."

Ali wished she could lie and tell Beth she would never encounter another trigger, but sugar-coating life wouldn't make death any prettier, or easier. "You'll find out in time," she said, steering her friend in the direction of the lunch hall. If nothing else, she could at least fix Beth's low blood sugar level.

"Or die trying." Beth's laugh sounded suspiciously like a sob.

Ali couldn't deny it. There was that possibility too.

She gently pushed Beth towards the buffet and put a plate in her hands when she made no move to do so herself.

"Are you going to tell Sam?" Ali asked, wondering which foods wouldn't make them both gag at a time like this. She settled on an apple for each of them.

"Oh yes, I'm sure he wants a psycho girlfriend who will run into a hovertruck whenever she gets the chance."

"You mean as much as you want a psycho girlfriend who daydreams about slashing her own wrists?" Ali grabbed a knife from the cutlery holder and waved the blade close to her skin.

Beth grabbed the tool out of her hand. "That's different," she said, putting a kiwi and spoon on Ali's plate.

Ali snorted. "How is that different?"

"It just is."

"That's not a very good explanation, Ms Psychiatrist. I don't think I'll believe that."

Beth rolled her eyes and stomped to a small table at the back of the hall. Ali took a relieved breath. Anger was better than shock.

"All I'm saying is that you should give him a chance." Ali hurried after her friend. "Maybe he'll be willing to help you." She lowered her voice as they sat down. "You'll need someone to look out for you...when I'm gone." It hurt to say the last few words, but they had to be said. Her expected life span was less than twenty hours now.

"I thought you said Rob had a solution for you."

"A potential solution. A very dangerous solution. And don't divert from the subject."

"I'm not."

"Yes, you are."

Beth shut her mouth.

"Sam," Ali said, to pull her friend back to the original point she had been trying to make.

"What about me?"

They both looked up in unison.

"Beth wanted to tell you something." Ali kicked her friend's leg under the table.

"I did not," Beth mumbled looking anywhere but at Sam.

The Assassin grabbed a chair and sat down. His arms

resting casually at his sides, his feet stretched out in front of him, he looked as if he had all the time in the world.

Beth glared. "Don't you think I know what you're doing?" she asked, when the silence stretched to a full minute, then two. "I'm a Psychiatrist. I know all about psychological pressure."

"And still you don't order me to leave," Sam replied evenly. "You aren't the only one who reads people for a living, Beth? More importantly, I know what it looks like when someone is desperate to confess." He leaned forward, until Beth's face was mere inches from his. "Are you afraid of someone, little one?" He flexed his shoulders, drawing Beth's attention to the strength in his combat-ready body. "I'll kill them for you. I promise."

"Then you have to kill me."

Sam reared back. "What are you talking about?"

Beth shook her head, then buried her face in her hands and sobbed. "They've turned me into a ticking time bomb."

"Bastards," Sam said, when Beth fell silent, after recounting the events. "You'll move into my quarters, where I can take care of you."

"I will *not*," Beth answered, "be a liability to my friends." Short, curly hair bounced in outrage.

The Assassin simply ignored Beth's comment. "And I will request for us to be linked."

"What's 'linked'?" Ali asked, having followed the conversation in silent amazement. *So much for asking Beth for some idle time,* she thought.

Sam shot a glance in Ali's direction. "Hybrids are linked, when two or more people share a direct wireless connection between their respective chips. You should know that. You're linked to Aiden."

Ali choked. "What?"

Sam studied her intently. "Aiden didn't tell you? Oops. I guess." He didn't look apologetic in the least.

Ali cleared her throat. "What does this link include?" And did she really want to know?

"It's how he keeps tabs on you. He wouldn't let you out of his sight, if it wasn't for the link."

All blood drained from Ali's face.

She had wondered before at Aiden's impeccable timing when he had come to save her the day she first looked into the Abyss. Was that why he'd had no qualms about sending her back to the complex alone, after Otis and his cronies had beat her up? "Can he read my thoughts?" The possibility was chilling.

"No. Nothing that advanced. He only gets an overall impression of your state of mind. Your emotions. He would, for example, know when you are experiencing one of your compulsions, when you are in danger, or hurt. Right now he probably knows that you are spitting mad at him." The corners of Sam's lips twitched at the expression Ali knew was on her face. Ali felt the urge to hit him.

He held his hands up in mock surrender. "Hey, don't shoot the messenger."

"What? Do I have a link with you as well?"

"We don't need one for me to understand *that* look on your face. So you'll move in tonight?" The last question he said seriously and directly to Beth.

"In your dreams."

Ali pushed back from her chair. She had her own battle to fight. It was a good thing Aiden had requested they start their double training session early, because she doubted she would be able to wait until after her study class.

***

Ali waited for Aiden in front of the training hall. She had spent most of the afternoon trying to find out how she could unlink. What she had found had only fuelled her over-boiling temper. Only Aiden could unlink them.

She saw the Protector coming down the hallway, his stride as sure as always, even though he had to know how she felt, if maybe not why.

"It was for your own safety," he said as soon as he reached her. So much for not knowing why.

Ali refused to be comforted by his words. Her welfare was a compulsion for him, nothing more. "Have you ever thought of telling me?"

"Yes. We decided it would be impractical."

We? Him and Doctor. Could it get any worse? "I want—"

"It's irrelevant what you want," he interrupted her. "I will not unlink. And you will not ask me to."

The chip processed the order, shutting her mouth. She was, once again, a prisoner in her own body.

Ali forced her jaw open, trying to break the compulsion.

"I want you to..." Her mouth felt like a foreign body. *Unlink.* She couldn't say it. Her brain provided the word, but her lips felt numb. *Unlink.* Her mouth worked, but no sound came out. Tears poured from her eyes as she gave in. She had wanted to disobey his compulsion so badly, but it was just too strong.

"Why are you doing this to yourself?" Pain flashed in Aiden's dilated eyes, and Ali realized her distress hurt him, too. Her Protector.

She shook her head. How could she explain to him that every time she gave into compulsion she realized that her only true freedom lay at the bottom of the Abyss?

***

After the training, Aiden accompanied Ali back to her quarters. The harsh workout had succeeded in dispersing most of her anger. There was just no energy left inside her.

Aiden, on the other hand, seemed unusually tense. Fury radiated from him in powerful waves, pushing against Ali like a living, breathing thing. Ali shifted to put more distance between them, her shoulder bumping into the wall of the outhouse's narrow corridor. It didn't help. His big body and ominous presence had taken over the whole hallway.

"Is something wrong?" She was almost afraid to ask.

"I've heard about the incident with the atracillin." Another wave of anger rolled off him. "It took us a while, but we've finally found the perpetrators."

Was that why he hadn't been able to make the morning training? "Who was it?" she asked, almost certain of the answer.

"Otis, Jay, and Mace."

It was still a shock to hear her suspicions confirmed. "How?"

"One of the Medics here at the Sanatorium is a member of the Chosen."

And Chosen stuck together. Everyone knew that. "So if you've found them, then what's the problem?"

"Eric and I disagreed on the disciplinary action. The Marshal who just came into the hall to speak to me informed me that my proposal has been denied."

"What was your proposal?"

"I've asked for them to be terminated."

Chapter 19

Ali watched the sun slowly chasing away the remnants of the night. It was a glorious new dawn, worthy to be the first of her new life, or her last. She took a deep breath, trying to calm her fraying nerves.

Did she really want to go through with this? Could she postpone it at least another day or two?

"Electra, mirror."

Her face appeared on screen, her eyes the darkest grey. In a few short days they would turn to black, true windows of her soul. At that point, her death would be almost upon her. And she would be too far gone to care.

No, she couldn't risk waiting that long.

Ali finally pulled on her Recruit uniform – possibly for the last time – and padded into the bathroom for her morning ritual.

She had another half hour before Rob expected her in his room. Thirty minutes. It had always seemed like an eternity when Aiden had put her through her paces. Right now, it felt like no time at all.

Even so, her mind went blank when Ali considered what

she wanted to do with the rest of her life. There was so much, yet so little that counted. And the few things that mattered were far too dangerous to contemplate in earnest. Like saying goodbye to Beth.

The thought of never seeing her exuberant friend again, cut Ali deeply. Still she didn't dare explain her impending defection to an inaugurated Psychiatrist, who would be more than likely compelled to report their plan.

Ali couldn't risk it. Not for herself. Not for Beth. And definitely not for Rob, who had been her rock over the past couple of weeks, steadfast in his decision to support her no matter the danger. Rob who would still be there until the bitter end.

Ali could almost taste it in her mouth. The bitter end.

She wished she could say goodbye to Aiden too, but that would be beyond foolish. She might have grudgingly accepted that she cared for the Protector, but to him she was still only one thing: his assignment.

Leaving the bathroom, Ali looked out the window once more, trying to take in the world, wondering at the same time why she even bothered. It wasn't as if she could take her memories with her, should she truly die.

The sun had climbed higher over the horizon, colouring the sky a bright red. She feasted her eyes on the beautiful display until her brain suddenly overlaid the natural spectacle with an image of her own body lying on the floor, bright red blood dripping from her ears as she struggled for breath.

Ali tore her gaze away from the gory sight.

That wasn't going to happen. Everything was going to be

fine. But the ice crystals of fear running through her veins refused to be thawed.

"Ali, it's time to go."

A tremor started in her toes at the sound of Electra's voice. It slowly worked its way up until her teeth chattered in time with her footsteps as she walked out of the room.

Goodness, she wasn't ready to die yet.

Seeing panic lurk in the recesses of her mind, Ali tried to implement the breathing pattern Aiden had taught her so long ago. Two beats in, four beats out. It didn't help. Neither did the frantic biofeedback commands she sent to slow her galloping heart. By the time she reached the first floor she was hyperventilating. Air, she needed air.

Ali pushed open the door to the gardens and stumbled outside. She found the ironbark tree she had sat under with Rob and braced her hands against the tree trunk. The rough wood bit into her skin. Ali pushed harder.

Her breathing finally slowed.

Allowing her legs to give out under her, Ali buried her face in the crook of her arm and silently cried.

She didn't know how much time had passed, when the sound of footsteps startled her out of her misery. A group of Hybrids was walking on the nearby stone path towards the training grounds.

Checking the clock on the chip, Ali struggled to her feet, trying to pull her courage up the same way she did her body.

Five-fifteen. Rob would be expecting her soon.

She took a long last look around the grounds she had hated so much when she had first arrived, almost three weeks ago. Now she wished she could stay here forever.

Even prison was better than the alternative. How unfortunate that the choice had been taken away from her.

She turned her back on the sight, before new tears could delay her and allowed her feet to find their way to Rob's quarters by themselves.

The door to his room slid quietly open, as soon as she approached, depriving her of one last chance to change her mind. *Maybe it is better this way*, Ali thought, her palms covered in cold sweat. She felt too close to running as it was.

"Ready?" Rob asked, when she stood in front of him.

Never. "Yes."

He looked at her for a second, as if the sheer force of his will could make her change her mind. Then he turned back to the screen of his DID, snapping commands at the device.

Feeling more nervous with each word that left Rob's lips, Ali drowned out his voice to give her biofeedback another shot. This time, she managed to slow her heart rate and breathing, as she stored the panic in the farthest corner of her mind.

"Ali."

Her name pulled her back to reality. "What?"

"The DID is ready."

She swallowed hard.

"I..." Rob ran a hand over his head and swore. "I wanted to say so many things to you, but I seem to have forgotten every single one." He gave a little self-deprecating laugh. "I still have to say them, though." He gently linked their fingers. "So I'll tell you the only way I remember how." With that, he pulled her close, his lips sealing hers, his arms circling her in a crushing embrace. The contact jolted Ali, and she pressed harder against him, until the room receded and her mind stopped spinning with images of death.

"I can't do this," Rob whispered long minutes later, his hands framing her face, his forehead a welcome weight against her brow. "I can't bear the thought of you being gone."

Ali touched her fingers to his lips. "I'm terrified," she whispered back, "but if I have to die, I'd rather die here in your arms, with the memory of your kiss fresh in my mind and the taste of your mouth on my lips."

A single tear slid over her cheek. "Please, Rob. Help me. Don't make this harder on me than it is."

He finally let her go, and the battle he was fighting with himself was plainly written on his face. "Engage," he said eventually, his voice thick with emotion.

Ali's mind reached out to the bioservers.

Darkness descended in front of her eyes as data poured into her mind. She knew that Rob was giving commands to his DID, but couldn't hear any of what he was saying. Then the flow suddenly changed. The dark fog lifted, and her muscles unfroze. She looked at him, and he nodded his head. The altered transmission had started, and it didn't seem to block her bodily functions like the usual data update would. Keeping the path to her mind open, Ali allowed the new information to pour into the chip.

She could feel chaos building inside her mind, as the infinite loop gathered momentum. Her movements turned jerky, her vision wavered – a sign of the chip struggling to deal with too many commands at once.

Then she felt a jolt, like a lag in the chip and knew the

power-feed had cut out.

"Five minutes," Rob said, grabbing her hand. "In five minutes you'll be free."

"Or dead." Ali attempted a wobbly smile.

"Don't say that. Don't even think it." He pulled her onto his lap.

Ali buried her face in his neck. "How can I not think about it, when death is all that's in my mind, lately? They've turned me into a freak." She bit her lip. Too hard. Blood tasted metallic on her tongue. The loop was overloading her brain as well. She couldn't coordinate her movements properly.

"You're not a freak." Rob shook her gently. "Do you hear me? You're ill. You're not a freak."

"I have black eyes." She lifted her head, her vision restricted to his face alone.

He stared back at her, his own eyes pained. "Dark grey," he said. "I love them like that. I love you, Ali. The way you are. I just want you to stay here with me. I just want you to fight. Will you fight for your life, Ali?"

She blinked away her tears. "I don't know if I'm strong enough to fight for myself," she said, and it was the truth. The daily battles with the Abyss had worn her down. "But," she felt the chip glowing hotter inside her brain, "I'm strong enough to fight for us. For you and me."

The sheen of tears she saw in his eyes was her undoing. She crushed her mouth against his, taking everything he offered and giving it back a hundredfold.

"You're my rock," she whispered against his lips, her voice shaking with the effort to speak.

"You're my sunshine, Ali." Rob answered, holding her tighter. "The darkness inside you doesn't have a chance."

"Cut the connection." Doctor's voice at the door shattered the moment like glass. The chip complied, but for once the compulsion was powerless in its attempt to make *her* comply.

"She can't." Rob set her gently on her feet.

Ali's mind felt like it was splitting in two. "Too much," she groaned clutching her head at the conflicting orders the chip and Rob's program fired at her.

"Then stop the transmission." Aiden stared Rob down.

"I can't do that either. I built it that way. Once it has started, it will finish."

"She will die, if you don't stop it, now."

For the first time, Doctor sounded truly concerned. *Probably concerned that he wouldn't be able to test his anialbus serum*, Ali thought angrily. How had they found out anyway?

Her eyes snagged on Aiden's triple helix and another groan escaped her mouth. *The link.* He must have felt it.

"Dieanyay." The words were garbled, her brain finally too busy to form a coherent sentence. It couldn't be much longer now.

The chip was working furiously inside her brain, as its emergency energy started running low.

"Alana, look at me."

Aiden had focused on her. His pupils almost swallowed his irises, until his eyes appeared to be black.

"Go to the ledge."

The order was so unexpected, the chip so busy,

compulsion curled through her with a second's delay.

"What are you doing?" she heard Rob's question and thought she saw him jumping out of his chair.

A dull thump followed, and Rob fell to the floor.

Ali's eyes opened to the landscape of her mind.

No, she screamed into the void beneath her, her heart beating double-time in her chest.

"I didn't kill him." A tingle circled around her wrist. "Do you hear me? Focus." The tingle shook her slightly. "He's just unconscious. He'll be waiting for you."

Panic receded, if only marginally, until she heard him speak again.

"Jump," he ordered, and her feet on the precipice took their last fateful step.

Her body dropped.

I'm going to die, Ali thought, strangely detached.

She closed her eyes and waited for the end that they always described as a peaceful event.

It seared through her brain in a flash of agony. Her head was splitting open. Her ears roared loudly over someone's scream. Her body bucked, snapping hard enough to break her spine as she felt her head smash into the ground.

Chapter 20

Ali swam in a sea of black.

Her limbs were tired from struggling in the thick molasses for too long. She wanted to rest, but something kept her going. She didn't know where. There was no light or warmth, no up or down. Only voices in the distance. She tilted her head. They sounded familiar, but her brain couldn't recall a face to match.

Her arms and legs kept pumping as she tried to swim closer.

The syrup pulled at her, trying to hold her down, but the voices were stronger.

She felt the softness of a bed underneath, clothing covering her skin, and still she was struggling in the liquid.

Her eyelids fluttered, though they wouldn't open as she slid back into her own body. Her ears latched on to the insistent sound of a Biomonitor next to her.

Beep... "injected a sensor to measure her brain waves" *...beep...* "still showing the required brain patterns" *...beep...* "entered the testing phase a few hours ago" *...beep...* "likely to die" *...beep...beep...beep...beep.*

The thick molasses dragged her back under.

***

A needle bit into her arm, and Ali jolted awake – not from the pain, but the voice that accompanied the shot. Her brain made the connection almost instantly this time. Anthony.

"That's the correct dose, sir. If she reacts like a Hybrid, we should see the effects within a minute."

"It seems she might be conscious enough to enjoy it as well." Doctor's voice.

"Enjoy what?" Her throat hurt as she tried to speak.

"Your freedom."

The Abyss. She had jumped. Was she dead?

Ali opened her eyes to the glare of medical lights. She doubted death looked like the medical facilities. Or that Anthony and Doctor would follow her into hell. And wasn't death supposed to be painless? Her whole body hurt. Ali tried to request an injury report from the chip and found she couldn't.

The magnitude of the failure registered a second later.

The chip was gone. She was free. No more compulsion. No more black soul.

In exhilaration, Ali danced over the ledge in her mind.

She froze in midstride.

The Abyss was still there. Hovering in the distance like a shining black beacon. Beckoning her.

But…

"I think the scan was correct."

Anthony stared at her, but she couldn't drag her eyes from the Abyss.

Ali licked her lips. "Why is it still there?" she asked,

feeling hysteria gathering inside her. Maybe she was wrong. She had to be hallucinating or something. She blinked her eyes. The Abyss didn't change.

"It seems that the activation is irreversible."

Irreversible? She was going to die anyway? She had gone through all of this for nothing?

Each thought pushed her closer to the edge. She felt the insane urge to laugh. Cry. Stomp her feet. Scream. "Why is it still there?" She settled for growling, a feral sound she hadn't known her throat could produce.

Anthony stepped back, holding his hands up in a defensive gesture. The Medic was afraid of her.

Good. Served him right for turning her into a dog. "Why is it still there?" she repeated.

"We don't know. It seems the short circuiting has only slowed the progression. You've gained a few more months to live."

Not good enough. Ali growled again.

"Calm down." Her head whipped around to Doctor. No compulsion.

"I'm not your pet any longer," she snarled at him. Snarling felt almost as good as growling, she realized.

He jiggled the steel around her wrists.

"Your mind may no longer be, but these shackles say that your body is still mine."

"You can't own my body."

"But I can use it."

Doctor pointed to the inside of her elbow where a black line was slowly crawling towards her shoulder.

...entered the testing phase a few hours ago...

Terror sliced through her.

Ali scrambled back on the bed, as if her body's retreat could stop the advance of the anialbus serum. The shackles bit into her skin.

"It shouldn't be long now." Doctor looked at the clock.

Ali's breathing hitched as panic blossomed. Nobody had survived the administration of the drug so far.

"Screen on, mirror."

Ali could see the black line crawling up to the back of her neck. It prickled under her skin.

"Make it stop." The panic jumped and dove into her voice. She felt new fog drifting into her mind.

"It works."

Ali's gazed flickered to Anthony, then back to the screen. Dark-grey eyes stared back at her. Light-grey. Grey-blue.

Disbelief wrestled the panic to the ground.

She looked into her mind. The Abyss was gone, a rocky platform covering the formerly gaping hole.

Ali gasped. "How long does the cure last?" she croaked, almost unable to control her excitement.

"Thirty minutes."

But time had lost all meaning. She was finally free.

***

Ali didn't know how long she had been sitting there, staring at her own eyes on the screen, oblivious to the people around her. She was savouring every fearless, free minute.

Suddenly, a storm ripped through her mind, tearing at her clothes, pushing her to the rocky ground. Ali felt the skin on her knees tear. A crack appeared in the rock in front of her, causing her to jump back in shock as it grew bigger and bigger. Far wider and longer than it had been before. Darker than ever, the pull towards it was stronger than anything she had experienced.

"She's coming down. Get Aiden."

She heard the voice as if from a distance, but her mind held her captive.

Cold air swirled from the depth of the Abyss as it drew her in, one step at a time. Her eyelids closed, but she forced them open, falling straight into the midnight black of her eyes on the screen. This was the end, she knew. There was no light left in her.

A tingle touched her arm. "Stay with me." Aiden's voice. But where was his face?

"She won't know you. She's too far gone." Doctor. She searched for him too, but her mind was lost.

The tingle on her arm grew stronger, grounding her. An anchor in the swirling black of a world that could be her mind or reality.

"Back away from the Abyss." Aiden's voice was calm. Firm. Familiar. He had used the same voice when he had trained her. Focused her.

Ali tried to step back, but didn't know how. She only knew how to jump.

She hovered on the ledge, torn between the voice coaxing her and the dark pull that tempted her to fall into oblivion.

"Back away from the Abyss." The tingles were almost painful now, driving home the point he was trying to make. She was able to focus on the face attached to the arm. The face of a stranger.

"We've done this before, Alana." He sounded certain.

As if his words had the power to reach into her mind and pull up a forgotten image, she remembered. The day in her room.

Ali stared at the Abyss in front of her. She had stepped away that day. She had lifted her foot and stepped away. But it had been so much easier back then. She hadn't known how hopeless it was to fight.

"Why should I?" she asked. "All that awaits is more horror. More death. If I die now, at least it can't get worse."

"No, Alana. If you die now it can never get better."

The words...they were her own. "It was you," she whispered. "It was truly you in that assessment."

"Yes."

Ali frowned at the gorge. "But it also wasn't. Not really. Was it? You were impersonating the Abyss. You were trying to entice me to jump."

"We needed to test your resilience. After that brain scan, we knew you were a dormant carrier. The blood test only confirmed the results. You surprised us, Alana. You passed the test with flying colours. You fought me, successfully. You chose slavery, instead of death. Have you changed your mind, now that you know your master is none other than the darkness inside you?"

Ali lifted her eyes to the stranger, but it was the face that had appeared next to him that pulled her in. One so deeply anchored in her mind, not even the Abyss was strong enough to make her forget.

She held Rob's gaze. "Not as long as I still have something worth fighting for."

On the screen, Ali could see the black of her iris crack, a

small flash of lightning shooting out, as she slowly shuffled away from the gaping hole. More and more white flashes appeared in her iris.

The swirl of smoke seemed to be less voracious the further and further away she walked, the pull towards nothingness still overpowering but less so.

She concentrated on her eyes. *Biofeedback*. Only this time it wasn't her heart rate she was trying to slow down. This time she was trying to save her own life.

The colour of midnight faded to grey.

Turning her back on the Abyss, Ali leaned against the tree that stood sentinel over the ledge.

Out of sight, out of mind. She snorted. A desperate sound. If only it was that easy.

"She's done it." Ali heard relief in Rob's beloved voice and realized that he hadn't been there when Anthony told Ali that the activation of her illness was irreversible and the serum lasted only for thirty minutes. Did Rob believe Ali was cured for good?

She tried to sit up, to tell him not to hope. That she still had only gained months to live.

A large hand settled heavily on her shoulder. Tingles raced over Ali's skin.

"She's not *done it*. She's still doing it," Aiden said above her, pressing her firmly down on the bed. "Her fight isn't over. She's still insane. The Abyss is biding its time at the back of her mind."

***

Ali stared at Aiden sitting in the corner of the room. He hadn't left since she had come down.

She would have preferred Rob's company, but two Marshals had hauled him back to his room a long time ago. Another punishment for helping her. It didn't matter that he had also saved her from jumping a second time.

"Were you a willing participant?" The question had been burning inside her, since Aiden confessed to having taken part in the assessment. He had known she was a dormant carrier and still he had hunted her down and brought her back to be inaugurated.

She didn't want to examine why the thought hurt quite so much.

Aiden seemed startled by the sound of her voice, after so many hours of silence.

"At first."

"What has changed?"

"I found out I'm your Protector."

A Protector who behaved against all rules of logic.

"Why did you order for me to jump?"

He studied her quietly for a few seconds, and Ali had a feeling he was weighing how much to tell her. "It was the only way to save your life."

She had deduced as much herself.

"I've had interactions with carriers from a young age," he continued in a low voice. "When they go…insane, the chip exhibits erratic behaviour, in particular during episodes. It malfunctions and won't allow compulsion."

Memories crashed into Ali's mind like surf against the rocks.

Anthony, unable to stop her from screaming. Her hand crashing into the wall after Beth's order to sit down.

So many times her own chip had malfunctioned, and she had never once realized it.

Ali looked at the Protector in front of her and felt another piece of the puzzle slide into place. He had made her listen, even whilst in the throes of her worst panic attacks. But what she had mistaken for compulsion had been her own instinctual reaction to the power Aiden exuded.

It had been his self-assuredness that had talked her back from the Abyss, his calm assertiveness that had snapped her out of her first panic attack in the training hall so long ago, and his natural authority that had allowed him to silence her when he stormed into the examination room.

"Research," Aiden said, pulling Ali back to the present, "is still underway to determine the exact cause of the malfunction, but it is believed that the attempt to control an uncontrollable state of mind – namely insanity – is highly irrational. As a purely logical entity, the artificial intelligence of the chip doesn't understand irrationality, can't deal with insanity, and treats the resulting erratic brain activity as a potential threat. The chip shuts down the connection with the brain completely to protect its electronic circuits. When your chip was about to overload, I used the same technique to protect your brain instead. Hurling you into madness seemed the only way to ensure the chip would shut down the connection before electrical currents from the overload could damage your brain matter."

"And what if I had hit the bottom, before you could pull me back out?"

"Your erratic brain activity would have escalated and triggered a chain reaction of misfiring neurons. You would have died."

"So you took a gamble."

He didn't like the word. Neither did she.

"I prefer calculated risk. I've done it before."

She knew there was a question she should ask, but her mind took a different path. "How did you do it?"

"I slammed a mindlock on you, as soon as I knew the chip was gone, then took it back off, when you were stable."

"At which point you risked my death yet again, by letting them test the anialbus serum on me. Tell me, would Doctor have allowed you to mindlock me again?"

A muscle started ticking in his jaw. "No. It would have tampered with the test results."

Of course. And his chip would have ensured Aiden obeyed the command. He would have stood there watching her die. Her Protector.

***

Ali heard the clock strike ten.

They had brought her back to her own room a while ago. Now she was alone. No nurse to keep an eye on her. No Aiden. Rob and Beth didn't even know she was out of the medical facilities yet. She had to tell them. Especially Rob. He had been devastated, when Aiden had broken the news of Ali's continued illness to him.

Ali pinched her arm. It hurt, and relief flooded her senses. She was still alive, even though she had to remind herself repeatedly. She hadn't given in to the Abyss.

This time. The Abyss's malicious hiss was still there, quieter now that they had given her some sedatives. They hadn't trusted her to be fully conscious in a room by herself, so shortly after the anialbus serum had been administered.

The serum. She was the first one to survive it. They had confirmed it after she had come down.

Thirty minutes of freedom. It had been the most wonderful experience, but the aftermath had been worse than she could have ever imaged. She wasn't sure what she would have done had Aiden and Rob not been there.

Anthony was certain that she would have made it anyway. The drug was stable, he said. But Ali thought he was wrong.

He might be a Hybrid and a Medic, but that didn't make him the expert in all aspects of life. Certainly not her life. She knew what she had felt, and she knew how close she had come to jumping.

She pinched her arm again.

Now she was useless to the Program. She had fulfilled her purpose. They had discussed inaugurating her with another chip, but the risk of permanent brain damage was too high. Instead they had decided on keeping her sedated for a while until they found a better solution.

She looked at the needle piercing the back of her hand then followed the hose up to the bag, where a steady drop kept her floating just above the bed.

She had to get out of here.

Whatever happened, she didn't want to spend the last few months of her life in a prison. In a cell, as a guinea pig, poked and prodded whenever Doctor felt like it.

Ali carefully pulled the needle out of her skin. It hurt.

She tried to stand up. The room spun. Slowed. Then ground to a halt.

So far so good.

She wavered over to her wardrobe and pulled out some clothing. Camouflage gear? No, running wouldn't work. She had tried that before. Her normal uniform then.

Ali grabbed her duffle bag. Two bottles of water. Some extra clothing. Not much to start her new life with, assuming she would even have one after speaking to Doctor.

She looked around the room. Electra. The device had saved her life. After a moment's hesitation she shoved the DID inside her backpack.

Two stops, before she had to face Dr Evil.

Rob opened the door the second she appeared on his intercom.

"Ali, they released you? Why aren't you resting in your room? You could have messaged me. I would have sneaked out." At the familiar sound of his voice her throat constricted, making it hard to breathe. When the pain had started, she had thought that she would never see him again.

"Come in. I'll call a Medic for you."

She shook her head, choking on her own emotions.

"Ali, you need medical attention."

"I need to leave." She sounded as if someone was strangling her. She didn't want to leave her friends. Him. But... "I can't die here."

She saw that he wanted to protest.

"I'm going to see Doctor now. I'll try to come back before I leave, but in case I can't say goodbye…"

Her feet started moving towards him, her hands curling around his face. She lifted her eyes to his and, for a moment, she lost herself in the depth of them. She touched her lips to his.

"I'll be fine." It was a whisper, because she could barely stand to lie to him.

She forced herself to release his face and move back. One step. Two.

He looked as miserable as she felt.

He grabbed her, and then his arms were around her. He squeezed her too hard, but she didn't care. Tears gathered in her eyes. He had done so much for her. He had risked his life. More than once. It just wasn't fair.

"Thank you for being my friend when I needed one," she choked. "Thank you for being…so much more."

Ali pushed away from him before he could answer, tears streaming down her face. "Until next time..." She ran out of the room as the first sob tore from her chest.

Why did she have to leave now, when she had finally found people who she truly cared for? Who truly cared for her?

Ali sniffed, trying to blink the tears away, but there were too many of them.

She doubted the next stop would be any easier. She turned in the direction of Sam's quarters.

"Is Beth here?"

The Assassin took one look at her tear streaked face. "Beth!"

Brown curls appeared around the corner, and a smile lit her friend's face when she saw Ali – then disappeared when she *saw* her.

"Ali. What's wrong? Why aren't you in bed, resting?"

A laugh escaped through her tears. Had Rob told her

what to say?

"I-I have to leave. Don't—" She stopped her friend before she could protest. "I have to. Please, don't make this harder than it already is. Rob can explain." Ali bit her lip to stop it from trembling.

"Okay," Beth sniffed.

Ali gave her a hug. "Promise me that you'll keep fighting."

"I could say the same to you."

"I will. I promise."

"Then I will too."

"Sam will take good care of you." She looked at the man who most people, Hybrids and humans alike, would give a wide berth.

He nodded at her. "I will."

"Thanks." Ali unlocked Beth's arms from around her neck, allowing Sam to move in instead.

"Are you going to see Aiden before you go?" Sam asked, gently rocking Beth.

Ali shook her head. He would either keep her here, or let her go too easily. She didn't think she could handle either.

Ali took a last look at the couple standing in the door of Sam's quarters then turned around with a heavy heart.

This is what it has to feel like to leave a true family behind, she thought.

Still there was one man who could force her to stay. Ali rubbed away her tears as she made her way to Doctor's Office. She couldn't show any weakness.

The receptionist was gone from her post so late at night, but Ali could still see light shining through the frosted diamond door.

She knocked.

"Rt2120, you don't believe in appointments, do you?"

The question was supposed to discourage her. Ali read the intention clearly, but death had a way of putting things in perspective.

"No, sir," she said without missing a beat. "I have a request."

"And that would be?"

"Freedom."

He blinked. "You are free. Free to roam around the compound, free to think your own thoughts. I would think you have more freedom than most members of the Program."

She nodded. "But—"

"Some Hybreeders would betray their own child for that much freedom."

For a second, Ali was taken aback by the anger in his voice. Then she remembered that he was a master of mind games. He played them, like a computer would play a round of chess. Calculated. Purposeful.

Ali pushed her pawn out. "I'm useless to the Program now."

"That much is true."

It still hurt to hear the words.

"So why keep me here? Why lock me up and care for me instead of washing your hands clean of any responsibility?"

"And have others following your example, begging for freedom? I don't think so."

"They don't ever have to know. Hybrids are sent out on

assignments all the time."

"You are not a Hybrid anymore."

"And only a handful of members know that, or the fact that compulsion can be overridden. Insane Hybrids without a leash – what would the human population think?"

He didn't flinch. Not one muscle moved. She had surprised him. Ali sent the knight to press forward while she was still ahead.

"Of course I could stay here and tell my story to everybody who is willing to listen. I wonder what the Investors would say, or the Human Council, if word spread that compulsion wasn't the end, that control over a Hybrid could be lost at any second?"

"Are you blackmailing me?"

She stared into his piercing eyes.

His gaze dropped. Ali took the queen.

Chapter 21

Ali lay with her eyes open, looking at the twinkling stars above.

"I can't believe I'm really leaving."

She turned to Rob, who was lying beside her on the balcony, his arm under her head like a pillow.

She had come straight to his room after she had finished speaking to Doctor, relieved that the hovercoach for her *assignment* wasn't due to pick her up until the next morning.

Rob had greeted her with a hug and a look on his face that said he knew.

"Please don't make me cry again," she had begged, and he had hugged her even tighter, burying his face in her short hair.

"I never want to make you cry, Ali. I just want to make you happy. What will make you most happy?"

"You and me…," she had said and felt his smile against her temple.

"That makes me most happy too."

Without letting her go, he had grabbed the blanket off his bed and carried it out onto the balcony. That had been half an hour ago, and Ali was still working up the courage to finish the sentence.

"I wish you could come with me," she said, stalling for a little bit more time. She shifted closer until she was lying more comfortably in the cradle of his arms.

"Yes." Rob's hand traced random patterns over the naked skin of her arm, raising little hairs in his path. He kissed her forehead. "I wish that too."

"But you can't. I don't want you to."

"Ali—" He tried to pull away, but she held him fast.

"I'm dying, Rob. In a few months, I'll be gone. Where will that leave you?"

The stubborn set to his chin said he didn't care. Ali did.

"You'll live in a world that you don't understand, and you'll have lost everything. Your family." She gestured at the compound. "Me. You'll be all alone. On the run. I don't want you to run again."

She could see he wasn't convinced. Ali forced herself to be blunt. "I don't want you to see me with my brain leaking from my ears."

Pain flashed in his eyes.

Ali told herself it was better this way. Denial didn't help either of them. "I want you to remember us the way we are now. Happy together. Maybe you can even mess up some of the suicide microchips the Program wants to implant into the next generation of dormant carriers. Didn't you say you've finally received your inauguration date? You could save lives, Rob."

"I wouldn't even be able to appreciate what I'm doing."

Of course. Emotions were suppressed in Ai Specialists.

How could she have forgotten? Something squeezed inside Ali's chest. She couldn't imagine Rob's quick smile and compassion buried under layers of compulsion. "Why are they doing it?" she asked, as if an answer could make a difference. "They don't do it with any other designation."

"All other designations work with people. Ai Specialists work with machines. Machines deal better with logic."

A fact that had saved Ali's life. At least temporarily.

Ali exhaled a deep breath. "The Hybrids you save will appreciate it. I will appreciate it."

Rob hung his head. "You're asking me to give up my life for the lives of a handful of strangers."

"I'm asking you not to give up your life for me."

Rob shook his head and gathered her closer. "Why does loving you have to hurt so much?" he whispered against her skin. "And why do I wish, anyway, that I could always feel like this? Like you're the most important person in the world?"

Ali's breath stuck in her throat. "You won't forget your memories," she said.

"No, but I won't be interested in making new ones." He tilted her head back on his arm, studying her, as if he was trying to memorize her face. "Will you help me make one that will last me a lifetime? Will you let me make love to you, tonight?"

"Yes," Ali said, warmth spreading over her cheeks. She still wasn't convinced that she would enjoy what she had been too shy to propose. But neither was she worried about it, the way she had been before. How could she? She had braved certain death, and yet she was alive.

She traced her fingers over Rob's beloved face. She wanted to give this to him, after all he had given to her.

Rob closed his eyes, banishing the pain of separation. When he opened them back up a soft smile was on his lips as he pulled her back against his body. "I love you, Ali. I always will." The kiss he gave her, was the sweetest Ali had ever received.

Eventually, Rob's arms loosened, and he pulled her up, off the ground. "We better go inside."

They slowly undressed each other in the nightglow of the room, soft music drifting around them. Rob kissed every inch of skin he exposed. When he finally took off her top, he sucked in a breath. He cupped her breasts in his hands. "I've dreamt of this every night, since the night of the massage," he said hoarsely, lowering his head, stopping short of pulling her nipple into his mouth. His questioning glance met Ali's.

She grabbed his head and pulled him closer, until his mouth closed over the nub. Ali whimpered.

This wasn't what she had anticipated, at all. This fire. This urgency. The sensations rushing through her body, as Rob laid her back on the bed in only her panties.

He trailed his hands down her bare stomach. When he slowly pulled off the last piece of fabric, Ali experienced a flash of embarrassment. She fought the urge to cover herself, as he stood at the foot end of the bed looking at her.

"You're beautiful." The reverent tone of his voice stifled any denial that could have crept out of her throat.

Ali blushed, then blushed some more when he pushed at his own trousers. He was much bigger than she had imagined.

A sliver of anxiety stole through her body. It must have shown in her face.

"We'll fit. I promise," Rob said, a warm smile tilting his lips. The words reminded Ali of another time, another place.

"I thought we've established that our definitions for this particular phrase are vastly differently."

He chuckled. "Not in this regard." He moved back over her.

She felt the hard length of his arousal press against her thigh.

"It will be another perfect fit," Rob whispered into her ear, as he rubbed himself against her. Ali felt moisture pooling at the friction. Her hips lifted off the bed to meet his, and another whimper escaped her throat.

He kissed her mouth and positioned himself at her entrance then slowly started to push inside her.

Ali squeezed her eyes against the uncomfortable feeling of fullness. This wasn't going to work. "Too much," she said, trying to escape the overwhelming sensations. The headboard stopped her retreat.

"Give it a minute," Rob said rocking back and forth in tiny increments.

Her muscles slowly relaxed. "Ready?"

"Yes."

He plunged inside her.

Ali strangled the scream that rose in her throat. She had known what was coming. She had just never imagined it to be this painful.

Rob held perfectly still above her, his forehead shining

with sweat.

The pain slowly receded, and she wiggled experimentally, sending little sparks of pleasure through her body.

"Don't." Rob's face was drawn as he kissed her again, until Ali was breathless. When he nipped at her lower lip, her stomach clenched. Rob groaned. "You're going to kill me." He rocked against her, unable to stay still any longer. "You okay?" he asked.

Ali nodded and wrapped her hands around his shoulders.

"Does it hurt?"

"Not anymore." *Not quite.* She still felt too full, but the pain was slowly changing into something else. Something more pleasurable. Ali knew where it would ultimately lead. There were some things in the dark that not even the Program could breed out of Hybrids. She just had never imagined to experience it with another person. With Rob.

This wasn't about her giving him a memory to hold on to, she realized. This was about them holding on to each other.

Rob stoked the fire with slow strokes. Sensations zinged through Ali's body. She could feel the tension building, fuelled by the rhythmic friction inside of her and Rob's incoherent jumble of words as he strained towards his own release. "Ali, I can't…," he mumbled, drawing in harsh breaths of air. "I can't."

She looked at his face drawn in concentration as he tried to prolong his release – for her. She lifted her hips until she felt her eyes roll back in her head with every stroke. "You don't have to," she mumbled, feeling like she was hovering on the edge of a different kind of abyss. "One more," she said, and Rob obliged, the way he had obliged her in every way over the past three weeks. Ali's eyes filled with tears. Happy tears.

She felt him withdraw, then pushed inside her again. Ali let go.

The abyss engulfed her in colourful sparks of pleasure. Her muscles spasmed, and Rob shuddered over her, as his own climax rolled through him.

"You were right," Ali said, hours later when they once more lay under the twinkling stars outside. "In this regard we *are* a perfect fit."

Rob laughed.

***

The hovercoach wouldn't be here until six to pick her up, but Ali had been unable to stay with Rob for a second longer, without spoiling their perfect night together with tears.

She had almost anyway, when he had kissed her sweetly on the lips, before pointing towards a shooting star from his balcony, as she made her way to the parking lot.

Ali sniffed. She would miss him more than anything else at the Program.

A Guard turned at the noise. Ali disregarded him. He was the third one to notice her lying in the soft grass next to the concrete. If Doctor had changed his mind about her *assignment*, the first two would have already hauled her back to her room.

Ali wondered what the next few months would hold in store for her. Thanks to Rob, she now knew a whole lot more about the world outside the confines of the Program than she had mere days ago. In fact, she knew exactly as much as the other Hybrids, who were slowly gathering around the parking lot.

She still couldn't believe Rob had thought of downloading the relevant information into her long-term memory before he blew her chip to pieces with the infinite loop.

Still, there would be a lot to learn. She had forfeited all help the Program would normally give to its members on assignment. She was on her own. Flying blind. Only this time it had been her own decision.

Her own decision. It sounded good.

The horizon slowly changed to dark blue, then light blue, then crimson as the first rays of the morning sun shot through the clouds in the sky.

The start of her new life.

Ali pushed herself up from the grass, to get a better look at the spectacle, when she heard his voice behind her.

"You're leaving."

"Yes." She tried to turn around, but a tingle on her upper arm stopped her.

"Don't."

Compulsion threaded through her mind. Not the chip. He didn't need it. His authority was absolute. Even now.

"Why not?" she asked.

"I won't be able to let you go."

"Of course. Your compulsion." How could she have forgotten?

The tingle spread to her nape, pushed her uniform aside to expose the column of her neck. Goose bumps rose all over her body.

"No. Not my compulsion." His lips pressed against the naked skin on the back of her shoulder in a shower of sparks. "You, Alana. It was always you."

She felt herself tense at the confession.

"Why are you here, Aiden?"

He hesitated behind her, just for a moment.

"To help you fight the darkness inside you."

"It can't be fought. Stop saying that." She was through with him giving her false hope.

"It can, Alana. Your mother is doing it. She's fighting the Abyss like you, every day."

Her knees would have buckled, had he not grabbed her arms. "My mother is dead," she said.

"She is alive."

"How do you know?"

"I saved her life the day you were born. Fight the compulsion, Alana."

She whipped around.

Aiden was gone.

S.G. Lovell lives in Sydney, Australia with her husband and their two dogs. She spends her days reading, writing, and enjoys connecting with her fans online.

Visit S.G. Lovell on the web at:
www.sglovell.com

www.ingramcontent.com/pod-product-compliance
Lightning Source LLC
Chambersburg PA
CBHW052017240626
47153CB00006B/1846